WHITE ANVIL

SASQUATCH ONSLAUGHT

MATT BETTS

SEVERED PRESS
HOBART TASMANIA

WHITE ANVIL

WWW.SEVEREDPRESS.COM

ISBN: 978-1-922323-10-1

EARLY PRAISE FOR *WHITE ANVIL*

"White Anvil delivers an engaging tale of experiments gone deeply wrong. The diverse cast of characters quickly grip you as you journey along their disastrous train journey. Not only must they recover from the crash, but something else is haunting their chances of survival – each character must overcome their personal challenges and differences with each other in order to outlast the uncontrollable monsters aboard the train. Betts plays off a well-constructed environment of isolation; the contrast of witty technology and an untamed myth of a monster, alongside the harsh winter environment outside of the derailed train, combine to create an action-packed adventure that you don't want to miss." — **Sara Tantlinger**, Bram Stoker Award-winning author of *The Devil's Dreamland*

"What happens when you are stuck in the middle of no-where Canada with genetically modified Creole bigfoot? An action-packed book that leaves you turning pages, that's what!"
— **Jonathan Lazar**, author of *Zachariah Lars and the High Elf Mystery*

"A story with a fresh take on a classic legend, full of suspense and action. This one had me on the edge of my seat and loving the characters." — **Michael D. Nadeau,** author of *The Darkness Returns (A Lythinall novel) Book 1*

DEDICATION

Thanks to all the libraries that carried books about mysteries, monsters, cryptids, UFOs, strange science, witches, curses, codes, lost civilizations, ghosts, spirits, magic, and all the other weird stuff that enthralled me as a kid. You continue to be appreciated.

MICHAEL DENTON

The walls of the White Anvil Prison were easily six feet thick and soundproofed, yet Sergeant Michael Denton was sure he could still hear the beasts howling inside. Of course, sometimes he could hear them in his sleep when he was off-base.

Denton walked past the plow train as it was warming up. He checked under the engine out of habit, searching for any sort of explosives or unauthorized passengers. Both this engine and the other train had been examined three times for issues mechanical and man-made; in fact, the protocol was one that Denton himself had developed in his early days with the Army Rangers.

The other train was much more complicated than the plow with the single engine. This one had seven cars: three for personnel, two for storage, and the last two were delicate. The cars themselves were quite the opposite of delicate; they were built to withstand the rough temperatures and more. They were designed to hold very nasty things, and, in Denton's experience, they'd done a great job of that. But that made them delicate, at least as far as security and visibility. Generally, they told passengers without clearance that they were refrigerator cars. But that only got them so far.

He checked the engine, circling it, focusing in on shadowy spots with his flashlight. He'd made a checklist in his mind of what areas needed close examination on each type of car and vehicle in the Anvil's motor pool, including train cars, engines, pickup trucks, SUVs, forklifts and more. They also had a number of small boats and rafts, just in case the nearby creeks or ponds needed to be secured—he had a protocol for those as well, always careful to consider where an explosive, a communication device or a weapon might be stowed. He had his crew refer to a printed checklist each and every time a vehicle of any type came in or out of the Anvil. The guards at the checkpoint were required to use a tablet to record footage of each of the items on the list, stored on a hard drive for daily review.

As he ducked to examine the first storage car, he was joined by Sergeant Healy. "They went over all this, sir. You can check the movies up in the guardhouse." Denton noticed she was standing back a good distance so as not to block his light, something she would do whenever she found him deep in an inspection.

"Today could get a little crazy. I just want to triple-check these things."

Healy laughed. "They've already been triple-checked. What you're doing is borderline obsessive."

For as long as he'd been at the Anvil, he'd been known as a stickler for detail, which isn't unusual for military personnel, but it was only recently he'd discovered that the soldiers under his charge considered him a little too anal about his checks. They kept up their duties and didn't complain, likely because he was lax about a lot of other things, and they didn't want to rock the boat and get stuck with a real hard ass for a captain.

"Do you know what we're taking today?" Healy asked.

It was a question he asked himself once a week. *What's on the train today?* "It's fifty-fifty. Half are your prisoners, the rest, 'other.'"

Healy's mouth tightened. "Any idea what that 'other' might be?" She looked over at the special cars at the end of the line.

"Yeah. I'd tell you but then I'd have to… Blah, blah, blah." It was a big day for Denton, the 'other' was certainly not something he was at liberty to discuss. On today's paperwork, it would read as *equipment and materials for military deployment*, requiring an increased armed presence for the run. Healy had clearance for a lot of things, but not for what was riding at the back. She would generally handle security on the transport trains, whether that meant watching out for visiting brass, keeping an eye on sophisticated equipment, or providing an escort for prisoners on their way to trial. She was in charge as soon as the train left the station.

"Will you tell me, so I can be prepared?"

Denton sighed. "You always ask that."

"And you never tell me."

Denton nodded. The nature of The Anvil's business required layers of security that ran so deep it was hard for him to explain exactly what they were doing at any given time. A soldier might be detailed to guard a door with no idea what was behind it, even if that meant they could be in grave danger because of it. "Back here at oh-nine-hundred." Healy checked her watch, gave a salute, and walked away.

After he'd checked the other cars, Denton found himself staring at the final two. Unlike their predecessors—passenger cars with rows of seats equipped with seatbelts and headrests— they each had four separate pods on one side, with ballasts on the other side for stability. The pod doors were open, forming ramps that extended to the concrete dock beside them.

Denton climbed up on the dock and walked up one ramp into the first pod. Inside was stark white, with lights filtering in from the translucent ceiling. There was a dark spot on the far wall; a small window that allowed the scientist tending to the pod to see inside. The whole wall was smooth and seamless, all one molded piece, which deterred the subjects contained within from tearing the pods apart.

"I appreciate you being thorough." Nara Takada was standing on the ramp behind him. "We'll be loading the assets in just under eight minutes."

"That's why you picked me to work here. I'm thorough."

"Mostly," Nara laughed. "That and you didn't seem to mind wild beasts trying to kill you." With anyone else, it might have sounded like a joke, but Denton knew she had hit the nail on the head.

"Speaking of which, how is our cargo?" Denton asked, moving on to the next pod. He walked around it, looking for cracks, imperfections, or potential malfunctions, trying to appear casual as he waited for Nara to reply.

She followed along and spoke only when they were close enough for him to hear her hushed tone. "They're getting prepped. They've fed, and the team has administered the pre-stasis medications. All of the subjects are reacting as expected. It's all going just as we practiced in the trial runs. I've contacted Ops Site Twelve. They'll be ready."

"You're not nervous?" Denton asked. "I mean, those trial runs were *just* trial runs. This is the real thing."

"What's the problem? Are you not prepared?" She raised an eyebrow.

"We're prepared, of course we're prepared," Denton said, moving to the next pod, realizing he'd wasted some time talking. "*I'm* prepared."

"Then what?"

It was hard to emphasize to the scientists how tough logistics were in these situations.

"You've done it before. Plus, the rugarus will be my problem—well, mine and the doctor's. There will be one subject in each of these pods. Total of eight. I'm monitoring four in the first car; Doctor Morley will watch the other four. Your job will be easy. Sit back and make sure no one comes into our cars. Then, you supervise the offload at the site. Easy."

Denton rolled his eyes as he moved to the next pod. "Doesn't make it any easier. Plus, we're a little rushed to get moving earlier than planned because of the storm."

Nara smiled; Denton guessed she saw him as a child babbling about inconsequential things. "You'll get it done. You always do." She left him to move on to the next car. "And thanks for being thorough."

Denton heard the nearby gates open to the Anvil's science hemisphere. It wouldn't be the prisoners, not this early, and they'd come from the other side. The cages with the rugarus would be rolling down the ramps in seconds. Denton sped up his pace to finish the last car.

The familiar hiss of the cage tender preceded the vehicle as it slowly made its way out of the tunnel and down the ramp. The driver guided it easily onto the platform, gently pulling eight cage cars behind. Denton watched the small caravan wind easily toward him and had a twinge of hope that everything was going to go smoothly with the run and they'd all be back after the storm ended, and once they'd enjoyed a little time in the United States waiting out said storm.

In the opposite direction, Lieutenant McElroy approached from the communications room. She saluted. "Sir? We've just got word our spotters at the ranger station recorded another small avalanche on the tracks between here and there. No idea how bad, sir."

Denton was not surprised. It was feeling like that kind of day. "Locate Healy and have her get everyone out here. Let her know I need her to ride with me up to the station. And tell Red I need him to fire up Big Daddy. *ASAP*." Big Daddy was one of the huge rotary plows that sucked in snow off the tracks and spat it back out in a great fountain. Most of the rotaries had been retired long ago, but Big Daddy got a great workout in the mountains around White Anvil.

McElroy nodded and hurried back to the comms room.

"Everything okay?" Nara called from the back of her train car.

With a forced smile, Denton replied, "Everything is fine, ma'am. Just fine." He watched the cage tender line up with the pods and wondered just how bad today was going to be.

MARGO HAWKINS

Margo Hawkins did her best to hold the equipment in place while securing it to the concrete base with the drill. It wasn't working. The angle was all wrong. "Can you help me lock this down?" she said. "I just can't quite get it."

"One sec. Almost done with this level." Reggie didn't even look up from her tablet.

She'd been playing some video game Margo didn't recognize, for hours on end. In hindsight, Margo realized that bringing her sister along wasn't her finest decision.

Margo had her master's degree in geophysics from UC Berkeley and was taking significant steps toward her doctorate when the position at The Brooks Group materialized. It was hard to say no. They offered on-the-job experience: actual field experience setting up seismic readers all around North America.

Reggie, at twenty-eight years old, was very good at Halo and Gears of War. That was about all Margo knew about her sister's current life; such was the extent they'd grown apart over the last few years. Reggie had gone to college for a couple of years before starting a band, touring, getting a few tattoos, and then quitting music altogether to work for a trucking company doing God-knows-what for three years. She had absolutely no interest in science or seismology, but she could drive just about anything, including a Sno-Cat like the ones Margo's group used on expeditions. When another team member fell ill, the expedition might have been scrapped if they hadn't hired Reggie to fill in. She had some cold weather experience from the year or so she thought it would be fun to be a mountain climber, plus, the rest of the team loved her, which drove Margo nuts. Reggie had visited for the holidays a few months earlier and everyone was enamored with her crazy, free spirit, and matter-of-fact attitude. The fact that she was constantly borrowing money from Margo and their parents really wasn't a factor in the team's love for her —they got to enjoy fun-loving, constantly-swearing, no-responsibility Reggie.

Not that Margo was bitter. "Seriously, just give me a hand. It'll take a second. Less."

With a sigh, Reggie put the tablet on the Cat's treads. "Fine. I'm done. Just a minute." She came over and stopped just short of the equipment, with her hands in her pockets. "What is this thing anyway?"

"It's a support for some of the equipment. We want it on level ground to run separate tests from the sensors we install." She'd gotten so used to Reggie's eyes glazing over that she made sure to use plain language whenever possible. "Can you just hold this in place? Or take the drill and tighten the bolts? Something?"

"It's not a drill. It's a hydraulic torque tensioner," Reggie said, grabbing the tool from her sister and making short work of securing the three bolts. She smiled and revved the tensioner. "That it? Can we get out of here?"

Margo allowed herself to be impressed by her sister. *Slightly* impressed, at least. "We have one more site to set up and then we're done. I told you that. Repeatedly." It was getting tough for Margo to tell when her sister was being serious from when she was just trying to piss her off. "Start loading the equipment, I'll calibrate these instruments and we can go."

"Got it." Reggie picked up her tablet, tossed it in the cab, and gathered the tools.

Tapping away at her laptop, Margo could feel the cold getting to her fingers. She tried to keep them covered as much as possible, but delicate actions required them to be exposed from time to time.

"Hey, Go-Go," Reggie shouted.

Margo hated the nickname. She'd hoped it would wear off by adulthood, but that didn't happen. When she was a baby, Reggie hadn't been able to pronounce her sister's name, "Margo", so she just called her "Go-Go" instead, and it stuck. Everyone thought it was adorable, even Margo herself. But it wore tiresome after twenty-some years.

"I'm getting some bulletins from the local weather service. That storm is advancing. It's going to get here sooner than we thought," Reggie said. "The satellite images back that up. It looks nastier than we expected."

The clouds were sparse, but the few that had made an appearance were puffy and white. The sun lit up the morning sky virtually unimpeded. "Really? How much sooner?"

"Hard to say. One of the models shows three hours earlier than expected; another shows almost four." Reggie shrugged. "I don't know, I suppose it could accelerate even more."

They were supposed to finish up their placements and head back in the morning before the storm hit in the early afternoon. Even three hours too early would throw them off. Margo unplugged the laptop and sealed the sensor. "Great. We were cutting it close to begin with." She put the laptop in its case and slid it in the back with the rest of the equipment. "What do the other teams say?"

"Looks like they're headed back already or getting close."

The other survey teams were closer to the home base, mostly on the west, northwest and southern areas of the zone. Margo and Reggie were in charge of the extreme eastern placements, which meant far more miles of travel than everyone else. They'd opted to camp an extra night in an effort to make up that travel time, but the terrain didn't cooperate much. They'd had to detour around an area blocked from a recent avalanche, which had cost them nearly two hours right off the bat. Normally, the entire area could be set up in a day using a helicopter to ferry people and equipment out and back, but a good part of the region was under heavy airspace restrictions from the government for whatever reason. That left Margo and the other BGSE teams no choice but to head in on the ground.

"Good for them." Margo had no idea how she'd drawn the short straw and been sent so far out on this one. She was by no means new to the team, having joined nearly three years earlier, but she was still technically the 'new guy' as everyone else had been around for a decade or more. "Can you figure out where that puts us? We're going further east for this next one, almost an hour, then we'd have close to four hours back from there."

"My guess is we're screwed, but I'll still do the numbers," Reggie said. She grabbed her tablet, took a few deep breaths, and blew on her fingers to warm them as she worked.

Her sister focused her attention back on packing, so they could at least get to their next site before the snow started to fall. The Cat roared as Reggie started it to warm up —a loud growl that spewed smoke into the air and the stench of diesel all around.

Margo secured the tailgate and climbed into the passenger seat. The portable radio was already blaring some almost-heavy metal of Reggie's choosing.

"There's supposed to be some kind of ranger's outpost about another..." Reggie held her fingers on the map for measurement, "Another ... ten or so miles east of your installation site. Could be wiser than going all the way back to town."

Margo took the map and inspected it closely. "Drive." They'd punched in the coordinates for all the sites into the tablet, and with the touch of a digital button, they were on their way to the site. It required Reggie to keep an eye out to make sure the GPS wasn't taking them into terrain that had changed or wasn't quite how it appeared on the satellite images. There was definitely a point marked 'Ranger Station R14' on the map. It was hard to tell if it was functioning, or a relic of the old days of trappers and furriers. There was surely nothing around it. No roads, no houses, *nothing*.

If they chose to seek shelter there, and the station was a decrepit mess, it could be worse than trying to make it back to town.

ADAM KALVAK

After climbing the front steps, Adam Kalvak hefted the paper grocery bag into one arm and knocked on the front door.

After a few moments, the door swung open and the elderly face of Emma Camm cautiously peered out. "Adam? What are you doing here? I thought you were going out of town today."

Adam smiled. "I was. I mean, I *am*. I just wanted to drop off your groceries before I left." He held up the large brown bag. "I brought milk and bread." He pawed through the bag as he talked. "I found some of those little crackers you like from that store all the tourists crowd into."

"I'm not completely helpless. I could have done this myself," Emma said. "You don't have to treat me like an old lady. I am fully capable of walking into town."

Adam felt himself blush. "I know, but with the storm coming in, I wanted to make sure you didn't get stuck somewhere."

"But you were leaving today, weren't you? You'll be late. Where were you off to? Montana, was it?"

"Yes ma'am."

"What for?"

A smile came across Adam's face. "Visiting my daughter. She's having a baby."

"You never mentioned your daughter before. We've known each other for years and you haven't said one word." Emma reached out and took the bag. "Go, then. Stop worrying about me." She practically shoved him down the steps. "You be careful and enjoy yourself in Montana."

"Thanks." Adam trudged down the walk and opened his police truck's door.

"Adam?" Emma called.

"Yes?"

"What is your daughter's name?" Emma barely stuck her head out of the open door.

"Rosa," Adam said.

Emma smiled and waved. "Lovely name. You have a safe trip, now."

With a wave of his own, Adam got in his SUV and drove off. He steered the vehicle off the narrow lane and onto a slightly wider street that meandered by the fields for a few miles before bringing him to the few buildings that made up the town of Waggoner's Crossing. Adam cruised past the storefronts, some empty, some still filled with people-mostly shoppers getting ready for the big storm.

Adam scanned the streets and sidewalks for any sign of crime, litter, or the potential for either, but he found nothing. Almost everyone would either be at work, school, or home. After a turn down the alley that skirted the library, Adam pulled the truck into his space behind the Royal Canadian Mounted Police Barracks. He shoved his gloves into his pockets and gathered up his belongings before heading inside.

He stopped at the sergeant's desk and pulled down the clipboard to check in his vehicle —careful to note the miles; added his signature and hung the board back up.

"What in God's name are you still doing here?" Sergeant Frazier asked. "I thought you were catching a bus an hour ago."

Adam checked his watch. The sergeant was right. The bus had left an hour and thirteen minutes earlier. "I missed it. I'll see if there's another." He headed for the locker room.

"There isn't," Frazier yelled after him.

Locker twenty opened with a little force and Adam stared at the duffel bag inside. He could've made that bus easily, but he wasn't ready. Things had taken such a bad turn the last time he'd seen Rosa. She'd said things that had made him examine himself, his choices in life. It wasn't something he wanted to repeat; better yet, he didn't want to put her through that again. He put his hand on the bag and let it rest there.

"You can still make it." Captain John Longtree stood in the doorway, staring. "You'll regret it if you don't go. You've been talking about this for a solid month."

"I wasn't really invited."

"Bull."

"Look—" Adam started.

"No. You can make the train if you get the hell out of here," Longtree said.

"What train?" Adam was confused. There was a train that crossed into the mountains, but it departed even earlier than the bus.

Longtree smiled.

"What? A ghost train? Come on." Adam laughed. It was no secret among the locals that the government, *somebody's* government, had a secret facility somewhere in the mountains. The miles-wide no-fly zone that extended all the way down toward British Columbia was a big hint. Adam hadn't seen an airplane over the mountains for years. "We aren't supposed to know about those, why would they take me?"

"Take my ATV. Drive it up the slope, leave it at the old cabin. You'll have to hike from there, but you're a big boy. You can do it," Longtree said. "Besides, Win owes me a favor. He'll let you on their train. He's a good guy."

"He's really not."

"Okay, he isn't. But he still owes me. But you need to go now. And I mean, *move*. You get yourself to Montana and you can be indecisive there, don't do it here. If you stand around here, you're going to regret it."

"It is a monumentally bad idea."

Longtree patted him on the back. "Do it anyway. Regardless, I don't want to see you back here before your time off is up. You can go see your daughter and meet your grandchild, or you can stay in your apartment and stare at the walls. Whatever you decide."

Adam watched Longtree leave and thought about what he had said. It would be an hour's drive to the trail, another forty-five minutes on the ATV up to the pass; that would be easy. After that, there would be no trails or roads. He'd have to hike over the ridge, around the lake, up another good-sized hill, and down the other side, all in snow that would be up to his shins if he wasn't wearing his snowshoes. Then on through the forest on half-hidden paths over to the ranger station.

As tough as it was, he loved the view of the mountains that the route gave him. He just wished they allowed helicopters or something over there.

Adam took another look at the poorly printed sonogram and sighed. If there was ever a chance to work his way back into his daughter's life, this would be it; maybe even his last chance. He folded up the paper as neatly as he could and tucked it into his jacket pocket. He left the locker room with his heavy gloves, an extra sweatshirt, and his duffel bag.

Longtree was waiting at the back door with a beat-up pair of snowshoes and a smile on his face.

MARGO

"I swear, if I have to listen to this guy much longer…" Margo said. "I won't be held responsible."

"Take it easy," Reggie mumbled from behind her tablet. Her latest video game obsession blipped away just inches from her face.

They'd made their trek to the last monitoring station in what Margo guessed was record time, with Reggie operating the Cat in the redline nearly the whole trip. Although, what Reggie played off as nothing when they hit half-buried rock, turned out to be a severed fuel line that they didn't discover until they'd stopped to install the sensors. They had backup cans of fuel, but try as Reggie might, she couldn't stop the leak. She slowed it, but even the smallest leak put their journey back in jeopardy. As Margo finished the setup of the sensors, and Reggie had exhausted every idea, snow began to fall lightly on their position. It only made sense to push on east to the station marked on the map.

It wasn't easy to get there, either. There were no roads, no trails, and the thick underbrush seemed like it grew just to make passage more difficult. Every time they thought they'd found a way around the wild-growing foliage, a line of wide-trunked trees diverted them off on some other directional tangent.

By the time they arrived, the snow was coming a little thicker, though it still didn't seem like anything to be alarmed by.

Margo and Reggie were surprised by the size of the station. What appeared on the map to be a dot that might or might not still be there was not only there, but it was a buzz of activity. There were a number of snowmobiles, track vehicles, and plows parked around the flattest area, which Margo assumed had a parking lot of some sort buried under all the snow. And another surprise: train tracks, which weren't on the map. Though trains were nowhere to be seen.

"Holy shit," Reggie said. She'd stopped the Cat on the ridge just to the west of the station. "This is some real Twilight Zone stuff. I was expecting a treehouse or something all the way out here."

Margo agreed, though she thought her sister was being overly dramatic. This was no old ranger cabin in the forest, though. Margo was still fixated on the train tracks. "I wonder where the hell those go?" She looked down at the map she had sprawled across her lap. "I mean, they look usable. They aren't some old mining rails, are they?"

Reggie held her tablet up. "Check this out. You can't even see them when you zoom in on Google Maps."

"You really think Google sent a car out here to take a bunch of pictures?" Margo shook her head and folded the map. "Let's just get down there and see if they have some floor space for us to sleep on for a few days."

The Cat roared to life again as Reggie applied the gas. "Google doesn't have to send a car out to take pictures. They have other ways of doing it."

"What other ways?"

Reggie shrugged. "I don't know. Satellites?"

A receptionist showed the sisters to a waiting room, where they sat for nearly an hour.

Margo stood with her mug and walked over to the silver coffee urn to pour another half cup. She sat down with her back to the older man—who introduced himself as Frank Caplin— and took a deep breath. It was one thing to be isolated out in the wilderness, but somehow being stuck in a room with this man's constant whining made it worse. At least if someone bothered her out in the wild, she could leave the tiny research base and disappear into the woods for a while. Here, she was stuck. A sterile unisex restroom only accessible from a curiously blue door on the opposite side of the room was the only escape —and she'd used it twice already.

"If we don't get out of here before the storm, I'm going to start cracking heads," Frank said, in his grating voice. Margo shook her head. The man exuded egghead rather than a fighter. He'd probably never punched anyone in his life, and it was doubtful he'd start with the military personnel here.

For almost two hours, the three of them had been sitting on plastic orange chairs in the white waiting room, with no word from anyone, though they'd watched people walk by in the hall the entire time. Other than the coffee, cups, creamers and sugar, there wasn't much else to see. No magazines, no television, no Wi-Fi.

The only other person in the room was a short, dark-skinned man wearing a dark uniform mostly covered up by a heavy, dark blue coat with Royal Canadian Mounted Police emblems on his sleeve. He'd been sitting in a corner chair, lightly snoring away since they'd been brought to the room. He propped his feet on a huge army-green duffel bag and rested his head on a wadded-up sweatshirt.

Reggie grumbled and turned up the volume on her tablet so everyone could hear the explosions in her game. Thankfully, it threw Frank off enough that he shut up, reducing his complaints to the occasional sigh. Normally, Margo would bitch and insist that Reggie wear headphones, but right now, anything that annoyed Frank was just fine with her. She could feel her leg bouncing, partly with impatience, partly with too much coffee.

The doors opened and yet another soldier entered the room wearing a crisp khaki uniform and carrying a clipboard. It was their third since they'd arrived. They'd all asked virtually the same questions, but this one at least smiled. None of the others had given them an answer as to whether the group could hitch a ride.

"Chapman?" the man asked, scanning the room.

Frank stood and extended a hand.

The men shook hands. "I'm Captain Irwin. I'm tasked with security here at the center." Irwin checked the paper on his clipboard. "It says you're requesting transportation back to the States on the next train. You want to avoid the storm." He squinted up at Frank. "Is that correct?"

"Yes," Frank said. "I've been told this snowstorm could strand us here for as much as two weeks, and that's unacceptable."

"The last civilian train pulled out early this morning from Chivington. Do you know where Chivington is, sir?" Irwin asked. "It's about five miles due east of here. And it left..." he examined his watch. "Nearly six hours ago." He stopped and stared at Frank.

There was a moment or two where Margo was shocked that Frank wasn't sure what to say, but he soon fixed that.

"I was doing a training module out in the mountains. There's this certification I wanted to get, but I was so lost that I wasn't going to get back to the base camp in time for the pull out. So, they just left without me. You know? They just took off."

Irwin tried to look concerned. "You were doing a certification of some sort, and your instructors just left you?"

"Yes."

"Lost out in the wilderness, your instructors… *left* you?" Irwin acted like he was writing something on his paper, but Margo could see it was either terrible handwriting, or just random scribbles.

"Yes. They made it to the civilian train you mentioned, I guess," Frank said.

"We issued this warning more than a week ago. Posted the train schedule in numerous places. Social media. Websites. News. Radio." Irwin stopped, seemingly waiting for an answer, even though he'd asked no questions. "We contacted any and all civilian expeditions that checked in with us, and personally visited a number of others we were aware of." He flipped a few pages and slid his finger down a list. "We also sent the information directly to any parties that were registered through our office. We sent a text and an email to the address provided." He held it out for Frank to read. "I don't see you or any certification organization registered here."

"There was no signal in the valley where we were camped. Look, I'm sorry I missed the other train. I'll pay a fine or whatever. But I need to get out of here." Frank folded his arms, though he had some trouble doing it because of the thick coat he was wearing. "*I* need to leave."

He was aware that Margo and Reggie needed to get out away from the storm too. He'd heard them answering the same questions, mere moments before him. But he seemed insistent on putting an emphasis on the word 'I' instead of 'we' when he spoke. Margo didn't buy his 'lost in the woods' story. He was certainly dressed like a hiker or park ranger or something, but she found it hard to believe he was out in the woods alone, only to be left by the people who were supposed to be training him. What kind of course was that?

"Look, I'm sorry." He waved to the sisters and addressed all three people at once.

"I just can't allow you on the train," Irwin said. "We have a barracks here. We can put you up for a while when the storm hits. They're co-ed, so everyone will have to stay in the same room—it's a big room—but we don't have anything more private." Irwin smiled again. "It beats sleeping out in the snow in some tent, right?"

"Co-ed? Same room?" Frank sounded like he might swoon.

"It's the best I can do." Irwin held up his hands and backed toward the door.

"I'm sure it is. And we appreciate the effort, and if it comes to that, we'll gladly accept," Margo said. "We just would rather get out of here."

"Sorry. The last civilian train already left. This is all I can do." The soldier turned, walked over to the other man, and lightly tapped his leg. "You too, Adam. Sorry we can't help you out."

The man stretched and yawned, then stood, revealing that he was nearly a foot smaller than the soldier. "You sure we don't want to go talk about this somewhere else, Win?"

Irwin looked puzzled. "No. I can't help you here or anywhere else. Sorry." The soldier held his hands up in finality. "Let me know if you decide to use our accommodation. We'll prep some extra beds and linens." As he reached for the door handle, Irwin was interrupted.

"Look, I'm not some dumbass lost hiker, or a climber that couldn't handle the hills around here. I'm certainly not…" Adam gestured to Margo and the others and shot them a questioning look.

"Oh, we're badass seismologists," Reggie said, without looking up from her game.

"I'm certainly not one of those, either. But I'm local. I know a lot about what goes on here."

Irwin took his hand off the door. "So?"

"I took a shortcut up the ridge on the way here. I saw a train up the tracks a ways. Looked blocked by a small avalanche." Adam turned his head and stretched some more, cracking his neck a little. "That was only a few hours ago. I've been sitting on that bench the whole time and I haven't heard anything go by on the tracks since I got here. So don't treat me like another idiot and tell me all the trains are gone."

"Thanks," Margo said. She certainly felt like a dolt suddenly. She didn't want to see a couple of guys get into a pissing contest, but if one of them got her a ride with their macho banter, she decided to let them piss as much as they wanted.

"No offense." Adam nodded.

Frank's expression soured even more.

The room was silent for a few moments while he and Irwin eyed each other.

"I'm sorry. There's no way you're getting on that train." Irwin opened the door and held it. "If there was a train on those tracks, it would be one that was owned by the military, and therefore would not allow civilians on board."

"There *is* a fucking train?" Margo stomped toward the door, but Frank bumped her as he charged for it too.

"I don't care if it's the national Canadian syrup reserve. If it's headed away from the storm, I want on that train," Frank said.

"From what I've seen, it isn't necessarily a Canadian train," Adam said. "I've seen the Stars and Stripes on some of those uniforms."

"Christ, Constable, you're a little far out of your jurisdiction to be spying on things that are none of your business." Flustered, Irwin slammed the door. "Just shut the hell up. It doesn't matter what you know about that train, or anything else, I'm not letting you on it. I don't care if you are with law enforcement or not."

"Look, I wasn't spying. It doesn't take a genius to make a few deductions when groups of soldiers are dumb enough to come into my town and drink while still in uniform, or their fucking Georgetown t-shirts and marine tattoos." With a thud, Adam dropped his duffel on a row of chairs and stuffed his sweatshirt into a side pocket. "Guess I'll just stand out by the tracks and thumb a ride, then." Once everything was settled, he pushed past Irwin, bumping him with the bag as he left.

"I kinda *would* like you to stand on the tracks for a bit. That would make my job a little easier." Irwin sounded resigned to let the man go, rather than drag him back again.

Margo glanced over at her companions, who were staring and waiting for the liaison's next move. She gathered her own things and raced after Adam. "I don't know who that guy is, but I'm going to follow him. At least he has a plan."

Reggie laughed, but gathered her stuff too. "Thumb a ride on a forbidden train? That's not really a plan."

"No, but it's something I can cross off my bucket list." The sisters chased after Adam. "Hey." Margo struggled to remember his name. "Adam? *Adam*, is it? You seem more in control of reality than anyone we've met. Any chance you can help us get out of here too?"

They walked down a white hallway, carpeted in grey, back toward the entrance to the building. The walls were covered in pictures of park rangers, constables, Mounties, and other oddly thrown-together hero-types. Occasionally there was a framed newspaper clipping, a sign up (or sign out) sheet, and other things that Margo didn't stop to clarify. At the end of the hall, the sun shone through the front door so brightly that she couldn't believe the reports were saying snow would start falling soon — and that it wasn't going to stop for days.

They got to the lobby area and the woman at the front desk was still there. Only now she was wearing a thick blue snowsuit that covered her from the neck to her ankles. A fat pair of gloves and a hat with a ball on top sat on the left side of her desk. A large suitcase was stashed near the seating area. As the sisters followed Adam out the first set of doors, the woman gave a wave.

Adam finally stopped to slide on his own gloves and pull on his hood. "Look. I'm sorry if I was an ass back there. I just need to get out of here. Irwin is supposed to be able to make that happen, but he's being a douche canoe because my boss beat him in poker one time. One time, that's it. So, I'm sorry. *Everyone* gets to freeze." He pushed open the outer door and stepped out.

The air hit Margo hard. It had been cold when they'd arrived at the outpost, but after a few hours in the warm waiting area, and drinking terrible yet super-hot coffee, her body wasn't ready to endure it again. She pulled on her hat and gloves, zipped her coat up to her neck, and shoved out onto the walkway, chasing Adam down the left fork that led to the railway station and train tracks. He moved at a purposeful pace, fast enough to display a long mane of black hair that twisted in the light wind. He seemed determined, and from the little bit Margo knew of him, she thought he might just stand on the tracks if it meant he could stop the train.

She caught up with him, nearly slipping on the icy concrete as she went.

They got under the cover of the station and scanned the tracks. All they could see was the lightly falling snow and two shining sets of rails.

“The maps don’t even show these tracks.” Margo stared at the beauty of the pass and the thick snow on the top of the Misinchinka Ranges. “Nothing for miles.”

“The maps? They aren’t always right,” Adam said.

ADAM

Adam felt stupid getting into it with Win yet again. The man was a jackass; no doubt about that, but Adam couldn't figure out why this one person consistently rubbed him the wrong way. Even picturing the man's face gave him an instant headache.

Worse still, his fellow lobby dwellers had followed him outside and toward the tracks. The older man, who was the one most likely to annoy Adam, stayed put, so at least it wasn't a total loss. One of the women shouted to him and he stopped his trudge up the steps to wait for her.

"Look, you really think we can get a ride on this thing?"

Adam shrugged. "Who knows? It might work out if we wait by the tracks and give them puppy dog eyes."

The woman stared at him for a moment, unsure how to take his words. "That's my sister, Reggie, behind us, and my name is Margo." She slid off a glove and held out her hand.

Adam obliged, without removing his own glove. "I'd leave those on. Conserve your body heat. Just in case the train doesn't stop for us. We could be out here for a spell."

"Thanks," Margo said.

"Nice to meet you." He took the last couple of steps quickly. "Let's get up to the platform and maybe it'll block a little of this wind and keep us from freezing so quickly, what say?"

They both took a step and nearly fell on their asses.

"You feel that?" Margo asked.

"What the hell?" Adam got his balance back and held his hand out to Margo in case she needed help.

"It was a tremor," Margo said. She turned to her sister. "A tremor. A goddamn tremor."

"No shit." Reggie braced herself on the railing of the steps. "Does this mean we got the equipment up in time?"

"Hopefully it's all working properly, but yeah." Margo could feel a smile coming to her freezing face. "We made it."

Reggie rolled her eyes and sighed. "Nerd."

He had no idea what the women were talking about, but Adam latched onto the railing and dropped his bag. The ground rumbled and started to shake harder and faster until the earth felt like water beneath his feet. The snow shifted and tumbled away down the slight hill. Still clinging to the rail with one arm, he reached out and took hold of Margo's coat, seemingly to her great surprise, as she looked up at him with the widest pair of eyes. She grabbed her sister's hand, and the three of them clung to the metal rail. Ahead, a window crackled and broke as the building shifted from the burden of a changing earth.

Behind them, a half dozen people fell to the ground, gripping whatever was nearby and solid. The station where he'd been waiting for the last few hours appeared to be caught on some sort of wave, rising and falling in rapid succession until part of the roof bowed too much and cracked near the middle of the structure.

The rumble lasted nearly a minute, and as it subsided Adam checked again on Margo and Reggie. Neither appeared frightened of the quake but energized by it instead. They went from holding on for dear life, to standing and starting back down the steps toward the damaged building behind them.

"Where are you going?" Adam stood up on unsure legs and followed cautiously. The outpost didn't look like it was done falling apart. "Let's wait."

"For what?" Reggie shouted.

"That was a pretty bad quake, maybe…"

"Bad?" Margo laughed. "That was a baby. A five, at most."

"I make more than a five falling out of bed," Reggie said.

The snow on the roof slid off in chunks, landing on the ground with heavy thumps. The women continued to the doors, reaching them just as several people were coming out. Two uniformed men carried another, who appeared to have an injured leg. Margo held the door for them.

"The power's out," a voice said behind them. "Pretty hard to find your way around unless you have a light."

As the last of the group exited, Adam caught up with Margo and Reggie. "It could still be dangerous; maybe you should wait outside." He couldn't help it, his law-enforcement training had kicked in, and he desperately wanted to get people away from potential danger.

"We can help." Margo pushed her way inside with her sister not far behind.

"Wait." Adam fished around in his jacket until he found the small travel flashlight he always carried with him. He flipped it on, and it cast a pale glow into the dark building ahead. "I'll help you, but if it gets too dangerous, we leave. Okay?"

The trio ventured into the dark building. The receptionist was gone, her desk at a different angle than Adam remembered, and all the things that had adorned it were now on the floor. As they approached the hall beyond, their shadows slid along the walls while emergency lights began to flicker. A long crack in the concrete floor extended down part of the hall and disappeared under a wall a few yards down. "Hello?" Adam called out into the empty passage. A thumping at the end of the hall caught their attention and he led the others toward its source. There, a door was blocked by fallen debris, and it was opening only a centimeter or so. "Hello?" Adam called again.

"Hey," a voice responded, muffled by the door.

"Are you okay?" Adam asked.

"Everyone seems to be fine. It's just there's no other exit from this room, and the door is jammed pretty good."

"Hang on, there's some junk over here we can move." Reggie was the first to try tugging the material out of the door's path.

The door rocked as the man on the other side continued to try to open it. "There's a good chance the doorframe is fucked, too."

It was something Adam had worried about as well. The structural damage on the roof was a bad sign and didn't give him much hope for the rest of the building. "We'll see what we can do." He scanned the immediate area for something to use to pry the door open.

"What do you need?" Margo asked.

"A crowbar would be just wonderful, but I doubt we have one handy."

Reggie answered for her sister. "Handy? No. But we have climbing tools like rock hammers, pitons, and shit like that in our equipment outside."

"Reggie? Reggie, is that you?" Frank's voice was coming from the room now. "Is Margo with you? It's me, Frank. Frank, from the waiting room?"

The sisters nodded weakly and Adam could tell they didn't want to interact with the man. "Yes?" Reggie finally said.

"Can you help me get out of here? I'd appreciate it."

Adam laughed and handed Reggie the light and moved back down the hall.

"Is there just the two of you in there?" Margo asked.

"This is our communications room, ma'am," a man said from behind the door. "There were a lot of us in here making calls and sending emails when the power went out."

"Got it. You sure there's nothing on your side we can use? A long knife? A flagpole? Anything?" Margo asked.

"Sorry, ma'am. None of us brought our scimitars or javelins with us. I radioed for help, so they should be with us before too long. But they did say there's some other people who need help more urgently than we do."

Adam found a folding chair and a mop in one of the maintenance closets. "Let's see what these can do." He wedged the mop handle through the crack and worked it back and forth. The soldier on the other side helped, and they managed to move the door a little more before a sudden snap left Adam with half a mop handle and a door that only slightly moved. "Okay. I guess we try the chair next." Adam sighed, slightly deflated.

"Move," Reggie said, behind him.

Adam found that she'd wandered off and found a fire axe and pulled it from its housing. "Whoa. Be careful." He stepped aside immediately as Reggie walked with determination, drawing the axe handle into both hands and pulling it back. "Wait, wait. You want to hit it near the…"

"You guys need to step back from the door over there." Margo didn't look surprised to see her sister advancing the way she was, but she had to warn others of her sister's impending violence. "*Way* back."

The axe landed with a thud, dead center of the door, but it didn't do much more than scratch it. "Look. Maybe it would be more effective if you hit near the hinges…" Adam wanted to take a minute to suss out a strategy on how best to weaken or unstick the door, but Reggie was having nothing to do with waiting. She wasn't the least bit fazed by the failure of the first strike and wound up for a second, which chipped a little more of the door away, and she landed a third and fourth, her lips curled up in an angry sneer. Her progress started as splinters, but quickly became flying chunks.

Adam shook his head. "Should I offer to help?"

"Nope. I think she needs an outlet for her frustrations. She's been cooped up with me for a little too long." Margo moved ahead, looking for anyone else that might need assistance, while the axe chewed away at the door.

Three soldiers approached with lights and equipment. "We were informed that some men were trapped in the comms room. If you'll step aside, we can get that door open quickly." Reggie turned around and gave the soldiers a death stare; her long brown hair fell into her face and sweat dripped from her brow.

"You've almost got it," the lead soldier said. "We'll look around to see if anyone else needs help."

A small pinprick of light started to shine through, becoming bigger with each strike. As Reggie took a break, a face pressed itself against the hole from the other side. "Hey. Thanks. We appreciate the help. I'm Captain Denton, by the way."

DENTON

Thanks to the efforts of the civilians, Denton found himself free to assist with clearing out the station. He sent the non-essential personnel out to the relative safety of the train platform while he and the leadership team assessed the damage to the structure. They sent survey teams to check the tracks for damage as well.

This didn't bode well for a day he was already anxious about. First, he had to help clear the debris off the tracks from what turned out to be a fairly minor rockslide, now a tremor, and he still had a transport train full of sleepy monsters sitting at the Anvil. Then, he had to take said monsters out into the field for the first time. And his teams had yet to even connect all the cars to the transport train. It didn't bode well at all.

Now, as he stood in the middle of the mess, he got more bad news from Major John Emory, the site liaison officer. "Look Denton, we don't have a choice. That tremor has caused significant structural damage to this barracks. No one can stay here. No heat, no communications, nothing," Major Emory said. "I'm sorry, I truly am, but we can't just leave the staff, or the civilians here. We can't even get the backup generators and lighting online, for shit's sake." Denton shrugged and went back to loading up his bag with things from his desk. "Now, can you hold the damn flashlight still."

Denton sighed and tilted the light so Emory could see into his desk drawer. "I get that, sir. I do. But to put people on a train with those criminals is a bad idea." He followed, shining the light as Emory began to walk to a filing cabinet. "Not to mention the *other* cargo."

"They're cyber-criminals. Computer nerds, right? None of them are Ted Bundy or The Green River Killer, now, are they? What are they going to do, cheat at PacMan?"

It was a marvel to Denton that the man in charge of security of a modern criminal facility thought so little of the potential his charges held for mayhem. And that his frame of reference for gaming was as old as PacMan. "There's a few that are more than that." He held up his clipboard and flipped through the pages. "There's a number that have weapons crimes in their files - Armed robbery, attempted manslaughter…"

"There's only three or four with firearms charges. Out of how many are we transporting?" Emory asked.

"Seventeen, sir. That's a good percentage." Denton flipped through the pages, looking for more examples.

"You'll just have to keep an eye out, because there's no way we can leave them."

"We could take them back to the Anvil. Delay my mission or force the trials of those hackers. We can leave one group behind," Denton said.

"No."

At a loss, Denton tossed his clipboard on the desk. "Fine, that's fine. But how can I keep an extra eye on those prisoners, when I also have to contend with Doctor Morley? Christ, John, I need a whole train to transport him —and those experiments of his."

"They have two specialized cars. The things will be locked up tight in there." Major Emory dug through a desk drawer, waving his flashlight around inside. "Anything happens, those cars have sealed pods to contain each experiment."

"Okay. I get that, but what about having a second train? We have a helper engine that pushes trains when they can't get up hills; we use it for track clearing, so why not hook up Morley's cars to that, and keep them separate from the civilians and prisoners?"

"And have *two* trains to protect? And have your resources stretched that much thinner?" Emory asked. "Come on. We'll keep the civilians as far away from the experiments as possible. Put them and the staff toward the front of the train."

"That's not really good enough. Even if we have a car of soldiers between Morley and the civilians, that's no guarantee…"

"That's the way it is, Denton." He gestured for the torch to be focused on another drawer. "Now, I need to pack up and get ready to go. You should do the same and let the people from the waiting room know what's going on."

Denton stared at the major for a moment, then thought about the tone his boss had adopted —the conversation was over. "Yes sir," he said, saluting.

In the hall, he dodged a piece of ceiling tile that had come down in the tremor, then slid past a couple of soldiers carrying out some equipment.

Halfway down the hall, Sergeant Healy joined him. "Is this going to happen? We're taking everyone?"

"Yep."

"That sounds like…"

"A bad idea?" Denton asked. "Sounds really bad, but I've just been told it's happening, and we need to live with it."

"Emory?"

"Yeah. Listen." They stopped at the armory and watched the soldiers load out the weapons. "I know you're going to hate this," Denton said. "But I need you to get in with the civilians and keep an eye on them."

Healy lowered her voice. "Oh, no. Come on, babysitting the staff? You know that's going to be a mess from the word *go*."

"There's not exactly going to be a party back with the prisoners. It's all going to suck." Denton shrugged. "You could always stay here at the outpost, or back at the Anvil. The skeleton crew manning both will need leadership. And I know you are up to that challenge." It wasn't a real choice, he knew. Healy wouldn't want to miss the chance to get away from the cavernous prison if she could help it; plus, the power outage at the outpost was going to be rough on everyone who had to stick it out.

"No. Thanks."

"I thought so. It'll be a fun excursion," said Denton. "Like one of those Alaskan cruises that the tourists love so much."

"This isn't a cruise ship."

"Yeah, so it's on a train. At least it'll be pretty."

"You have the strangest priorities, Denton." Healy hefted a load of equipment and followed the soldiers up toward the loading docks.

Denton watched her go and hoped it would be more like a gentle, relaxing cruise than any of the other possibilities zipping through his mind.

MARGO

They stood in line behind the others evacuating the center. Margo noticed they didn't use the word *evacuate* but that was exactly what they were doing. Everyone in line had a suitcase or duffel, or both. At the head of the line were two machines similar to the type airport security used. One was like an arch you walked through, the other had a conveyor belt that dragged your luggage into a mechanical tunnel to scan.

"Listen up. I am Staff Sergeant Osborne and I have important information for you, so, eyes front. Put your gear on the belt. All electronics go in a separate bin next to the luggage." The soldier held up a small bin. "I need cell phones, tablets, watches, exercise devices, pagers, whatever. If it transmits a signal, or receives a signal, I need it powered off, and in the bin." He plunked the container in the pile with the others. The people in line started to grumble, and he shut it down quickly. "I know this isn't our usual procedure, but this isn't our usual ride. You will receive them when we reach our destination."

It looked like Reggie might throw up. It was tough to remember the last time she'd been seen without a device in her hands.

As Margo expected, Frank was the first stupid person looking for an exception from the soldier, who seemed to be getting sourer by the moment. "I need to let my group know where I am, where I'm going. There's no..." Frank held up his phone and moved it around. "There's no signal for calls or internet here."

"Put your phone in the bin. You'll get it back later." Osborne held out his hand.

Frank was still moving the phone around trying to get a signal.

"If you don't shut it off immediately and put the phone in a bin, I'll leave you and your party here. I can't say I'm thrilled you're coming along anyway."

Margo reached over and snatched Frank's phone. "I'm not in his *party*, thank you very much, but I'm not getting left here because of him." She tossed the phone in with the others.

"Smart woman. Listen to her," Osborne said. "I need anything trackable, hackable, crackable or pinging. You will take them out of your luggage, drop them in the bin *next* to your luggage, and then step back. Your phones will be kept in a secure lockbox in the supply car immediately after they leave this platform. They'll remain there until the transport reaches its destination. The only key to the box will be on a chain around my neck." Osborne pulled a chain out from under his shirt and rattled it around for all to see. "So you don't have to worry about anyone running up your data usage, looking at your browser history, or swiping through your vacation pictures from Branson."

The soldiers at the head of the line started the conveyor belt, moving the first bags into the scanner.

The rest of the line did as they were told quickly, and Frank finally joined them, with a roll of his eyes and one last sigh. And a slight kick in the shin from Margo.

Another soldier took a moment to scan the crowd and didn't look happy about it. "I'm Captain Denton. I'll be with you on this mission… trip. This *trip*. As you can tell, this isn't your usual transport. *Your* transport, the train you should have been on, is likely somewhere near the American border, almost safe and sound." Denton sized up Margo and her sister. "As I was saying, this isn't your normal transport. This is a military train, and as such we have areas you are restricted to. There are four cars that you may use freely. Two seating areas, one dining car, and a shared facilities car. The rest of the train is locked down and unavailable to you." He paused, and Margo wondered if he was waiting for questions, or if he was just confirming that everyone had heard him. He seemed fairly laid-back in a non-military way. He talked only as loud as he had to, without yelling, and Margo appreciated that.

He gave a cursory glance around at the silent room some more before speaking again. "Clear? Any questions?"

Frank opened his mouth, but Reggie mumbled under her breath, "Not a word."

"We have research equipment that needs to get back to the States with us," Margo said. "It's not much."

Denton acted as if the question was more annoying than anything, barely glancing at Margo to answer it. "We have already anticipated that request. I don't know exactly how much space your apparatus takes up, but there's some room allocated in one of the cars. Show our men your gear and we'll stow it. As long as it's powered off and it fits in our cubby-hole, it can go. If not, we'll see it gets shipped as soon as possible."

"As soon as possible?" Margo could feel a lump rise in her throat.

It wasn't a big deal; they'd have data that the others had already collected that they could analyze, but Margo worried she would be blamed if they fell behind. "Shipped?"

While Reggie normally loved to see Margo squirm, this time she grabbed her sister's arm and leaned in. "Don't freak out. Remember, we're talking about our lives here. I'm sure they'll fit it in the train. It's just a couple of laptops and a few hard drives. If they can't fit it, we'll FedEx it or something. We'll get overnight."

It made Margo laugh at least. "Sure, why don't we just ship *ourselves* home while we're at it?"

The woman from the front desk raised her hand. "Why can't we have our phones?"

"We have concerns about the safety of our cargo. We'd rather not chance anyone accidentally broadcasting our location." The soldier seemed annoyed to answer.

"To whom?" Reggie asked. Margo was surprised her sister was paying attention. "Who gives a shit where we are?"

"I really can't discuss that with you, unfortunately," Denton said. "Any more questions?" He moved on quickly. "Fine. Let's move out. These men and women will start scanning your gear and we'll get loaded up," Denton said. He tugged his helmet back on and pushed through the doors.

"Oh good, we're going to have to listen to this kind of crap for the next seven hours?" Reggie tossed her tablet and phone into a bin next to her bag. "And we can't even drown it out with music. Lovely."

They all did as they were told, with minimal grumbling. From what Margo could gather from snippets of conversation, the key to people's willingness to go along with the plan, was they were going home. It was that simple. They'd all be able to leave this beautiful—yet freezing—locale, and likely wouldn't be back in weeks, depending on how badly the storm hit the area and how long the cleanup took.

Margo was the first of their trio through the metal detector. She raised her arms and spun around as they told her to. Two men and one woman watched her do it, then waited for the additional men watching the monitor. One of the techs nodded minutely and the others waved her through. Margo collected her things and moved over to the side to reassemble her things. As she did, she looked out the small windows at the front of the station. The train was waiting.

She counted the cars - ten altogether, plus the engine. It was a sleek white train with white windows and small doors on most of the cars and larger doors on the last two. There were soldiers in white and gray camouflage at each of the doors and three more walking on top of the cars. They all held automatic rifles at the ready.

"Let's go," Reggie said. "Don't want to miss out on all the good seats." She shoved her gloves and hat in her pocket and lugged her pack up onto her right shoulder. "I'll sit with you, but I get the window seat." She stuck out her tongue and followed another soldier out the door.

That had been their travel arrangement as kids. Reggie and their brother, Alek, always got the window seats. Even though Margo was taller and sitting in the middle of the back seat of the car meant scrunching up her legs, their parents had always allowed it. She insisted for years that she wasn't bitter.

Margo gathered her stuff and made her way to the train. The men stationed at her car made an offer to help 'stow her gear,' but she declined. She was heartened when they offered Frank the same suggestion, and he took it—allowing someone else to carry his stuff.

Inside, the train cars were pristine, if not a little antiseptic. The mainly light gray interior was accented by maroon and black high-backed chairs, similar to the ones on Margo's flight from Philadelphia. Except these were roomier and more comfortable. Not at all what she expected from a military train.

Her sister waved at her from the front of the car. She already had her feet up against the wall in front of her, and a bag of trail mix in her lap. "How old are you?" Margo tossed her pack on the floor in front of them, sat next to Reggie, and marveled at how nice the seat was.

"What?" Reggie asked. "I'm just getting comfortable. It's going to be a long-ass ride."

To Margo, Reggie seemed like twenty-eight going on twelve, every moment of the day. It took only three days into the expedition for her to get on Margo's nerves and for them to have their first fight. It was downhill from there. "Put your feet down. Who does that?"

"Seriously?"

Not in the mood to navigate her sister's childish behavior, Margo stood and followed the receptionist and another man as they made their way into the next car. She tried to storm off, but the man was having trouble opening the door, forcing Margo to stand just feet away from her sister without moving.

"Oh please, don't go." Her sister's mocking tone made Margo even madder. Maybe they needed a train car between them for a while.

"It goes up. Pull it up. The handle." The receptionist was also getting impatient. She was waiting for Frank, who was having trouble with the door to the next car. "Pull up the handle." She pushed him and reached over to the door, pulling the handle up with a flourish, and opening the door inward. She walked by him without another word. Frank followed, slightly reddened.

The next car was already nearly full of soldiers. Each of them took their own seat and left their gear in the seat next to them, or made the bags into makeshift pillows, preparing to sleep the trip away. The man in front of her found an open seat and sat down, but Margo followed the woman to the next car, which was nearly empty.

In the middle was a soldier sitting alone. The woman stopped and handed him a fifty-dollar bill. He handed her a bag and smiled.

"Thanks, Jack."

"No problem." The soldier pocketed the money.

The woman continued to the front of the car and put her things down in the front row.

Margo decided to sit in an empty row near the soldier and suddenly realized she hadn't brought her pack with her. It was still way back with Reggie in the other car. She stood up and sighed, debating on whether she needed anything from the pack anytime soon. As she stood, she noticed the woman from the front desk waving her forward. Margo glanced back to make sure it wasn't someone else she was signaling, but it was obviously her.

Margo slid between the seats, then moved forward, curious what the woman could want to tell her. She got beside the row tentatively. The woman beckoned her closer. "Would you like to sit up here with me? This ride is going to suck." She opened the small bag to reveal a number of plastic containers filled with ice, and under those, she revealed a quart of orange juice, and several small bottles of vodka. "And I hate to drink alone."

Margo laughed —and considering how crazy her sister was driving her, she readily accepted the invitation. "Margo," she said.

"Hi. I'm Bria."

ADAM

Adam pulled his folders out of his bag and spread them out on his lap. He removed a plain piece of paper from one of them and stared at the fuzzy picture of his daughter. The whole thing was blurry and mostly pink because his printer had been running low on ink. He smiled, nonetheless. The bulge in Jules' stomach was nearly as big as she was.

"Hey, you look serious with all those files, you aren't planning on working the whole way, are you?" Frank sat across the aisle, smiling. His bushy mustache made Adam cringe a little. It reminded him of a pinecone. Adam stared for a minute and then smiled. "I hadn't planned on it. Just a little light reading on some things happening around the area." He held up a handful of files while he put away Jules' picture.

"You don't remember me?"

Adam shook his head.

"I'm Frank. Frank Caplin? The park ranger from over near Yellowknife? We met at that harvest festival a couple of years ago. You remember that party we went to? How could you forget? The cops showed up, we both got arrested."

"Ahhh. You didn't have the mustache then." Adam pointed at the sorry clump of hair under Frank's nose.

Frank stroked his mustache and smiled. "Right."

"You're remembering wrong, Frank. I wasn't at a party with you, I arrested you." Adam pointed to the Canadian flag and the RCMP patches on his jacket sleeve. "You had to pay damages for what you did to that totem." Adam could see the wheels turning in the man's head; the startled look, and the slow realization of what was happening. "And you totaled a rented ATV, too." Adam smiled. "If I'm remembering right."

Frank gave a weak laugh. "Yeah. I was pretty drunk."

Nodding slowly, Adam smiled back at him. "So, what are you up to?"

"I'm good." Frank grabbed up his belongings and stood back up. "I was up here for a couple of programs. Getting certified for stuff. I was shadowing a ranger out at Aurora College, getting university credit to learn about ice."

"Ice?"

"Yeah. See…"

Adam interrupted Frank before he could get any further. "Was there a party last night, Frank?"

Frank's face was red and had been since Adam had reminded him how they knew each other. He slowly rose and smiled. "I'm just…" He pointed to an open seat a little further back. "Good to see you."

Adam watched as Frank not only walked to the back of the car but carried on until he reached the next one altogether. Adam had lost track of how many whites he'd locked up for being stupid on the reservation. Most got drunk and loud, some got drunk, loud and belligerent, looking for a fight. Few ended with enough liquid mojo that they actually broke things. Once Frank mentioned the party, he was easy enough to recall.

The train jerked to a start and Adam watched the station as it quickly faded in the distance behind them. The scenery became the beautiful white-covered trees and the snow-capped mountains of the Misinchinka Ranges. It would be their view for a few hours, unless the storm hit, then there would be nothing but the gray-white blast of flurries hitting the windows.

Storms were nothing new. Adam had seen it all before, just not from a train. He'd ridden out one blizzard in an RCMP building, stuck in what amounted to a long metal hangar with a half a dozen inmates and two other officers. He'd travelled to Tuktoyaktuk, a place just as remote as the RCMP station he hailed from, to help with a prisoner transfer. Everyone else had the sense to get stranded in the comfort of their own homes. At the station, they'd all eaten vending machine snacks, sodas, and bad coffee for a couple of days. It could have been worse.

He watched as the train dipped slightly and found another postcard view around the next corner.

A woman's voice came from a few rows up and said. "I'm bored already. How about you?"

Adam held up his files again. "I've got these reports to read." He figured that was going to be his standard response for the rest of the trip.

"Eh, plenty of time to do that. We'll be on this thing forever, right?" The girl climbed over the row of seats and held out her hand. "I'm Reggie Hawkins. You were in the stupid ass waiting room with us, I think."

He shook her hand and nodded. "Yes. That was me."

"Police, huh?" She was leaning over the back of the chair.

"Yes, I am."

"Canadian?"

"You're not?"

"American."

"I see." Adam nodded thoughtfully. This could *not* be the conversation for the next seven hours. He couldn't allow it to be. "What do you do, Reggie Hawkins? What brings you out to this place in the middle of the Canadian Nowhere?"

"My sister is a seismologist. She's out here assisting a bunch of other scientists on a thing about the effect of something on the rate of whatever."

"I look forward to the results of that," Adam said. "But that's what your sister is doing here. What are you doing here?"

That took her aback some. She shrugged.

She appeared to Adam to be in her mid-twenties, maybe fresh out of college, maybe not. Peeking out of her collar was a neck tattoo that Adam couldn't make out, and there were more on her hands: a fanged unicorn on her left, a bat on her right. Letters across her knuckles spelled out "Gear Punk." Her hair was partially shaved at the bottom and long on top.

"You just came along?" Adam asked. "Into the butt-ass cold North for no reason?"

"I'm good with mechanical stuff. I drive anything with wheels — sleds, tracks," Reggie said. "There's not much call for that back in Miami, unless you're teaching tourists to jet ski, or you're doing something illegal."

A laugh erupted from Adam that he hadn't expected. "Enough people I know that are good drivers use their powers for evil rather than good. It's my line of work."

"Out here? Aren't they more likely to steal horses?"

Adam laughed again. He tried to be offended by her comment. "We have cars out here. They even have them on the reserve. People actually steal them." He set his files on the seat next to him. "When I was a kid, we used to have snowmobile races."

"No shit?"

"No shit. We'd spend our free time and money jacking up our rides, like city kids would pour money into their cars. We'd set up courses that went through some rough territory."

"I had no clue anyone did that. I figured everything up here was about dog sled races."

"Harder to really soup up a dog," Adam said.

"They're kind of what-you-see-is-what-you-get, I would imagine." Reggie smiled and nodded.

"So, you're just along for the ride, or rather, the drive?"

"I fix things, I drive. I'm paid a little. Better than looking for a real job, I suppose. It's not terrible." Reggie got quiet. "Not too terrible." She nodded out the window. "It's cold." She watched out the window. "You probably knew that."

They talked more, watching the snowfall increase as they went. Adam thought about how different the two of them were. He guessed they were maybe ten years apart in age, but their worldviews were much farther away. Life on the reserve, or way out in the Yukon, was a far cry from growing up near the beaches of Miami, although she hadn't actually said that was where she was from. He felt himself being a constable—

questioning everything she told him, like she was a suspect or a witness. It was hard to shut it off.

A pair of soldiers walked into the car with rifles slung across their chests. "They eyed each of the passengers as they went but moved briskly to the back door and left.

"What do you suppose makes them so pissy toward letting us hitch a ride?" Reggie asked. "And what did they mean when they said we could be located by our signals?"

It was a question Adam had asked himself, especially in the face of the stupid lies they'd told when he'd confronted them about it. It was another case of his law enforcement instincts kicking in. He wondered but decided he probably didn't want to know.

MARGO

She wasn't crazy about getting day-drunk on a train, so Margo took it easy on the alcohol. As much as she wanted to get blitzed out of her mind and sleep for the rest of the trip, she was still —technically— the responsible one of her little group. She had no idea which car Reggie had ended up in and didn't care. Hopefully she was driving someone else batshit at the moment. Her companion had no such reservations. She downed her first plastic cup full of screwdriver in minutes and made a fresh one.

"What exactly do you do, Bria?" Margo sipped her drink.

"Technically, I'm a public liaison. Kind of a glorified secretary, kind of a public information officer, a little bit of a mother to the idiots who come in and out of the station without putting on their hats and gloves. Just once, I'd like to let one get frostbite, lose a finger. Then they'd listen."

It was funny, but Margo couldn't tell if Bria was serious or not. It could've been the alcohol, she supposed.

To pass the time, they continued to talk; nothing important, which suited Margo fine. They discussed television shows they missed, significant others —Margo was single, never married; Bria was twice-divorced.

"I'm going to find the washrooms," Margo said. She stood and swayed back and forth a little. It had to be the train, more than the booze, but she latched onto the back of the seat to steady herself. The fun and camaraderie of the last hour or so soon faded as Frank spotted her and waved.

"Hey, you're in this car too? Great." He came up the aisle and stood next to Margo. "What are you two doing?"

"I'm looking for the bathroom," she said.

"Can I sit with you two? No one is any fun in the other car."

"We're not much fun, either." Margo stepped into the bathroom and nearly slammed her head into the wall as the train swayed again. She gave a sigh and closed the accordion-like door. She stood in front of the mirror and stared at herself for a moment. *It's just the alcohol.*

DENTON

"Everything good?" Denton asked.

"No issues, sir." The private moved away as Denton nodded. He was braced against the doorframe in the hall near the security door, watching the soldiers sitting in the military car, entertaining themselves as much as they could, wearing their clunky gear in the cramped car. He nodded to the guards and they unlocked the padlock on the door, then used a key on the deadbolt. They opened it and let him in. On the other side, he could hear them doing the same thing in reverse.

With a nod, Denton acknowledged the soldiers guarding the other side and stepped through to the seating area. Seventeen prisoners took a moment to gauge him and then went back to doing nothing. There were eleven men and six women, all spread out across the aisles and rows. None were more than two seats apart on all sides. It was a headache planning the seating. Worse than figuring out who would sit where at his first wedding. The last two rows were full of soldiers staring at the back of the prisoners' heads.

"What's up, boss?" One of the prisoners yelled. "We almost there or what?" The others laughed.

Not even close. Ignoring the prisoners, Denton moved up the middle of the train to the next door, also padlocked. He twirled his finger to indicate he wanted it unlocked. The corporal fumbled with his keys, looking for the right one. All the electronic locks on the trains had been retrofitted to only open with keys. The most advanced transport they had, and all of the electronics had been removed. Door panels, transmitters, entertainment systems, phones, the whole lot.

"Sorry," the corporal said, fumbling with the lock. The other guard unlocked the deadbolt from the other side and opened the door. Once inside, Denton got his own key out and unlocked the next door. He slid it to the left and then closed and locked it behind him. He'd grown up on Star Trek where doors opened automatically, and here he was, securing prisoners like it was the 1800s.

This car and the one behind it were the only ones with any sort of tech allowed in them. Denton required it. He'd rather that, than let these holding pods fail. He followed the hall to the right and stepped lightly around the sealed cells on his left. At the end of the train, Nara Takada, one of the scientists on the project, was checking a reading.

Normally, he would have refused to transport these experiments at the same time as his prisoners, let alone throwing civilians into the mix, but the imminent storm was a strong persuader, at least to higher-ranking people than Denton. "Where's Doctor Doom?"

"Hello to you as well, Captain," Nara said. "Happy to see you again, Captain. Yes, I agree, the weather we are experiencing is wonderful." She didn't bother to look at him. "Doctor *Morley* is in the next car doing the same checks on his subjects as I am, thank you."

With a deep sigh, Denton started again. "Sorry. It's a crazy day here. Hello, Doctor…"

Nara interrupted. "Too late now. Besides, I'm busy." She pointed to the rear door with her pen.

"But…" Denton tried again and was shut down by a sharp look and an additional thrust of the pen toward the door. He didn't have the patience for being delicate with Doctor Takada, and wasn't in the mood to talk to Morley, but he needed an update from him. He passed Nara and used his key card to open the door to the next car. He followed the short hall to find Morley sitting on an overturned bucket, eating an apple. Upon seeing Denton, he bobbed his head and chewed up his last bite.

"Ah, good. I was wondering how things were going up front." Morley stared for a second. "So, how *is* it going?"

"Everything is going slightly behind schedule, because of the avalanche covering the tracks earlier, but otherwise, no problems." Denton motioned with his key card to the pods. "How are things here? That's the real question."

"Everything's fine. Just fine. There's no reason for anyone to be concerned." Morley seemed indignant. "What about those civilians I heard were onboard? What's that all about?"

"Necessary. We couldn't leave them behind because the tremors rendered the outpost uninhabitable," Denton said. "They won't get in our way."

"I don't like it. Any one of them could be a spy or a saboteur, here to wreck this experiment."

Denton was nearing his limit of crazy people. The researcher and his axe-wielding companion were bad enough; he didn't need the man overseeing the volatile experiment getting paranoid on top of everything else. "All the non-military personnel on the train are confined to certain cars, and believe me, from what I've seen, they just want to get home."

"I hope so. What about those prisoners?"

"I assure you; they're all being watched carefully," Denton said. "Just concern yourself with everything back here."

Morley shook his head. "No problems here."

"Good. I'll be thrilled when we part company with all these other people once we get across the border." Of course, what followed next was going to be much more difficult. The first mission with these beasts was going to be more than nerve-wracking, even without the distractions. "I'll check in with you again in an hour or so." Denton waved over his shoulder and moved back to the previous car.

"Good talk?" Nara asked as he passed.

"The best. We bonded. We laughed, we cried." Denton stopped at the door and sighed.

Nara waved at him. "Rough day?"

"Rough day."

"Look at it this way, all the craziness is behind you," Nara said. "You can relax for the rest of the trip."

"I wish I could be so optimistic."

"We're all ready for the mission. We turn them loose, they do all the hard work," Nara said.

Denton did the security dances to get back to the prisoner car and he sat in a seat in the back row. He thought about how much it felt like a jinx, rather than a compliment, when Nara said the bad stuff was behind him.

"Everything five-by-five, sir?" one of the soldiers asked.

"It's great."

"Good to hear. Want me to wake you when we change guards?"

"I'm not going to sleep," Denton said, crossing his arms in front of him. "Thanks anyway."

In a matter of seconds, he faded out to the sway of the train.

MARGO

As Margo left the lavatory, she heard a sound up ahead, like a clap of thunder followed immediately by breaking glass, and then the metallic scream of metal scrunching against metal. It was a noise the likes of which Margo had never heard before. It was like the world was angry and taking it out on the train. She was airborne then, like the train had floated up off the tracks, taking flight. She could see the car headed for the edge of an embankment, though with all the snow, it was hard to make out any other details. Another thunderclap and the whole car swayed to the left, dropping Margo to the floor. She slid a few feet before slamming into the back row of seats just as the train car ground itself to a halt.

Most of the shouts stopped on the impact of the car.

The interior lights went out, and she flailed about in the new darkness until she grabbed the legs of one of the metal chairs. Margo didn't want to sit up. The metal piece had kept her from slamming into the walls and drifting freely around the cabin to endure more injuries, but she had still been knocked around against the frame of the seat and the floor. Her side hurt. She tasted blood in her mouth, and her lip was throbbing. Her left arm stung from where it had slammed against the underside of the seat. She finally opened her eyes to see the small emergency lights flash below her, and sat up slowly, trying to judge how much her body could handle. She determined that the car was upright, but in poor shape. From where she was sitting, she could see a huge tear in the wall toward the other end of the car —as if it had split open. Snow was blowing in with thick flakes tossed by a heavy wind, and the cold air hit her face hard.

From somewhere in the distance, she heard more sounds of crashing and destruction. She assumed at least one other car was suffering the same fate as hers, sliding down the embankment with sudden ferocity.

"Hello?" Margo called out, sliding across the floor and propping herself up against the wall. The sting in her arm had lessened, but the pain near her ribs lingered. "Anyone? Hello?"

"Here. Over here." A man's voice, weary and small, floated from the other side of the train. "I'm okay." In the almost-dark, Margo saw a shadow of the man as he moved in the unlit alcove of the far exit.

She got to her feet and steadied herself against the wall.

"Hello?" She made her way forward, using the wall as she went. "Where are you?" She remembered that the car wasn't terribly crowded; only a handful of people had been sitting nearby when she'd sat down with Bria to drink. She checked her pockets for her cellphone but quickly realized she'd handed it over before getting on the train. In addition to calling for help, she could've really used it for its flashlight right about now.

Margo carried on moving forward, one row, one headrest at a time, feeling her way. When she got midway to the rip in the side of the train, she remembered that Bria's supplier—the man who'd handed her the bag of booze—had been sitting nearby. She found him another row up. His body was laying across the seats, but he was still strapped into the first chair. His torso was twisted at an unnatural angle, and against her better judgement, she reached out to feel his pulse. His skin was still warm; warmer than she expected it to be in the frigid temperature. She moved her fingers to his neck, repositioned them when she found nothing, and then tried one last time to find some sign of life.

No luck.

She stepped back and inhaled a deep breath. A heavy feeling began to spread through her stomach, and she was terrified that she was bleeding internally. Most likely, she hoped, it was fear.

To keep herself from staring at the man, and freezing —literally— to the spot, she reminded herself again of Bria, and moved forward, looking for survivors. She came to the gaping hole that protruded inward, its jagged metal shredded, like teeth reaching into the carriage. It was hard to tell what was outside as the flurries twisted and snaked their way inside on the wind. Margo could feel the temperature dropping in the car as she moved on. She remembered the man who'd responded to her a few moments earlier. "Hello? I'm Margo. I'm coming your way. Can you walk?"

"Gantz, ma'am. I'm standing. Walking is not quite as easy. I think I've broken something. Ankle, maybe." She heard him shuffle a little and she could see him then, in the low light coming from outside. "I hope that's the worst of it," he said.

Margo moved cautiously toward him, watching for any debris. "Do you see a woman near you? In that front row?"

The soldier leaned against the wall and peered around the corner. "Yeah. She's here, on the floor. Looks like she's in bad shape." He slid himself along the wall toward her and knelt down with an audible groan.

Margo arrived at the front of the car, right behind him. She stood looking over his shoulder.

"She's breathing. Pulse is pretty slow."

Carefully moving down to the floor, Margo found a line of blood on Bria's forehead, coming from somewhere under her hair. "Bria?" Margo gently put her hands on her new friend's brow, to try and assess the severity of the wound. She pulled her hand away, covered in blood. "Is it bad? Can we help her?"

The soldier, whose name tag read 'GANTZ' gave her his own terrified look. His eyes were wide, with dilated pupils. "I don't know what equipment we have here." He was in a full panic already. "Jesus. I don't know. How many other people are here? How many were in the car? Are they dead? What about the other cars?" He pulled himself up using the seats, and shouted, "Anyone? Someone please answer. Someone help us!"

A groan on the other side of the aisle caught their attention. On the floor, another soldier was getting to her knees.

"Shit," Gantz said. "MacGregor. I didn't see you in the darkness." He hobbled over and did his best to help her up.

"Wait." The soldier was already sitting up and grabbing for the chairs, to get to her feet. "Don't stand up right away," Margo said. She scrutinized the soldier as best she could in the dim light but didn't see any blood. "Everything feel okay?"

"Big headache," the woman said. Margo saw her nametag read "ALLEN". "And my left hand. Hurts like hell and I can't move my fingers."

"Here, let me help you." Margo reached under the soldier's right arm and lifted her up, afraid to touch anywhere on her left arm. "There you go. Lean against the wall."

"What the hell happened?" Allen held up her left arm and looked at her hand, as if staring at it would somehow reboot the hand's systems. "I was standing here and then I was on the floor. What happened? How long was I out?"

Gantz helped her steady herself. "Not long. At least I don't think so."

"Good questions," said Margo. "I don't know if I was out for a little while too. Could've been a minute or two, maybe five. I remember a thud, and then the train went off the tracks, then there was some tumbling before we came to rest." She remembered Bria around the corner. "Come on, you two can sit down in these chairs while I try to help this woman." She knelt and tried to get her mind to stop racing from one thing to the next. She had to help Bria and the soldiers, so she hadn't even checked the rest of the car for other casualties. Margo put her hand on Bria's forehead and tried to wipe the blood from over her eyes. She succeeded only in smearing it around and making it worse.

"First aid kit's in the closet by the door." Gantz pointed back where he'd been lying and started in that direction.

"Great, stay there. I'll get it. You take a minute. I'll find it." Margo waved him back to the seats until he sat down next to his fellow soldier. She stepped around the corner and into the alcove for a second and put her hand over her mouth to avoid freaking out completely. The blood all over her hands was almost more than she could bear. She wasn't a doctor, had little medical training, and certainly had no idea how to handle a train wreck.

She wondered if the other train cars had fared any better, and if they were still attached. Once she'd tended to Bria, she'd go check on them. She hoped one of the cars would have a doctor that could help with the three casualties here. Her hand smeared blood across the cabinets as she opened them one by one to find the medical kit.

"Shit."

Margo noticed Gantz standing in the middle of the gaping hole in the side of their carriage, bracing himself against the jagged ribbons of metal there. "What?" Margo pulled out a small first aid kit and moved to join him. When she got next to him, she understood. The car was on a sharp incline, leading down into the trees and rocks below. From their vantage point, they could see there were no other cars in front or behind.

The snow melted as it hit their faces.

DENTON

CONGO RIVER REGION - SEVEN YEARS EARLIER

Denton watched the back of the man ahead of him in line. It was the best way to keep himself on target in the pouring rain. The jungle along this stretch of river was particularly thick, and some soldiers had to keep one hand on the soldier in front of them just to keep in line. What had started off as a joint operation with the local government to track down a particularly violent terrorist cell had gone sideways in a hurry and became a struggle just to get back to their base.

The weather was the worst of it; torrential rains had come in from nowhere. There had been nothing in the forecast about precipitation, but it came anyway, carried by a wind that drove the rain hard into the men's faces as they moved on their target. All of that water quickly made the ground a slippery, sucking mess; it forced them to work twice as hard just to make progress.

To Denton's mind, they were in the storm for a week, but on the other side of it, he learned they'd only been out for three days. So much darkness day-to-day, as the storms moved in and disappeared, made it seem like a constant cycle of day and night one minute to the next. They rested when they could, stopping at safe rally points. But no one got to relax or sleep all that much; they all complained about an uneasy feeling that made them tense and unable to sleep. Denton felt it too. Starting on the second night, he felt something watching him the moment he closed his eyes. He half-expected to open them and find someone or something standing over his bedroll, ready to pounce.

Their targets were terrorists who'd lived in the area for years and knew their way around the terrain, so everyone figured that was why they were on high alert. It felt like something else to him, but surely it was just nerves.

The signal came for everyone to stop in their tracks, and Denton stood like everyone else and listened. There was the sound of water, but not just the ever-present rain, it was something else. The river was rushing along nearby. Maybe their scouts spotted some of the cell crossing the river, or fishing? They waited five minutes before Denton heard the strains of a murmured argument. "What the hell?" He leaned forward and asked the soldier in front. The man shook his head.

While they waited, Denton noticed a smell. It was a cross between a grease fire and a refrigerator full of spoiled milk. Word came back that they were finally closing in on the encampment they were searching for, but there was some problem causing them to hold, a few meters out. The scuttlebutt was that the camp was empty. No one speculated as to why. Denton assumed the delays they'd experienced getting to the target may have allowed the cell to clear out.

"Let's go," Captain Brewer called. "Looks empty, but we'll clear it by the numbers."

Everyone paired off and moved where they were told. Denton and his partner, Hammond, were directed toward a single-room structure that was little more than a hut, covered with fronds for a roof, but with mismatched lumber for walls. They quietly pushed the only door open and entered to find a half dozen sleeping bags, and clothes and cooking utensils scattered about the dirt floor. Near each sleeping bag was a backpack, each still full of gear and supplies. Denton and Hammond exchanged looks, questioning where the people would have gone without their equipment.

The men headed back out into the compound, regrouping with the others. "Clear," each pairing said as they were assembled again. Brewer appeared to be as confused as anyone. He stared out at each building, and then into the trees beyond.

"Maybe this isn't the right camp?" Hammond offered.

"No, this is it. We found some of their ordinance and other markers we were told to secure." Brewer waved his finger at the ground around him. "Start policing the area. I have a lot of boot prints here that aren't ours. See if anything else turns up. Stay in pairs, don't wander out too far."

Everyone did as they were ordered. They drifted off, making their way out from the center of the encampment. Denton and Hammond's course took them to the riverbank, and they both scanned the water. The center was littered with large rocks and boulders, making it a difficult area to navigate by boat. "Maybe they crossed and took off?" Denton asked.

"Why? So, they can watch people when they arrive? Do you think they have this place rigged with some kind of alarm?"

It was a stretch, seeing as the camp was pretty low-tech, but it was a possibility. "I don't know. It would give them some warning, and they could clear out." Denton stepped into the water, splashing as he walked up the shore. He scanned the opposite shore for signs of life until he tripped on something in the water and nearly fell on his face. Hammond chuckled while his partner got his balance back. He was drawn back to see what had tripped him up. Unlike all the dark rocks around it, this object was white and stood out in the relatively clear river. "Hammond?" Denton asked. "Does this look like a femur to you?"

Hammond stepped closer. "Maybe, but that..." he pointed further away from the riverbank, "...that is definitely a skull."

It looked like another rock to him, but as Denton changed his angle, he discovered Hammond was right. Walking further into the water, he spotted another skull, this one half-crushed and missing the jawbone. Denton felt his stomach tighten. "Cap?" Denton shouted. "We've got something over here." Brewer walked with purpose to Denton, the others perked up their heads as well.

"What is it, sergeant?"

"We're finding pieces of multiple skeletons in the water here, sir." The three of them walked the shoreline and spotted more bones and fragments within the water, just a few feet from shore. The rest of the team kept scanning the trees for signs of any enemy presence, though they all stole glances to see what was happening.

Brewer inspected the nearest skull as cautiously as he could, nudging it carefully with the barrel of his rifle. Denton moved away, just in case the piece was somehow booby-trapped. When nothing happened, the captain waded into the water and picked up the skull. "I don't know. It's hard to say how long this has been here. I can't tell if the river has polished it clean or if it's relatively new, or what." Hammond moved in closer and peered over the captain's shoulder.

Behind them, some movement caught Denton's eye. One of the boulders in the middle of the river seemed to be rocking back and forth. It took a few seconds for Denton to convince himself that he wasn't seeing things, and at first he thought it was being moved along by the river, but the current wasn't strong enough to move something that size. Still, he could plainly see the rock was slowly rising as it turned. "Sir?" Denton said, loud enough to be heard over the river. When he got Brewer's attention, Denton pointed to the rock. "I'm not sure what's happening but that thing has moved a couple of times."

He didn't need to explain; from the other side of the rock came another, smaller grey object. This one a slender head met at its far end by a long neck that held it aloft. The other end of the neck was not a boulder, but instead an enormous lumpy body. The head was something from a nightmare-all teeth and dripping gums.

Denton felt a scream somewhere in his throat, but it only buzzed around him like a bee that would never quite sting.

"Holy shit," Hammond said. He fell on his ass in the water and stayed there while he stared at the beast that was unfolding itself in front of him.

Denton got the idea that it resembled a dinosaur he'd read about as a kid; a brachiosaurus, though this one seemed to have a slightly shorter neck and wider body. The rest of it looked to be one part dragon and another part hippo. And as it glared at the men, that head began swaying and turning, taking everything in with its enormous green-and-black eyes.

"Move back, let's give this thing some room," Brewer said. He sounded unsure of his orders, and just as confused as Denton was.

Hammond got up and backed away, but the monster had already chosen to fixate on him. It ignored the captain and Denton's retreats, following Hammond with its eyes and adjusting its neck with each of the soldier's movements.

"What the hell?" Hammond shouted. The creature reared back, and a hood snapped out from around its head. The beast's massive lips curled back, revealing jagged teeth dripping with fetid river water.

The thing lunged forward, snapping its jaws as it attacked.

DENTON

The explosion of sound woke Denton from his sleep. His car slammed into the one in front of it, and he was sent hurtling forward. He'd only intended to sit for a moment and hadn't buckled his seatbelt or put on a helmet. He was dazed from the blow as the car tilted and landed on its side. He fell to his right, slamming into the train wall. His ears were filled with the sound of metal-on-metal as the cars struggled to stay on the tracks, then struggled to stay upright, and failed at both.

His car shook as it was hit by the next. The interior lights flickered and died as it rolled onto its roof and began to tumble. It teetered for a moment, not going over, but threatening to.

Something in the air dared everyone to move, to breathe, lest the whole thing start rolling even more. Defying that fear, Denton grabbed a seatbelt and clicked it together. With the train upside down, he couldn't get into a seat, so he wrapped it around his arm and managed to grab hold just as the car made good on its promise and began to roll for real—quickly, side-over-side. The whole frame of the carriage creaked and groaned with each rotation and landed with the crushing sound of metal. The buckle kept him from flying around freely, but it also whipped him into the walls as it went.

He could hear shouts now, over the ripping and tearing of metal; the thuds of the hulking train. The outside was a blur, barely visible through the shattered windows. The light of the evening sky flashed by over and over, but he couldn't make out any details of the location.

As they continued to flip, the limp body of a soldier flung itself into Denton, and his arm slipped from the seatbelt. He and the soldier went to the floor just as the car fell on its side and stayed there, still sliding down whatever hill they'd landed on. There was more screeching as the car met something that slowed it down and eventually brought it to a halt.

Denton lay face down on the side of the carriage, his head resting on the cold, unbroken glass. He wanted to yell out to see who else was still conscious, but his body told him to stay still. And there, amid the debris, next to the dead soldier, Denton let time pass. He struggled to stay awake, afraid that the thudding in the back of his head might be a concussion —or something worse.

He breathed deeply, and his lungs seemed fine. He moved his hands, to find that they seemed to be responding well. He rolled over onto his back and checked his legs. Other than a pain in his left knee, they worked.

Shouts of terror broke through the other noises. Three of the prisoners were hanging by their hands in the cuffs that held them to the chairs that were now oriented on the top of the train car. He made his way in the low light, walking along the opposite windows which made his floor now, almost tripping over the soldier's body in the process. He leaned down with two fingers on his neck, frantically feeling for a pulse, but found nothing.

"Shit, help this guy, he's choking."

"Get me down," one shouted. "This dude is bleeding all over me."

"What the fuck happened?"

Denton stumbled toward the voices. "I'm coming, just hold on." He tripped over another body before he made it to the row below the prisoners. Two of them were alive. The third had a patch torn right out of his face, from his ear to his nose. Denton didn't need to check for a pulse.

"Christ, get this guy off of me," another inmate said. The body of the first was hanging up against the man who'd been sitting next to him. There was no way for the second inmate to get away from the dead man.

Denton climbed the seats until he could get to the cuffs and released the survivors, doing his best to let them down carefully. They sat where they could, and tried to regain their wits, or as much of them as possible.

Sitting next to them, Denton wiped the blood from his forehead and nose. He had no idea what kind of injuries he'd sustained and considered whether it was just adrenaline that was keeping him moving now. "Hello. Anyone else need help? Anyone else there?" He half-hoped nobody would call out. He was beginning to feel the pain in his head already, and he realized that might bode poorly for him staying mobile.

But, if no one answered, it meant he and the two prisoners might be the only ones alive in the car.

"Back here," came a man's voice.

Another followed, "Here, sir."

Denton mustered his strength and stood, ready to go in the direction of the replies. He moved a few steps toward the back, keeping his eye on the prisoners. Before he got any further, he was stopped by a noise from somewhere outside.

It was a shrill screech, almost like a woman's scream, but higher. It was an animal, he guessed, but it sounded fairly big. The guttural howl continued for almost a minute straight before fading out.

"What in the fuck was that?" A quiet voice somewhere on Denton's left asked.

He noticed one of the female prisoners hunched over and hiding, still cuffed to the seat and staring at him.

"I don't know," he said, though he had a very good idea. He unhooked the woman from the seat and helped her down. "Are you hurt?" He didn't really wait for her answer. "Go over and sit with those two." He pointed to the other prisoners.

He continued on, climbing over debris and looking for people. He stopped at the man he'd stumbled on —a private from the base— and checked him for vitals. Not finding any, he moved to find the next person in the mess. Further back, he heard stirring, and saw a soldier rising and helping another man to his feet.

Denton helped half a dozen soldiers that were well enough to stand, and two that weren't. "See if you can find a medical kit and help who you can," he told the most able-bodied among them. He found a torn duffel, pulled out a scrap of a shirt, and used it to wipe the blood from his face.

"Once we get these soldiers squared away, we need to organize a detail to keep an eye on the prisoners and make sure they get patched up." Denton moved to check on them, but there was no one there.

"What prisoners?" One of the men looked in the same direction. "How many of them survived?"

There was too much to think about. Denton's head was still spinning, and he hoped it was just his brain overloading with sensory input. "There were five of them. Right over there."

The wind buffeted the car hard enough that Denton felt it sway. Snow blew in through the far end where the prisoners had made their escape. The nearest soldier mumbled, "Good Goddamn luck to them. It'll get worse out there long before it gets better."

Denton was more troubled by the development. He hadn't had time to check which prisoners he'd gathered, so he had no idea who'd left. It only mattered in that he wanted to know how dangerous the escapees were. He immediately thought he should go after them. The idea that the elements would finish them off wasn't something he wanted to think about, not to mention that he was in charge of the prisoners. It was his ass that would be held accountable; he would have to explain all this in the near future.

His thoughts focused on the scream outside. He knew exactly what it sounded like. He'd heard it before. He hated to consider the possibility that Doctor Morley's experiments had escaped, but if the prisoners could, then why not the monsters?

There were so many variables, and Denton's head hurt. It seemed stupid to run out into the snow, especially with night approaching rapidly. He had no idea where the other cars were, or what condition they were in. Did he think they could just wander out and transport everyone back here? How would they navigate in the storm? How many people would they have to carry? How many trips would they have to make; how long before something attacked them? It might be wiser to find the doctor and Nara and find out what they were dealing with —and how to stop it.

"You okay? Denton?" the soldier with the medical kit asked.

“Yes. Sorry,” Denton said. “I just spaced out trying to wrap my mind around all this, that’s all. I swear.” He wondered how many men and women were unaccounted for out in the snow, and how many were more than likely dead in the other cars.

ADAM

When their car began to tilt, Adam grabbed Reggie and pulled her close. He'd never unbuckled, and Reggie was still sitting on her knees on the seats in front of him, leaning over the back to talk.

They both shouted as the car went on its side and slid down the side of a hill. They were spared any tumbling as the car stayed sideways, but it managed to hit trees and rocks as it went, violently jostling the car as it slid down the hill.

Adam clung on, even as luggage and people flew from the back of the car, landing in front of them, on top of them, all around. It came to a halt after what was probably only a few seconds but felt longer; like an eternity, with each scream stretched out to an absurd length. Now, as the transport came to rest, the screams died off, becoming moans and whimpers around him.

"You okay?" Adam asked. Reggie nodded.

"Good. I'm going to let go of you now, can you find something to hold on to?"

Reggie felt around, and soon Adam felt her weight supported elsewhere, so he released his white-knuckle grip on her jacket. He took a breath to clear the bad air festering in his lungs. There was smoke coming from somewhere and a low buzzing alarm was repeating in the distance. He took another deliberate breath to clear his mind, and after exhaling, he reached down to unbuckle his seatbelt. No success. It was either damaged, or his weight was still on it at an angle that kept it locked in place somehow. He tugged again, but the lever wouldn't budge.

In a moment, Reggie was standing in front of him. She stood with the wall beneath her and analyzed the buckle. "Hang on," she said. "I told you I was good with mechanical things."

"It's a seatbelt."

"Still counts. Hang on." She tugged upwards and Adam felt the restraint loosen and give way. As he was falling out of the seat, Reggie supported his arm and stopped him.

"Thanks," Adam said. He did a quick self-check to see how badly he was injured. His arms hurt from gripping Reggie so tightly, his waist ached from the seatbelt, and his jaw hurt from having clenched it so hard, but from what he could tell, he was spared any serious injury. Just a few feet away, he saw Reggie doing the same —rubbing her shoulders, moving her arms around. "Are you hurt?" he asked.

"Mostly bumps and bruises," Reggie said. "Thanks to you, I think. Thank you."

Adam noticed a few more people moving about, assisting others. "Let's see if we can help anyone else." Reggie followed as Adam made his way around the seats up toward the ceiling, which now made the wall. Here, they found belongings strewn around, and people being assisted by soldiers and anyone else who was mobile. The stench of smoke bothered him, as he couldn't determine its origin. He thought about the orientation of the train and considered the fact that the main doors were now on the top and bottom of their car which would make leaving difficult, especially with any injured. There were the connecting doors to the car behind, but he assumed they were still padlocked.

"Is everyone alright?" Adam asked. "Does anyone need help?"

Near the front, the roof of the car looked like it had been crushed by a giant fist. When the carriage had impacted something along the way, it had created a ripple effect of ridges that went twenty feet back. A number of people waved from that area and Adam climbed over to help, carefully avoiding the sharp metal edges sticking up.

One of the front door guards, Lieutenant Healy, was trying to free a civilian from two seats that had bent close together and trapped his arm. "I've tried on my own, but I just can't get the leverage to pull it apart," she said.

"If I pry it open, can you get him free?" Reggie found an armrest that had snapped off, and wedged it into the seat.

"I think that'll work," Healy said.

Positioning himself opposite Reggie, Adam grabbed one of the seats to help get it loose. "I'll pull as well."

Together, they pried the seat apart enough to pull the trapped man free. His arm was crushed just above the elbow, though the skin wasn't broken and he wasn't bleeding.

"Can you immobilize this?" Adam asked.

Private Healy nodded. "I'll need some wood or metal and something to tie them with."

"I'll find something," Reggie said.

On his feet again, Adam moved further to the front, but stopped at a noise outside. He immediately thought it was a wounded animal; something in pain, but the sound lingered, getting higher in pitch, ending with more of a growl.

Everyone froze and scanned the area as if they could find the source somewhere in the room. In the back, a group of soldiers lifting a row of seats off a casualty finished what they were doing, set the debris aside, and scrounged for their weapons.

"What the fuck …" Reggie asked, "… was that?"

Adam could feel his head shaking before he formed the words, "No damn clue." He'd spent his entire life in the wilderness—growing up in the hills of Montana, then as a guide in Saskatchewan near Black Lake, and now as a constable. He'd encountered every type of bird, badger, moose, canine, and creature the land had to offer, and that sound was nothing like anything he'd ever heard. In summer, about five years earlier, he'd been called to assist with a coyote that had gotten itself caught in a bear trap. The metal teeth of the device had slammed shut on the animal's hindquarters, and the shrill cries of pain could be heard a mile away. It was a terrible thing to hear; difficult to block out the pitiful sounds of pain, rage and fear. That was the nearest thing Adam could compare today's sound with, only today's was louder and more filled with rage. This thing sounded angry.

He thought twice about moving any closer to the front doors. They appeared to still be shut securely, but he had a bad feeling about standing too close to them. "Let's get all the casualties moved over to this side," he said, pointing to the roof. "We can figure out what we're dealing with and what kind of first aid we still need to apply. And then we can work on our next move, okay?"

The soldiers looked at each other, wanting to do it, but they each had that nagging *chain of command* light flashing in their eyes.

"You heard the man, let's move out," Private Healy's voice boomed in the car. Seeing she was a private, he assumed she was low on the chain of command, but hearing orders from someone else in a military uniform must have snapped the others out of their need for leadership, because they all moved quickly and carefully immediately after.

"Thanks," Adam whispered to Healy. She smirked and went back to working on the man's arm.

Despite his misgivings, Adam moved to the door leading to the next car. The padlocks were still secure. He scrounged in the closets and cabinets next to the doors until he found a portable first aid kit. "Heads up, Reggie," he said, tossing her the kit.

Since he'd had to leave his gun with the guards before boarding, he felt useless without a weapon. When they'd encountered the coyote in the trap, they'd put him down, dispatching it with a merciful shot as soon as they had assessed its situation. Now, with that howl outside, his hands felt empty. He'd beg one of the guards for a sidearm as soon as he could, but in the meantime, he continued digging, finding a toolbox with a hammer and screwdrivers, tape, a ratchet set and more. In a box, he found cleaning rags, paper towels, napkins and toilet paper. He took a pack of unopened cleaning rags and brought them out to each group of people working on the injured. He kept checking, finding lacerations, a few broken limbs, and a cracked tooth, but no one was dead. He was glad of that. The head wounds could turn nasty, he knew, but for now, he counted a small victory.

Reggie and Healy joined him as he surveyed the scene.

"Lieutenant Lowenstein has medical training; he's taken over with the broken arm and some of the more pressing casualties. He thinks there's a couple of concussions from the people that slammed into the walls or the seats in front of them." Healy pointed to a few men nearby, tending to bandaged patients. "But he's doing his best."

"Okay." Adam checked out the side door, which was now part of their ceiling. "No idea when —or if— anyone is coming for us, so I guess we need to figure out how to get an entryway open at some point."

"True, but most of these people aren't going anywhere —not in their condition, and not if this storm is going to hit," Reggie said. Some of the windows above her were intact, but several were cracked open and snowflakes were already streaming through.

"Just as easy to get through one of those, if we're looking for an exit, I suppose," Adam said. "But if we're staying here, we need to cover those to keep the snow out and maybe shield everyone from the cold just a little."

The three of them stared upwards for a moment, and then they each scanned for something that could provide a way up, but nothing presented itself immediately.

"I could give one of you a boost up," Healy said. "You both look to be pretty light."

Adam nodded. "Probably right. How about the two of you boost me? I think the sound we heard was just a wolf, but if there's any danger, I'd rather face it than the two of you." He heard the words come out his mouth, but couldn't suck them back in.

"Excuse me?" Reggie asked. She pointed at Healy. "You don't think maybe she's a little better off to fight off a wolf with her pistol and body armor than you are with your hammer and screwdrivers?"

"Not what I meant. Sorry it came out that way." Adam held up his hands in surrender. He didn't want to blurt out that he thought whatever was outside wasn't a wolf, but didn't mean to sound like a chauvinist. He just believed that whatever was lurking out there was going to be a lot to handle and he wanted to give the others a chance if it came to fighting something unknown. "I'm happy to go up, but I still don't know what we can use to cover those windows."

Reggie motioned to one of the injured soldiers. "You got those towels and first aid kit out of cabinets near the back —could we take the doors off and cover the windows with them? Maybe some clothing or something to fill the gaps? You could use your newfound screwdrivers and hammer to get them off their hinges."

It wasn't a sure thing, but Adam assumed it would work. The doors would be almost the right size to cover the windows, and they wouldn't need that many. "Let me take a look." He moved off toward the rear of the compartment.

"We'll see if there's something to help us get up and out of that door while you work on that." Healy nodded to Reggie and the pair started walking through the car as carefully as they could, stopping to help along the way.

MARGO

The only thing that kept Margo from losing it entirely was the sudden injection of something new into the already terrible situation. It was just enough to stop her from getting suddenly hysterical, though it should have made the situation worse. Outside, *just* outside, a shriek filled the air and cut through the cacophony of the storm. It wasn't from any of the people on her train car, certainly, and she was sure it wasn't human, but she knew that whatever it was, the thick wall of the train car was the only thing between them.

She pivoted to return to Gantz, but tripped over another soldier that lay on the ground.

"What the hell was that fucking sound?" Gantz yelled.

"I don't know." Margo felt around for a makeshift weapon. She found one of the soldiers' rifles, but had no idea how it worked, and had no chance of figuring it out in the dark. She leaned in to the soldier on the ground and whispered, "Hello? Can you hear me?" and felt for a pulse — with no luck finding one. As she rolled the soldier over, the hilt of a large knife strapped to his chest caught her eye. She unsnapped it, and gripped it tight.

There was another sound outside; the crunch of footfalls in the snow. Margo slid herself backward, trying to disappear back into the alcove, moving away from the man on the ground. A shadow fell across the dim light coming from the gaping hole in the train, a shadow that became the outline of a person approaching. Margo sighed in relief and smiled, knowing that she wouldn't have to deal with the emergency at hand on her own. "Hang in there, Bria," she said. "You too…" She stopped. Gantz had frozen in place while staring at the shadow.

Margo turned back and saw that the simple outline was larger than a man, and as it got to the hole, it was nearly as tall as the train car - maybe eight or nine feet- and wider than any man should be. She clutched the knife as if her life depended on it.

The thing raised a hand and steadied itself on the train, then moved forward, stepping into the car. It lowered its whole body in order to pass through the hole.

The shadow slowly gave way to the details of what had stepped into the train. It was covered in thick, stringy hair; the first thing Margo noticed. The hair —mainly around the feet—had snow clinging to it. By the time the ducking head was in sight, Margo wished she'd taken her chances with the rifle. The face was more akin to an ape than a man, but even the eyes and snout were obscured by hair that drifted freely from its head and its body. The only area that didn't seem to be growing hair was a wide stretch of its chest and stomach that showed what looked like a catcher's chest plate of white and gray.

There was nothing like it in Margo's memory —or even her imagination, and she couldn't help but gasp. She hoped that the winds covered the sounds as she felt her body tense with each of the creature's movements.

It came another step into the car, and the metal floor creaked under its weight. It breathed heavy sighs; sniffing the air as it walked, still hunched, a few more paces into the train car. It was alert and scanning side-to-side, never stopping, not even when it seemed to look directly into Margo's eyes. Its whole body moved when it was looking around, like its neck wasn't able to turn independently of its shoulders.

In the cold, the thing's breath unfolded into a cloud in front of it. Margo stole a glance at Gantz and Allen, who were just as stiff as she was. Their eyes were wide, jaws set silently in a potential scream.

The beast finally rested its gaze in Margo's direction and in just a couple of long strides over crushed seats and other debris, it stood just a couple of yards from her alcove. It sniffed some more —pushing another thick cloud from its nose. The thing bent down, looking into her eyes the entire time.

It was impossible for Margo to understand what she was seeing in the monster's eyes. They were reddened around the edges; more human than not, incongruous with the rest of the thing. The tiny bit of humanity kept her still, thinking she couldn't possibly be seeing this thing, this monster before her. Her mind went dark, overloaded with the sudden intrusion of unknown data. Her legs weakened and she felt herself stumble. When it finally reached out for her with one of its long arms, it could have been days or weeks later for all she could tell. The only defense she could properly raise against the beast was a scream that rose from every molecule of her being.

The scream propelled Gantz into action and he leapt onto the monster's back in an awkward attempt to tackle the thing. While he seemed like a fairly muscular man, his charge didn't move the creature. It rose slightly and swatted away, grabbing at its assailant with its long spindly arms and thick fingers. The ill-conceived attack didn't last long; Gantz wasn't able to keep a grip on the beast when it swung around, and he was sent flying a few rows back.

The monster moved to see where Gantz had gone, when the train car was suddenly lit up by a series of flashes and Margo shied away as the sound filled her immediate space. Out of the corner of her eye, she saw the other soldier, Allen, pointing her pistol at the creature and firing. It was unbearably loud in such a small space, and Margo could immediately smell the smoky discharge of the weapon. The creature shielded itself with one arm, though the shots didn't seem to have the effect Margo expected. It flinched, but there was blood.

The gunshots seemed to startle the creature more than anything. It reached blindly toward Margo, grabbing her ankle with one hand, and then snatching the other soldier on the ground with the other. It put them each under an arm and navigated its way out of the train. Margo shouted, hoarse from her screams already. She heard a call from Allen behind them, and then they were in the thick of the snowstorm, tromping through snow that was up to the beast's knees.

She was still gripping the knife in one hand, unwilling to let go of it, even unconsciously. Left without any other option, and terrified about being taken further from the car, she tried to stab the thing—first in the chest, though the knife just bounced off the strange sort of plating there. She swung at the arms and legs next, but there was no reaction. The beast slowed, only because the snow had become deeper, or the hill steeper. She looked up at the monster's face and decided that it was the only other target she could reach. She swung the knife, and it bounced off the ridge of its nose, leaving a small slice across it. It wasn't a mortal wound, but it startled the monster enough to make it notice. It stopped and dropped the soldier, but raised Margo high, grabbing her with both hands. She shouted and lashed out with the knife, but it careened off the thing's hard chest. The strikes got a reaction this time; a raw snarl that sent the stench of the beast's breath washing over Margo, and then she felt the monster's arms wrap around her in a crushing embrace that took the wind out of her. She felt the muscular arms closing tighter until she couldn't inhale. She reached up, hoping to gouge at its eyes or slice its face again; she couldn't make it that far. She grabbed at its neck instead, trying anything.

She found it had next to no neck, rather, an elongated skull, which overlapped the thick chest plate. Underneath, where the two parts met, she found a loose layer of skin. It was obvious this close, she could feel it and touch it, and it was unlike the rest of the creature's skin. Anyone shooting at the thing from a distance wouldn't have the sudden insight she did.

Her head was swimming from the monster's grip and Margo's first attempt to stab its neck was feeble, and glanced off its chin. She was seeing bright flashes of light in her vision, as she felt she might pass out. *"This is it!"* she thought. She sucked in a last breath, her chest fighting to expand. As she did, she stabbed upward, under the thing's jaw. The knife slid easily into the side of its neck, bringing a quick trickle of blood and a yelp of pain.

The result invigorated Margo and she attacked again.

DENTON

The pounding on the door startled Denton and the others. It came just as things seemed to be settling down in the car. "Hello?" There were voices outside, and the sounds of scraping as they tried to force open the door.

One of the other soldiers was doing his best to bandage Denton's cuts, but stopped as soon as the pounding began. He paused and helped five soldiers come inside; they were searching for survivors. Denton recognized them even through the heavy gear they were wearing.

Once they were settled in, he started looking for information. "You men were up front, weren't you?"

"We were stationed on the engine and the supply car behind it," Cahill said. "Barely managed to get clear in time."

"In time for what?"

Carlson answered. "We careened down this side of the hill, and both the engine and supply carriage went into the river. We only managed to get free by pulling ourselves onto some ice and running like hell across it before it cracked."

Their story painted a more desperate scenario than Denton had imagined. He'd hoped that maybe the cars were all together or at least close by, not too far apart. The idea of losing the engine completely hadn't occurred to him. "Okay. You need to give me the full sitrep. Where the hell are we? And what the hell happened?"

"We were approaching the Mackenzie Bridge. Maybe a mile out, it wasn't visible in the snowstorm. Something exploded after the supply car and we all went off the tracks. I don't know if it was an actual explosion or another avalanche like the one near the Anvil. But the cars started slamming into each other. We were on a raised hill just before the bridge and some of the cars went one way down the hill and some went down the other side. That's as far as we got," Carlson said. "We made for the nearest car we could find, and that was yours."

"What's your situation, sir?" Cahill asked.

There wasn't much to tell. Denton had gone around to the men in the back rows and found that a thick section of the back wall had been crumpled and sliced through the seats, killing the passengers instantly. Denton pointed to the prisoners. "It's bad. We're it."

"Do you have your walkie-talkie?"

Denton nodded towards the crumpled-in portion in the back. "It was in there somewhere. I can't get to it. Did any of you grab one?"

"No time," Cahill said.

Without communication gear, they had no way of knowing if anyone else was alive. "You say we were the closest car you could find to the river? So hopefully there are more that didn't go into the water."

"On this side, we didn't see or hear any go in. No telling what happened on the other side."

Denton sat down on one of the chairs and held his face in his hands. The fact that the cars were split up was bad enough, but with everyone scattered on both sides of the embankment, things were going to be that much harder. He wondered if anyone was out searching. And then it occurred to him what —and who— should have been in the car with the men. "Wait. Your car was also the command car." The other men nodded gravely, as if anticipating Denton's next question. "What about Emory, and Irwin, and the others?"

"Never saw them," Cahill said. "We got out and we waited on the riverbank, hoping someone else would come out behind us or surface once the thing sank, but they never did, least not that we saw. Emory was in the storage area with the lockbox holding everyone's phones, last time either of us saw him."

It was a barrage of bad news all at once for Denton. Not only was his commanding officer and any other superior gone, every possible long-range communications device was in a box in a sunken train car. He rubbed his head in a futile attempt to massage away the headache he'd developed.

After a moment, Carlson set his pack on the floor and sat down. "Did you all hear that howl earlier? What do you figure, a wolf or something? Sounded close."

Yet another thing for Denton to worry about. Their car seemed in good shape, with no snow streaming in, so it was a good place for them to rest and stay out of the elements, and certainly to stay out of the way of any predators.

"Yes. Sounded very close. We're going to stay put. Let's clear an area toward the front for us to set up blankets and coats, or whatever we have for the injured, and we can try to set up an area in the back to put the prisoners. We'll prepare whatever we can in case any survivors come looking for shelter or medical attention." As much as Denton felt like he needed to help others, he couldn't risk the lives of the remaining prisoners to do it. He figured that once they got set up, he'd go out on his own and start searching. But it wouldn't do any good to bring survivors back if their car wasn't able to hold them. "Carlson?" Denton pointed to the crushed back of the train. "I need you to try to get through that section and see if you can get to our walkie, and maybe a first aid kit. I know it's a mess, but do your best."

"Yes, sir." Carlson moved off.

Outside, the wind picked up and rattled the walls of the train car. Denton wondered about Doctor Morley and Nara. He thought about the monsters they had in the pods and how they might have fared in the crash.

His car would need heat—a fire. He surveyed the wreckage and the increasing pile of debris that was accumulating as the soldiers cleared room for the injured. There was plenty to burn for a fire, he figured; it would not only provide heat, but would signal to anyone else that might be struggling nearby. There was very little ventilation, though. He evaluated the ceiling, and remembering that the car was on its side, decided they could easily bust out one or two of the windows to form a vent. He grabbed the nearest able-bodied soldier who wasn't actively helping the injured. "What do you think? If we build a fire at the far end, could we form a funnel out of something? Tarps, clothes maybe? I think these cars had blankets. Whatever it takes to keep the smoke contained and heading out of the car."

The soldier nodded. "That last window would work. Poke it out easily enough. It'd put the heat mostly at the one end, though."

"It'll be better than nothing," Denton said. "I'm putting you in charge of that. Take whatever you need and make it happen."

Denton walked through the car, checking up on the activity. The injured were getting the care that they needed; the car was being organized. He knew he was needed here, but he couldn't help but worry about all the other people out there that he could be helping. How many were out there, cold and alone, possibly dying in the snow? He'd been in combat situations overseas and his priorities were always spelled out for him on every mission. Now, he was torn. He was supposed to protect the people, and he was supposed to guard the experiments. How could he do any of that, with those elements scattered so far apart?

He got to the end of the car, leaned against the wall and stared at the door, weighing options and listening to the howl of the wind. Mostly, he thought of Nara out there fighting for her life against the elements and those beasts, those damned rugaru.

MARGO

Margo kept stabbing at the fleshy area around the neck until the beast dropped her. It howled in pain and swatted wildly around with long hairy arms. She scrambled backwards, sliding through the snow and flailing on her hands and feet, grasping the knife as tightly as possible, when she ran into a large rock. She stopped and held out the knife in front of her, ready to slash at the beast. Through the flying snow, she could barely make out the monster, though she'd moved backward only a few yards. She could see it reach down and grab the soldier and sling him over its shoulder with ease as it roared.

Over the din of the storm, she could hear loud footfalls, crushing the thick snow as they went. The sound faded into the distance as the monster vanished from Margo's sight. She pulled herself closer to the rock she'd run into, trying to use it as cover, slashing at the air when she thought she heard something through the curtain of white. She was shaking in the cold; she was shaking from fear.

"Hello?" A voice shouted from uphill, in the direction of the train car. "Jesus Christ, lady, are you there?" She thought it might be Gantz but she didn't want to take her eyes off the storm in front of her. And she certainly hated to yell for fear of attracting that thing again. She realized, though, that Gantz was shouting, and if that thing could hear him it might come back. Or worse, there might be more than one.

Like coming out of a freeze, she turned slowly and assessed the obstacles to getting back into the car: rocks, and twisted metal train parts. She mapped her route in her mind.

It wasn't an easy climb. A thin layer of snow slid off her sleeve and she could see how quickly it was accumulating. It was a choice of staying out here and freezing, possibly being attacked again, or heading back and risking another attack there.

Margo gathered herself and moved toward the car, driven by the fear of the cold and the terror that continued to swell. She could still smell that thing. Something about its stench reminded her of spoiled milk or rotten eggs—something she'd left in the fridge too long. The odor was almost overpowering now, although she'd hardly registered it while the thing was crushing her.

She crawled along as quietly as she could. Once she felt good about her footing, she started to run, falling after the first few steps, but then, finding her stride, she went on ahead, climbing upward, —pushing through the drifts that were nearly up to her waist in some spots.

"Hello?"

She heard it again but refused to give herself away. She wasn't sure who —or what—was calling.

The sulfur stench that Margo thought was just a memory of the attack became stronger and it spurred her on even faster, cutting through the snow like a city snowplow. This was a different smell altogether. It was close. And it seemed to suggest her fear was well-founded.

She saw the outline of the car, and the shape of Gantz before it.

"There's more than one of them. Get inside," Margo said. "Run." She climbed over the snow, pushed Gantz, and when he didn't move quickly enough, ran past him and pulled herself over the jagged tear in the wall. "Get in here," she shouted, but he stood looking into the white, his rifle raised. There was another roar outside; closer now, angry, snarling. Loud.

"Get…" She stopped when she heard a scream—a man's. It was Gantz, and Margo could no longer see his form. "Get in here." She ran back toward the gap in the car but stopped a few feet away. It had gone silent outside and Gantz, who'd been at the gap moments ago, was gone. On the ground, in his place, was his weapon.

It took just a moment for Margo to decide not to risk going for the gun. She fumbled through the dark again and found Allen and Bria at the rear door of the car. In a minute, she found a pistol on an injured soldier and pulled it from the holster. She moved around the corner to the floor next to Bria. She reached out and held her friend's hand. She could feel the injured woman's chest rising and falling. "We'll get out of here. I just need to think. I'll figure it out."

Allen slid down off the chair and wedged herself next to Bria. "What the ever-loving fuck was that?" She didn't sound frightened to Margo, just confused.

"I don't know." Margo shook her head minutely. She found her coat was drenched in blood; she hoped it wasn't hers. She wiped her hands on her pants, shivering so hard that she didn't want to even consider opening her coat to check for wounds as she wiped her hands on her pants, trying to get some of the blood off.

They both stared at the gap and watched the snow start to pile up inside the car. It was obvious that they'd need to do something; whether they needed to move to the back to get away from the hole, try to cover it, or move somewhere new. Although Margo knew very little about medicine or first aid, she was sure that Bria was in no shape to travel. It seemed like a long shot that they should even take her as far as the back of the train.

"Help!"

Margo heard the words drift weakly from the back of the car. She looked through the hole in the train, to see if anything outside had reacted to the noise.

"Please."

Margo and Allen exchanged a questioning glance. They hadn't heard any other voices since they'd crashed.

As quietly as she could, Margo moved toward the voice; it was tough climbing over seats and stepping around debris. The voice mumbled again, and she followed the sound to a tangle of seats that had accumulated on one side. She pulled aside some gear and found Frank in his thick winter parka, pinned against the wall by a broken wall panel.

"Shit, Frank." Of all the people to survive the crash, Frank was not the first person she'd expected, or really hoped for. "I didn't know you were even still in the car."

He didn't respond; rather, he glanced at the metal that protruded from his coat and appeared to have him pinned.

"Don't try to move," Margo said. "Let me look at it." She noticed she was gripping the knife in her left hand and realized she must have picked it up again when she heard Frank's voice. She took a second and placed it gently on a nearby seat cushion. She slowly followed the twisted piece of metal, careful not to move it for fear of making matters worse. "I'll get you out of this."

"I think it's through my lungs. I can't breathe." Frank sounded pathetic in his pain.

"Hold still." Margo looked at the hole in the train car behind them, thinking she heard something move. When nothing came, she focused on Frank.

"Oh, Jesus, get me out of this."

"Shhh." Margo found where the metal went into the jacket and tried to follow it into the down, but it was too thick. She slowly pulled the zipper of the jacket down to the waist and positioned herself so she could see under it. She was surprised to find the piece of metal took a sharp turn, and rather than going straight through his body, it glanced off at an angle. The thick heavy parka held the scrap in place, and it had barely nicked his side. "Hold on, Frank, maybe I can pull this out."

"What? No!"

They stared at each other, and Margo let go of the metal. Her hands were shaking. She sat back and took a breath. "What should we do, Frank? We can't leave you stuck to this train. We're going to have to move at some point."

"It doesn't have to be now." Frank's eyes filled with tears. "Does it? Oh Christ, help me out of this."

"You asked *me* for help."

Frank moved slightly and sucked in a gulp of air. "That was before…"

"Before what? Before you knew it was me?"

A cough made Frank's whole body tense up as it moved the metal and brought a new grimace to his face. "No, no. It was before I knew how bad this was. I'm afraid."

Margo knew she had to get him out, or they'd all be stuck in that car, with no escape from that thing. "You're bleeding." Under Frank's coat she found a light trickle of red. "Not too bad. But it could get worse."

"Yes. If you pull the metal bar out," Frank said. "Christ, if I get out of this, I'll never drink again, I swear."

Margo sighed. "What are you talking about?"

Frank started to well up. "That's why I missed the train in the first place. I wasn't on some training session, I'd come out to my buddy's cabin and we all got blasted. I wandered off to pee in the woods and just kept going. They all just left me."

Allen sighed. "Really? That's what you were doing out there?"

It didn't make any difference to Margo; she still had to get him out of the situation. She could make him feel guilty later.

She knew basic first aid, but that was it. Her instincts told her to pull the piece out, and then stitch up the entry and exit wounds, but she wasn't sure if she could do it. "Sit tight for a minute, and don't panic. I want to find the medical kit."

"Wait. Don't go. I don't want to be back here alone again." Frank reached for her, but the pain made him stop. "Please."

"I have to check on the others. I'll be right back." Margo picked up her knife and walked back to the other end of the car. In her mind, now, she considered the knife her own, rather than one of the soldier's. She guessed it didn't really matter, but it was odd to her how quickly her mind shifted in the situation.

The first aid kit was on the floor next to Bria. "Margo?" Bria's eyes opened. "Margo, is that you?"

Margo stopped and leaned down. "Yes. It's me."

"Are we getting out of here soon?"

The wind picked up again outside, buffeting the car. "I don't know, Bria. I'm still figuring things out." She sighed. If Frank's injuries were a stretch for Margo's skills, Bria's would be a leap. "Is there anything I can get…"

A squelch of static stopped Margo's questions. It was muffled and brief, but she was confident that she'd heard it with a voice this time, though the words were garbled. She opened a small storage door, and then another, until the sound brought her to a small case behind the back of a third. Inside: a small, yellow walkie-talkie. She held down an orange button. "Mayday, this is Margo Hawkins. I'm with the NyCroft scientific expedition. We're on board a train stuck in the snow. We have a number of casualties; no idea about the status of the passengers in the other cars. We need help."

"That's a hell of a lot to say," Allen said. "You need to be a little more succinct."

Margo let go of the button. "Thanks. I got this."

"Also, that thing is pretty small. I'm guessing it doesn't have much more range than a couple of miles, tops. This storm won't help reception, either. Whoever that is, they're probably not far away."

It had to be one of the other crash victims. "You're calling out to the world, Margo, when you'll be lucky to get the nearest train car. Talk to *them*."

With a deep breath, Margo tried again. "Anyone out there? This is Margo Hawkins." She stopped and waited. "Margo Hawkins calling — anyone copy?" She waited. "Nothing."

"Maybe you need higher ground or something. Bundle up and go outside, maybe climb up to the roof."

"Whoa," Margo said. "We can't go out there. Forget it." In that moment, she would rather sit there and freeze than head outside.

"Look, I know you're scared," Allen said. "I am too, but Bria isn't going to make it unless we get help."

"You know I'm scared? Are you fucking kidding me? You weren't nearly carried off by that fucking thing that attacked me." There was nothing Margo could do to steel herself to go out again. Not even the threat of freezing to death, or the plight of her friend.

ADAM

"I heard it, but couldn't respond," Adam said. Healy had pulled out the walkie-talkie after her excursion onto the top of the train car, and they'd tried to reach others to no avail.

"When I was up top, I couldn't see much, couldn't even see an outline of one of the other cars out there; could be we're out of range," Healy said.

"They'd have to be pretty far away, wouldn't they?"

Even in the mess of the weather, they should get a mile's worth of reception, Adam guessed. "They could be right under our noses and we wouldn't know. I hate to say it, but we're going to have to go out there and find the other cars. Maybe get our people into another coach or bring others here. If *we* need help, I'm sure there are others out there in worse shape."

"Copy that. And with night coming on, visibility will only get worse. If that's possible." Healy started up the rows, checking which soldiers were able and who needed to stay behind. Most of the troops were helping their comrades; bandaging their wounds, reassuring them, moving debris. She returned minutes later with three soldiers and some extra guns. "Here." She handed one of the rifles to Adam. "Know how to work one of these?"

"I'm familiar," he said.

"Excellent. I'm leaving a number of armed men here to look after everyone, and these three will come with us, if that sounds right to you, Constable," Healy said.

"Whoa. What about me?" It was Reggie. "My damn sister is out there somewhere. I need to get to her."

Healy gave her a quick sizing-up. "You don't have the survival or weapons training."

"I've been on more of these cold-weather science bullshit things than I've had birthdays, and they make me go through their fucking training every few years, since I'm not one of their university nerds and they need to do it for insurance or something," Reggie said. "And didn't you just say the howls we heard were only wolves? If you're worried about me handling guns, don't give me one. I don't want one. I would suggest the five of you badasses can handle some wolves with your automatic weapons."

Everyone in the little group raised their heads to look at Healy and Adam.

"I'm good with it." Adam was the first to speak.

"I'm not going to waste time debating this. If you can't keep up, we can't slow down," Healy said. "Copy?"

"Crystal clear."

They'd rigged up a rope ladder to the entry above them when Healy had come down earlier, making it less challenging to get up there, although still an exercise in upper arm strength. Healy went first and secured the roof with one of the soldiers, then Adam and Reggie, and the others.

The snow was thick on the roof, nearly half a foot already, by Adam's estimate. He did notice that the wind had lessened some, allowing for a little better visibility. He watched the soldiers spread out and begin scanning the area for the other cars. From that vantage point, Adam pieced together what had happened and why communications might be difficult. To the East was a massive hill with train tracks on top. Once they'd crashed, the cars rolled or slid down the side of the hill to lower ground. He scanned the area, trying to find cars to count, but didn't see any. He wondered if any of the cars had crashed on the other side of the hill.

"I've got an outline of something boxy to the north. Could be a car," one of the soldiers said. He pointed off in the distance and the others carefully made their way alongside him.

"I don't see anything," Reggie said. She ducked and tried to see from another angle.

It was there. Adam could see it; or rather he could see the absence of light, blowing snow around this darker void. "To the left of that tree." He pointed for Reggie's benefit.

"Still nothing," she replied.

"Let's move out. We can get over there while there's a lull in the storm," Healy said. She led the way, carefully finding a way down from what was the top of the train now, working her way out onto the wheels, and using their axles for hand holds. The other soldiers knelt, covering the area around them with their rifles. As soon as she touched ground, the next soldier made his way.

"Are they this fucking worried about wolves?" Reggie leaned close to Adam for secrecy.

It was a fair question, but he supposed that with the train having been derailed by an unknown source, they were treating it as a possible attack. It made sense, but Adam assumed it was just as likely that the weather had caused the crash.

DENTON

CONGO RIVER REGION - SEVEN YEARS EARLIER

The beast's jaws clamped down on Hammond's left leg and he screeched in pain. With a firm grip, the thing began to drag the terrified man back into the water.

"Sir?" Denton asked. His captain, Brewer, didn't respond. He was standing a dozen or so feet from Hammond, entranced by what he saw.

The monster wasn't something Denton understood, or *wanted* to understand; he only wanted to see it gone, and if shooting might make that happen, he was happy to try it. "Fire," he said. He raised his assault rifle and shot at the massive rock-like body, careful to avoid the head and mouth that was holding Hammond. He watched his initial barrage ping off the monster's hide and fall into the river. Maybe the rifle fire managed to rouse some reaction from the soldiers other than fear, but it was then that Denton heard more weapons firing nearby. The rest of the squad didn't seem as discerning as he had been. Their shots hit the thing's head, once it sustained a shot in the eye.

With a quick turn it dunked its head underwater, taking Hammond with it. A couple of the men continued to shoot at the stony grey hide that remained above the surface as the head and a good portion of the neck slid out of sight. Their random shots continued until they'd emptied their clips and had to stop to reload. Their nearest teammates reached out to stop them from continuing to fire everything they had.

"Nothing can hurt that hide. What should we do, sir?" a corporal asked. Denton didn't know him, and couldn't see his name tag.

"I don't…" Brewer stammered.

"How the hell do we get Hammond back?" The corporal spoke up again.

Denton stepped into the water and continued until it was almost up to his knees. He stopped when it occurred to him that they *weren't* getting Hammond back. Judging from the bones they'd found in the river, he assumed the creature either drowned its victims, or devoured them under the water. Either way, standing in so much water probably wasn't good for his own health. He found another soldier who'd wandered into the river and pulled him toward the abandoned buildings. "Fall back. Do it now, while it's occupied."

"What?" the corporal asked. "But we need to get Hammond." He moved up, charging into the water even deeper than Denton.

"Get out of the water," Denton said, dragging the soldier to safety. When they reached Captain Brewer, they stopped. "Captain? We can't stay here. We need to move out." Brewer looked at him as if he'd gone mad.

"We need to finish this mission. There's a terrorist cell around here that we need to eliminate." Brewer's eyes seemed to dart from object to object, not focusing on one thing for more than a second.

"Sir, we need to get out of here. The cell is gone." Denton pointed to the mound in the middle of the river. "THAT thing killed it. We need to call in an extraction."

Next to them, the soldier he'd pulled along began shooting his pistol. Denton saw the monster's head emerge from the water, bloody eyes locked on the nearest man. Brewer acted as if it were nothing. Denton grabbed the man's radio and ran for the scattering of buildings, making his way to the one furthest from the monster. He leaned against the wall and sat down.

He took a deep breath and held the radio up to his mouth before realizing he didn't know what to say. A message about a giant monster would likely slow a response while command asked a lot of questions and probably doubted his sanity. "Bloodhound-Three to Elevator, request immediate extraction. Coordinates to follow."

"Negative, Bloodhound-Three. Extraction denied. Your last location shows *restricted*."

The group was certainly in an area they were not authorized to be operating in, but that was kind of the point. If the military asked the local and national governments for permission, odds were the cell would have left long ago, tipped off by a paid siren in some office somewhere. "Elevator. This is Bloodhound-Three. We have suffered one casualty and…" Denton peered around the corner of the hut, to see the creature had advanced closer to the shore, and that more of the soldiers had dispersed to cover. The gunfire had slowed, likely because the men were running low on ammo, or they realized the futility of their actions, "...and we are in a firefight with an unknown hostile." He couldn't think of a better way to describe what he was seeing—unknown, and definitely hostile.

"Negative, Bloodhound-Three. Proceed to designated extraction zone." The radio squelched and Denton thought about what else could get a HELO to their location.

Nearby, one of the huts disintegrated as the monster shoved its head into it, and then extracted another soldier with its teeth. As wood and plastic debris fell from the beast's head, the man struggled and beat at the thing, desperate to get out of its grip. His screams ended in a horrifying gurgle as Denton ran behind the next structure.

From his new vantage point, Denton could see Captain Brewer standing partially behind cover. He still had a faraway look as he tried to focus on the monster devouring his men. He didn't want to shout and give away his position, but neither did he want to see the captain end up at the bottom of the river.

DENTON

With the thoughts of the Congo still on his mind, Denton stood up. He couldn't bear to stand by and watch as others faced danger. "Change of plan. I'm going to go out and see if I can locate anyone else. We can set this area up as a field hospital for the injured, and a safe place for any military to fall back to."

Denton picked up his rifle and checked the ammo, then checked the rest of his equipment. It was the report from Carlson that their injured parties were in a stable condition for now, that convinced him that he needed to go out. That, and the fact that the fire was working well. Smoke streamed out of the car, through a section of the windows, keeping it clear. Those were the reasons he could give someone if they asked why he'd abandoned the men, anyway. He wouldn't mention monsters to his superiors, at least not the ones who weren't cleared.

"You think that's wise? Going out alone? It's going to be dark in an hour," Carlson asked.

"Can't see anything now, really."

Carlson nodded. "True, but what if those animals we heard weren't the only ones out there? What if there's some that are nocturnal and looking for food for energy in the cold?"

Denton didn't reply, but his answer would have been no. If all of the cars had detached, then the two doctors would be trapped on their own in the storm. They'd be alone with their deadly cargo in those pods, and he didn't like the sound of that. "I count five prisoners on the run. We need to get them back." He knew that was probably even more reason to bring more troops along, but he wasn't about to risk anyone else to hunt down Morley's experiments in the storm.

He pulled down his face mask, cinched his hood tight, and pushed his way out.

The wind whipped at his face mask and pushed back at him with every step. Visibility had dropped to only a few feet and the snow had begun to fall in earnest, heralding the worst part of the storm. He'd left the car and started climbing upward, trying to get back to the top of the hill, where the tracks were. He stayed as close to the steep incline as he could, trying to put something between him and the worst of the winds, though he had little luck.

Ahead, he saw a large dark shape that grew larger as he approached it. He brought his gun up and continued to close the distance. He guessed it wasn't a creature, since the sheer size of the outline grew to ridiculous dimensions as he got closer.

He wondered if it was another car until the shape took better definition close up. It was a small grouping of pine trees in the side of the hill, one side coated in inches of precipitation, the other still showing some green-laden branches.

Denton stopped in the lee of the pines, letting them block the storm so he could rest. As he sat there, in the oddly shallow snow, he noticed some footprints that hadn't quite been snowed over. They led, as near as he could tell, into the trees. He pulled himself along slowly, with his gun once again raised, careful not to snap any branches or make any unnecessary noise as he went.

The tracks went further into the calm realm of the pines, and suddenly, one set of tracks split into two, then three. Denton knelt and examined them. They were definitely made by boots, not an animal. All three tracks were identical in their tread, but the sizes were different. One was smaller than the others by a decent margin. He surmised that if they were all identically-branded boots, they could belong to either prisoners or soldiers. And these didn't look like standard issue military survival boots; they looked cheap. He raised the rifle and swept through the trees again, following the tracks into a pine with thick hanging branches.

A voice came from inside the canopy of branches. "Don't shoot us! We didn't take any guns. We don't have any guns." It was a female voice, barely able to speak. She sounded like her whole body was shivering.

Denton wasn't convinced. "How many of you are in there?"

"Two," she said.

"Two?"

"Yes. Well, three, but the other guy is dead. Does he count?"

Denton ignored the question. "I'm coming into these branches. If I see anyone with a weapon, I'll shoot," he said. "Is that clear?"

Two voices confirmed their understanding. This time it was a man *and* a woman.

Denton kept the rifle in one hand and pushed away the foliage with the other. Beyond, branches heavy with snow and ice hung low, making what amounted to a small room at the base of the tree. Inside, two prisoners wearing orange ski caps were huddled under layers of coats, while another man lay nearby, unmoving, and wearing just an orange prison issue jumpsuit and boots.

"He was hurt in the crash. He made it here on his own, but he fell down when we got here. And wouldn't get up," the woman said.

The man nodded. "We tried to help him."

The man was nearly blue already, and didn't have the inclination to argue with them, or the ability to dispute anything they were saying.

Denton considered how long it had been since the crash, and how long the prisoners had been out in the cold in light gear. It had to have been hours. "Neither of you are armed?"

"No," the woman said.

"We counted five prisoners escaped from the train. Where are the other two?" Denton scanned for more tracks.

"There were a couple that took off when we did. They snatched jackets from some guards and ran up the hill," the woman said. "No clue where they went from there."

"Now, *they* had guns. They picked them up when they took the jackets."

It wasn't good news. Denton wondered how far the other two had got, and where they might be headed. He recognized the two prisoners before him, but without a manifest, he had no clue who they were. "What're your names?"

"Hall, Trudy Hall."

"I'm Tony Cook," the man stuttered.

"Okay. Let's chalk this little escape attempt up to bad decision-making and get you back to the car before this shit gets any worse." This certainly wasn't the way Denton had hoped things would go. He assumed the prisoners would be long gone, and he'd be able to keep looking for the cars with Morley and Nara and whatever they were transporting. He thought about the other man, half-frozen in the snow and decided he couldn't bring himself to leave him there.

He leaned down and rolled the prisoner over, finding frozen blood all over his chest and abdomen. A huge tear cut across the man's jacket. The tag on his overalls gave his prisoner number but not his name. "Looks like he must have been hit in the chest during the crash. It's bad; I'm surprised he made it this far."

"He seemed pretty goddamned determined," Hall said.

Bowers nodded in agreement. "Said something about the charges he was going down for when we got to the states." He watched Denton move the body and start to lift it. "You're not going to try to carry him back, are you? That's nuts. Listen to that wind out there. There's no way we'll make it with you carrying him. We'll all die."

"You think we should leave him here?"

"He's not going anywhere. When the storm ends, he'll be right here where we leave him," Bowers said.

The prisoner was right on both accounts, and Denton knew it. They weren't dressed to survive the cold and would likely die quickly. He wondered if maybe there was another train car closer than the one he'd just left. *Was there another just around the trees?* Could it be that simple?

"You two bundle up. I'm going to scout around to the other side of these trees and see if there's another car closer than the one we came from. Make sure you get as much of your faces covered as you can. Hands, too." The nearby trees crackled and their branches began to snap. Denton feared the trees were collapsing under the weight of the snow, but as he turned, he discovered the situation was much worse than that.

Thick branches snapped and fell as one of the giant grey beasts came crashing toward them, not slowed in the least by the prickly impediments. Denton only got a quick glimpse before he reached back and tried to move his rifle into firing position. It was definitely tall and wiry, dark gray-white from both the snow and the thick hair that covered it. Denton couldn't remember which one of the mountain peaks Nara had named it after.

He stumbled back from the dead prisoner. A rumbling growl caught the air and filled his ears. The rugaru closed to within ten feet of the trio before reaching out with one far-too-long arm and grabbing the dead prisoner. Once it had him, it leaned closer to Denton and the others, sniffing and growling.

Denton raised his rifle and pointed it at the thing that loomed before him. He noticed, even before he shot, that the hair around one side of its neck was already matted with blood—possibly an injury from the crash. Another crackling snarl spurred him to fire, aiming directly at the monster's neck, but nothing happened when he pulled the trigger. He tried again, only to be met with another empty click. He'd checked the weapon before he left, and it had been fully loaded.

With no time to resolve the problem, he stepped back and switched the position of the rifle so that he could use the stock as a bludgeon.

After the long growl was done, the beast leapt off through the branches. Through the stinging snow, Denton saw it jump one more time, headed in the general direction of his train car.

The three of them stood staring into the white wall of twisting, swirling snow.

ADAM

The group moved forward, led by Healy and the other soldier, staying in the order in which they'd left the train. Adam kept the rifle they'd given him slack around his neck, but the soldiers moved in formation, with their weapons up and ready to fire, should anything go wrong. They had trouble communicating, even though the snow had slowed and the wind had died down; it still required them to yell if they wanted to be heard. Otherwise, the soldiers used hand signals to give each other information. That didn't help Adam or Reggie, unfortunately.

They passed a group of trees, pines covered with inches of snow. For Adam, the going was tough, with the snow reaching over his knees in some places. He'd learned a long time ago to get taller boots than normal. In his line of work, he'd trudged through pretty high drifts to chase down criminals, and he knew the dangers of frostbite. It appeared that Reggie was protected as well. For all her complaints about having to go through refresher survival training, it seemed like something had been drilled into her head.

The leaders stopped and motioned for everyone to do the same, then one of the soldiers from the back went forward and conferred with them. The one behind them stayed alert and scanned the area behind them.

The three in the lead knelt and Healy pointed to an area to the right of the train car they were trying to reach. Adam followed the direction, and concentrated, trying to make out what they might be scrutinizing. Visibility was good at the moment but all he could see was snow, snow, and more snow. He took another look at the hill that the train had tumbled down and found it was steeper than he'd guessed.

"What're we stopping for?" It was hard to understand Reggie through her face mask and hood. "It's goddamn freezing when we stop moving for too long."

Adam let her follow his gaze, saving his breath.

In a minute, the soldier came back and talked to the ones left out of the conversation. Close up, Adam recognized him as a soldier named Pratt; he'd met him as he joined the group earlier. "We think we can see something off near the base of the ridge we came down. Could be just wolves, could be rocks, could be nothing but our eyes playing tricks on us. But I'm going to go check it out. I'll circle around to the right and flank whatever it is."

"Careful," Adam said. Even if it was 'just wolves,' those could be just as deadly as anything, if one wasn't prepared for them. "Need help?"

"No, orders are for you to keep on course and get to that next train car," the soldier said. He nodded to the other and moved out into the white world alone. Adam followed his progress for a while, until Healy motioned them all ahead.

"Can we just keep going?" Reggie shouted. "I'm freezing my ass off here."

"Patience." Out of the corner of his eye, Adam continued to watch the soldier. Soon they were at the next train car, though it was hard to tell what it was if you weren't looking for it. The snow had hit it hard enough from one side that it formed a thick drift up to the roof. They moved around to find the car correctly oriented with the wheels on the bottom.

Healy and her partner rounded the side of the train and stopped, motioning for everyone else to do the same.

Reggie sighed and watched the soldier behind her move up with the others. "Lot of stopping and starting here. Let's go."

"Patience." Adam was as curious as Reggie was cold. Why weren't they moving closer to the car to get a little shielding from the wind that was still blowing, even if the precipitation had taken a break?

When the other soldier caught up, he raised his rifle and pointed it at the unseen side of the coach, and they moved off, all disappearing from sight around the corner.

"What the fuck? They're just leaving us here?" Reggie stepped closer to the others.

"Wait a minute," Adam said. "There could be a problem over there."

"A problem that isn't over *here*?" The woman moved with purpose, and Adam quickly fell in beside her, rifle at the ready. As they came around the corner, they found the three soldiers standing around a hole in the side of the car. It began as a wide slice, maybe a foot across, and gradually got bigger as the car went along, until the far end of it was torn completely open. Healy was a step or two inside the opening, scanning with her rifle.

The other two moved in behind, so Adam stood where he was, watching their backs and keeping an eye out for wolves or other animals that might come from elsewhere looking for shelter. He squinted off in the distance to where Pratt had disappeared to check the movement near some trees, but Adam couldn't locate him.

A low whistle brought his attention back to the car, and he found Healy nodding for he and Reggie to join her. As they got in, another soldier, Lund, moved to a position beside the door and started keeping watch.

Despite a gaping hole in the side of the car, it was warmer inside, if only slightly, but it was noticeable. Healy motioned them forward again, more urgently. She'd pulled down her coverings and raised her goggles.

Moving into the car, Adam found what had the soldiers spooked. Not only was the whole left side of the car damaged from the crash, but so was the majority of the seating on that side, likely for the same reason. Further in, however, was more of a mystery.

The chairs there were torn more haphazardly, and Adam wondered if the passengers had done it in an effort to help the injured or free someone who was trapped. As the thought hit him, he looked around for people. "Where is everyone?"

"That's the question," Healy said. "We've found blood, but none of our people."

"How many were here?" Adam found some of the blood on the seats, but most of the floor and chairs were covered in snow.

"This was mostly a staff car. The paperwork is buried somewhere in this snow. I'd guess twenty."

"That's a lot of people to just vanish." Adam knelt beside one of the seats on the left side. The cushion was torn in three places. He guessed it appeared a lot like an animal had done it, clawed it clear through, but the marks were too big to belong to a wolf, and the pattern would be all wrong.

"We saw that too," Healy said. "Wolf? Wild dog?"

"I don't think so." There was hair embedded in the foam of the chair back. Adam took his glove off and pulled it free. He held it up to whatever light he could get from the outside, and figured the follicle was white, and fairly long. "I suppose this could belong to a wolf, but it doesn't seem like it."

"What else could it be?" Reggie asked. "I mean, it isn't a rabbit or a fox, right? So it has to be a wolf, right?"

Adam shrugged. "I couldn't tell you without analyzing it in a lab."

"If it attacked any of these people, what other options could we have?" Healy examined the room again.

"Look," Adam said. "We don't know if anything attacked anyone. All the people are gone from here. It's unlikely one animal attacked them all, and carried them all off. For all we know, those marks are from something that broke loose in the crash and tore the seat in a weird pattern. The hair could be human, or it could be something from inside the padding of the chair." Adam rose and pointed outside. "And I'm guessing that any tracks, human or otherwise, are now covered by snow. My guess is, these people decided they couldn't risk the elements with the storm, gathered up the injured, and set off to find somewhere a little safer and headed out. They might be in another train car right now."

Healy pointed out into the snow-covered landscape at the hill nearby. "That would be hard to climb if you were dragging or carrying the wounded. If they set out, they're likely still down here."

"*If* they set out," Reggie said.

"Let's not get too pessimistic just yet," Healy said.

It seemed like Reggie had a rebuttal for a second, but instead she changed the subject. "Hey, did they have a walkie-talkie like we did? And did you check to see if it's still there?"

One of the soldiers started to the back and opened the corresponding closet, and seconds later held up a small yellow device. "Still here."

"So what does that mean? Did they forget about it?" Adam asked. He knew it was unlikely that would happen. "Were they in a hurry to get out and didn't take the time to grab it?"

"Could be broken," Reggie said.

The soldier handed the device to Healy and she checked it before putting it up to her mouth. "This is Healy calling Lowenstein. Can you hear me? Over."

A scratchy voice came back. "This is Lowenstein. Have you found the others? What's the situation? Over."

At the very least they were able to raise the survivors in the car they'd just left. That at least proved that both devices were working. "They left quickly, maybe the guards that knew about the walkie-talkies were incapacitated," Healy said.

"Yeah." Adam looked around for any other possible clues. He was used to tracking animals back home when he was a kid; he'd learned to hunt by following hair, scat, prints, and sometimes a prey's unique scent. As he entered law enforcement, he honed his people-tracking skills by identifying footwear and shoe size. Over the years, he'd accounted himself a fair judge of signs, and people called him a good tracker. For him, it was knowing the surroundings —knowing what was *supposed* to be there and what was out of place. Was a branch broken? Were the weeds trampled? Had tree bark been gnawed on? But this situation was different. It wasn't a place he'd been before, so it was hard to know what was there that shouldn't be.

He regarded the slope all the way up to the top. There were high drifts and a few ridges visible. Any real evidence of passage was erased by nature. There was snow everywhere.

In the car, Adam was careful where he stepped, afraid to disturb it, like any crime scene he'd come across as an officer of the law. He didn't step in the blood that had frozen to the floor; he didn't touch the overturned packs. Each move was a sidestep, an exercise in avoiding something that might be important later.

He stopped at a broken railing near the door. Its sharp edges were coated in blood, another edge that had caught some soldier in the crash, but as he leaned closer, he found another hair; this one, long and white. "Did you say this car was mostly officers?"

"Yes, sir. And staff. Why do you ask?" Healy moved closer as she answered.

With the tip of his ungloved pinky finger, Adam pointed to the hairs that were stuck in the blood. "Any of your officers have long grey hair?" Healy leaned closer and examined it again from a different angle.

"Could it be an animal? A wolf?" Healy asked.

It was a question he'd been running through his mind since he first saw it. "I don't know. I guess if it's a big enough wolf, sure. But it's different than the other one we found. Different colors, different length." He didn't know how much he wanted to speculate on the origins of the hairs, but he figured it was best to get it out in the open. "I don't think it is, though." That got Reggie's attention, and she moved closer to see what had everyone's eye.

"Why not?" Healy folded her arms and lowered her voice. "I don't want to panic everyone."

"Look, I don't want to panic anyone, either. I'm just being realistic," Adam said. "There are bloodstains on the floor. If there was a pack of wolves, I think we'd see all kinds of paw prints in the blood. I bet it's still sticky, even as cold as it is. If it was a lone wolf, I don't see how it would have dragged that many people away. I think it would have taken what it could and holed up somewhere warm and safe."

Reggie appeared uneasy, but Healy wasn't convinced. "So, the troops left and a wolf showed up after. There's an explanation."

With a calming wave, Adam stepped away with his thoughts, not wanting to alienate himself from the military. He continued through the debris, replacing his gloves to fight the cold. There was nothing among the wreckage that pointed to anything other than people injured in a crash—until he got to the very back. As careful as he was, he still felt his boots stick to a particular part of the floor, which suggested he'd found some more blood. He glanced at the snow near his feet. Bending down, he carefully wiped it away until he could see the blood, still flecked with white. As he moved the snow, he found his was not the only footprint in the red pool.

"Over here," he said. "Careful."

Healy came to check, with Reggie trailing close behind. They both stooped to see what Adam was pointing to this time. "A footprint?" Healy asked. "That's to be expected."

"Look closer. This print is barefoot." Adam pointed to the top of the print.

It seemed to confound Healy for a moment before logic kicked in. "A soldier lost a boot in the crash. Not hard to explain."

It would've been Adam's explanation as well, if it wasn't for one additional piece of information. "Healy, look at the print in relation to my hand. It's almost three times as big. Do you have any officers with feet that big?"

"I don't understand. What in the fuck are you talking about?" Reggie sounded baffled. "Do you think some giant came in and took these people?" She smiled at Adam. "That's crazy. Right?"

There wasn't much Adam could say, he wasn't sure what it was they were looking at. Long hair, a big footprint.

Reggie's smile faded when she saw Adam's sullen expression. She turned quickly, "Hey, what happened to the other guy? The one who went to check out the thing outside?" She cleared her throat. "If we're worried about something attacking people, maybe he's found the culprit. Hopefully it's an oversized raccoon or some other simple, fucking explanation."

The soldier on watch gave her a glance, then Healy. "He went behind those trees a couple of minutes ago. Haven't seen him since." When Reggie gave him a dirty look, he said "What? It's been two minutes, for crying out loud."

With a quick jab, Healy pointed at the two soldiers. "You two, go back him up —but stay in our line of sight. The three of us are going to get to see what we can see on top of this thing. With any luck, we'll find another car. This one isn't going to help us when the storm kicks up. We'll join you when we're done. Move it out."

"Copy," the soldiers said, readjusting their covers as they hopped off the train, and moving as fast as the snow would allow them, toward the trees where their fellow had disappeared.

"Lowenstein, this is Healy. Over." Healy walked up the aisle of the car, assessing the damage as she went.

"Lowenstein, over."

"We're moving on to find the next car; contact you then. This one isn't suitable for shelter. Over."

"Should some of us come and help move the injured? Over."

Healy took a breath which puffed up into a white cloud in the train car. "Negative. I repeat: negative. Stay put. Out." She put the walkie-talkie in her coat and approached Adam. "We need to see if we can get some high ground and locate the next car." She indicated the roof of the carriage. "Think we can get up there?"

Together they moved around the car. "Should be a ladder built into the side, if we can locate it." They looked up and down at the edge of the carriage, packed with snow, from its ride down the mountain, and subsequent storm. Adam stared at the snow. "I guess we dig?"

"I guess." Reggie didn't sound thrilled. From the bits that Adam could see of her face, she appeared sick, and she constantly scanned the area around them, presumably to watch for danger. He hoped she could continue to be useful, and not fall apart if danger really came to them.

MARGO

"We stay put, if we can find a way to barricade that hole a little better, nothing can get in," Frank told Margo. "Someone will come find us. It's the best option."

"No. We'll freeze to death when the storm gets going again," Allen said.

The two of them moved about in the center of the train, Frank pacing and holding his side from time to time, Allen limping and hobbling to stay out of his way.

The snow had already picked up outside and the wind was buffeting the side of the car. Margo had recovered as best she could from the shock of being attacked, though she'd sat in the corner of the train for nearly an hour, silently processing what it was that had come out of the veil of the storm and grabbed her. She replayed the sensation of its massive paw wrapping around her like a vice and lifting her like nothing. Her head spun. The smell —something like cabbage or Sulphur— lingered on her body.

At some point, she'd found herself pulling on whatever cold weather gear she could find. There was an ache in her head that told her she couldn't stay in the car; if that strange thing could carry off soldiers, it could come for the others just as easily. "If that thing is out there, my sister is in danger. She can't protect herself from that." In the moment, she tried to convince herself that her sister wasn't a helpless child, but she couldn't do it.

Frank latched onto her arm, though she hadn't realized he was so close. "Look. I don't know what it is you saw, but if you're right, everyone is in danger. And I don't want to be the one to tell you this, but there's no one else here; we don't know who else is even alive out there. To venture out in the elements is stupid and unnecessary, not to mention all the other dangers out there. For all we know, the rest of the cars have slid all the way down this hill we're on. Your sister might not have made it, and wandering aimlessly in a snowstorm will greatly diminish your odds of survival as well."

The possibility that Reggie had died in the crash had crossed Margo's mind. But it had been pushed out by the timing of the attack and her inability to move. Considering the other fatalities, it was possible that Reggie had died, but she hadn't accepted it as fact. "I'm going out to look for her. We have no idea what our situation is, we could be close to other cars full of people that need our help."

"Ridiculous," Frank said. "What help are we going to give? If there are wild animals out there, the soldiers can deal with them. If people need medical attention, the soldiers have medics. Stay put, and don't become another person that needs saving." At first glance, Frank seemed angry, but Margo saw past that. She could see he was afraid.

"I've been on enough cold-weather and even arctic expeditions that I know how to survive in the elements. Hopefully that will be useful to someone. At the very least, it'll keep me alive long enough to locate Reggie."

"Your little sister isn't some helpless child. I'm sure she's fully capable of taking care of herself. She's probably sealed up in a car somewhere." Frank rubbed his hands together and paced away. His voice grew quieter. "*You're* the one who needs help. You won't last a few minutes out there. I'm trying to keep you from killing yourself."

"Then I'll find her wherever she's holed up." Margo pulled everything tight around her, velcroed her sleeves and pant legs, and zipped up the snowsuit to her chin. "Bria is still alive. I need you to do what you can for her while I'm gone."

"What?" Frank glanced over toward where Bria lay. "You said it yourself, we'll freeze to death."

"You two just do what you can." Margo pulled on her goggles and layered her scarf. The knife she'd taken from the soldier was lying on a seat nearby. She picked it up and walked back to the fallen soldier and pulled his belt off gingerly. She was overcome by the sudden possibility that the man would come to life and take it back. She buckled it around her waist, pulled it tight, and replaced the knife. It was heavy around her waist, pulling her down, and she seemed more off-balance without a huge pack on her back. The belt had a pistol in the holster, and she pulled it out.

"Margo, do you even know how to use that thing?" Frank shied away from her.

"Survival training, Frank. We learned on hunting rifles, but they let us shoot pistols in our free time." The gun was unlike anything she'd fired. It was an automatic, not a revolver, but she didn't want to let Frank know that. Reggie had used them on a range once, laughing, shooting targets and bottles, causing shattering little explosions and much louder booms when the pistols discharged. Margo hadn't admitted it, but she was afraid of those weapons. They seemed to have so much more uncontrollable energy for destruction than the revolvers.

She'd paid attention as her sister received instructions from the man on the target range. She looked for the safety, and it took a moment for her to find it. She made sure it was still engaged and placed it back in the holster at her side. She took the dead soldier's gloves, which had thinner materials around the trigger fingers. If she had to take off her own thick gloves before she could shoot, the gun wouldn't be much help.

The wind caused the snow to swirl like a tiny tornado, daring Margo to brave the elements. It was already getting difficult to see very far again, and she knew it would only get worse as night fell.

ADAM

On top of the car, the group could see slightly further. There was an occasional break in the wind, just long enough for them to scan the area. There was little to see, actually. A white sheet covered everything in their range of sight. Adam pointed off toward the outline of the trees where Pratt had last been sighted. There was a dark line of tracks that trailed the two soldiers sent to find him. With the snow somewhat abated, the soldiers were able to find his tracks; finding another car was not so easy. Up the hill there were lumps in the snow, which, from their outlines, Adam assumed to be trees. Others were rocks, outcroppings, and hills. None were even close to the boxy rectangular outline of a train car.

When Adam spun around, he found much of the same. White, with slight outlines. The hill sloped down for another quarter of a mile or so, and then rose on the other side of a valley, joining the mountains with a steady upward climb on the opposite face.

"Where the fuck is everyone?" Healy asked. "Not another single group anywhere nearby."

The curse word seemed out of character, but Adam supposed that without her subordinates around, she felt like she could let herself go.

"I'm worried the others may have all gone over the other side." Reggie was still antsy, scanning everything twice. "We could be wasting our time over here. Maybe we should just go to the top and see if we get a better idea from up there."

It wasn't a bad idea, as far as Adam thought. It might even give them access to emergency call boxes or other measures that were put in place along the railway.

"I'm for it." Healy looked over at the two soldiers as they got closer to the trees. "They always taught us to occupy the high ground." She nodded to the men in the distance. "We'd best collect them and Pratt and get to it. Maybe if we can get to the top before darkness falls completely, we can set up some shelter."

With no other carriages in sight, they climbed down and moved to find their missing teammate. The whole group went with them, reluctant to split up. They followed the tracks to the tree Pratt had originally left to check. Soon, they caught up with Maddox and Lund, and they all moved together. Healy and Lund led and Maddox followed Adam and Reggie at a distance.

Once they were out of sight of their train car, they found a spot where the tracks ended. The tree was on one side, and on the other was a long flat section of the hill with a ledge some twelve or so feet up. The ridge was high enough that Adam was sure the soldier couldn't have climbed it, at least not quickly or easily. And it made no sense to do so, because further north, the hill softened, and was easier to climb.

"Where the hell did everyone go?" Maddox swept the area, his rifle at the ready.

In the snow next to the end of the footprints, they found Pratt's rifle half-buried in the knee-deep snow. The soldiers dug around the tracks to see if any more of his gear had been left behind, but nothing turned up.

Reggie pointed upwards. "Did he move into the tree? Maybe he stepped closer to this pine and the snow fell off the branches and buried him?" She moved closer to the tree, where the drifts were worse, coming up to her waist.

"Doesn't look disturbed, but you could be right," Adam said. He moved toward the tall pine, trying to clear the way as he went. He joined up his path with Reggie's and they proceeded together, making better progress. Behind them, the three soldiers continued to clear around their missing comrade's trail, hoping to unearth another clue.

The flurries began to intensify again, becoming larger flakes. The wind remained calm, Adam guessed, because they were so close to the hill it was blocking the gusts. The other side was likely bearing the brunt of it.

"Hey," Lund said. "Over there." Adam saw the soldier was pointing further north on the hill.

He moved closer to the military trio but couldn't see anything.

"Further up the hill. About midway? Looks like a train car."

Adam still couldn't see it.

"Alright," Healy said. "I got it. Hard to tell. Looks like it, though." She pulled a small pair of binoculars out of her belt and focused in on the object. "Good eye, Lund. Definitely a car. Perched on a ledge about a half-mile back." She handed the binoculars to Adam and pointed it out. "Pretty concealed in the snow, but you can see some of the red markings on an exposed part."

It took a moment, but Adam found it. There was a number five and part of the letter 'E' visible in one of the few bare spots. The car appeared to be upright, though its condition was hard to determine.

"Could Pratt have somehow seen it and headed off to investigate?" Adam handed the binoculars back to Healy.

"He'd know better. He would have checked in with us right away," she said.

There was a shrill shriek then, Adam felt the noise rattle his spine. It was like a nail on a chalkboard played under the roar of a bear. When it was finished, the group moved almost as one to see the source. There, on the ledge, was the creature it had come from. Tall and muscular, its gray body rippled as the wind caught its long hair and sent it almost perpendicular to the ground. It was nearly ten feet up on a ledge, but it reached down from its perch and easily swiped at Lund, slashing his head, shredding his hood, and knocking his helmet several feet behind him. Lund fell to the ground, alive, but scrambling to get away from the beast.

It leapt from the ledge and landed on all fours, like an ape. That was the first image that came to Adam's mind as he tried to make sense of what he was seeing —a tall ape that stood up and walked easily on two legs. The thing moved quickly, gripping the rock and outcroppings.

Any further reflection was cut short when Healy and Maddox raised their weapons and shot several quick bursts at the monster. It recoiled at the attack, retreating several yards with two quick strides. It shied away, trying to shield itself by curling into a ball. Several rounds tore through the fur on the thing's back, disappearing into its flesh. Dark holes opened up under the skin before the hair whipped back in place with the wind.

When the firing stopped, the beast spun around quickly, and one of its long limbs snapped outward as it did so, flinging a huge rock. Frightening accuracy guided the small boulder, smashing it into Maddox's chest with a crack. Both rock and soldier fell to the ground with the crunch of snow and bone.

Adam realized that Lund had been screaming the entire time, and the beast turned its attention back to him. It charged forward, again closing the distance easily on its long legs, and grabbed Lund's ankle with one arm.

"Shit." Adam realized he'd been standing there, useless, mesmerized by the thing and its red-pink eyes. He'd been hypnotized by the fluidity of its movements; quite delicate for such a huge and imposing thing. He flicked the safety on his rifle and opened up on the monster, aiming for the chest. His shots connected, and it recoiled, still gripping Lund. But it didn't stop, and it didn't slow down.

"Help me," Lund said —over and over.

Healy fired as well, and the monster tried to block the gunfire with its free arm.

After a few more shots, Adam finally saw the dark blood begin to stain the light color of the beast's fur. It roared, moved back toward the ledge, and tossed a still-shouting Lund up onto it. It reached for an outthrust rock from the sheer wall and pulled itself up in an easy motion. It was back up on the ledge in a moment, and after a brief second out of sight, it reappeared, scrambling up a more forgiving slope with a now silent Lund over its shoulder.

Afraid of hitting Lund, Adam stopped firing, though he followed the thing's progress through the scope on the rifle. It disappeared toward the north, still running at full speed. Its path took it somewhere up the slope above the train car Adam's party had spotted just before they were attacked.

Healy quit shooting only when she ran out of ammunition. She too, watched the beast through her scope.

Adam turned to see Reggie on the ground next to Maddox. Her expression showed her fragile hold on her composure. She waved her pistol with each movement. "What the fuck is happening?"

Adam felt the same way. He passed the question on to the only other survivor of the group. "Healy?"

The army corporal was still staring off in the distance, where the thing had vanished.

"Healy." Adam grabbed her shoulder and turned her around to face him. "You have to help us. Where should we go? I don't want to be here when that thing comes back."

Her face was frozen in what Adam could only interpret as anger, but it was more than that. She had no idea what it was either, and she was just as scared as the others. "What?"

The train car they'd just left was no match for the storm that was about to hit, Adam knew that much. "Do we try to get back to the car we started out in, or head for that one?"

"The one in the same direction that beast just headed in?" Reggie asked. "Are you crazy?"

It occurred to Adam that there could be more people out there unaware of that monster and what it brought with it. "Who else is out there in its path?"

The three looked at each other and Healy seemed to regain a part of her composure. "If there's a chance Lund is still alive, I say we head in that direction. I can't just leave him. And I need to know if that thing took Pratt, too."

"What about Maddox?" Adam indicated where Reggie was kneeling by the man's crushed body.

Healy repeated the question bluntly. "Is he gone?"

Reggie nodded.

"Nothing we can do for him," Healy said. "When all of this is over, we'll come back and gather up his remains for a proper burial. We can't take the time now."

"What?" Reggie pointed at the man's body next to her. "Leave him?"

"Reggie?" Adam asked. He suddenly realized what they were all talking about. They were about to follow a monster into a brutal storm on the slim hope that the soldier was still alive. And on the even slimmer hope that they could stop the beast from killing anyone else. Adam's spine ached as he thought about it. "We won't go if you're against it. We can turn back."

Ignoring him, Healy moved on, and headed up the hill at an easier slope.

"I'll go, but…" She glanced down at Maddox's body.

"If you want, we can take him back to the first car," Adam said.

"We can't put him in there with the others. Hell, half of them were at death's door. It'd make morale even worse. She's right. We can come back later." Reggie reached down gingerly and pulled the soldier's pistol from where it had fallen nearby. She brushed the snow off and checked the action. "I have changed my mind about carrying a weapon, though."

If she hadn't done it, Adam would have suggested it for sure. Things had gone from the potential to fight wolves to the knowledge that something much worse was stalking them, and it was a hunter that was better at traversing the awful terrain then they were.

Adam lifted Lund and Maddox's weapons and removed the clips, stuffing them into his own jacket before gesturing to Reggie to take some extra pistol clips. They moved on, weighed down by the ammo, and heavy with the events that had just occurred.

They pushed through the snow as best they could, trying to catch up with Healy. She moved quickly, more used to facing the conditions and climate, while carrying all of the equipment.

By the time they reached the car, she was nowhere to be seen, but Adam found her tracks and followed her around the half-buried car to an open door on the other side of the carriage.

"Healy?" Reggie said quietly.

"Hello?" Adam added. Inside, Healy was staring at something, oblivious to the others' arrival.

"Healy, is there anyone in here?" Adam was encouraged that the car was in good shape, and that whoever had been in this one might have made it through the crash alive. But this car was different. There were no rows of chairs; nothing like the dining car. This one had a hall to one side, and several doors and portals on the opposite.

Adam walked up to where Healy was staring. The portal looked in on a small room, but the wall on the other side was torn away. On the floor lay a creature like the one they'd just fought; only this one was lying in a pool of blood, huge gashes lining its chest and torso. Its bloodstained head was caved in on one side. Adam assumed it was another victim of the crash.

"What is it?" Reggie asked, standing near the door and staring out into the world.

"It's another one of those things, but it's dead." Adam pulled himself away and moved to the next portal, and found a similar room, but this one was empty. The next one was empty too, as was the fourth. All the rooms were missing their far wall, except for the occasional piece of metal twisted up from the crash.

"Shit," Reggie said. She stood next to Healy. "Are there more over there?"

"All empty."

Adam came over to Reggie and slammed the door. "Let's hole up and regroup here," he said. Reggie helped him turn the emergency lock to seal it.

"Here? You want to wait here? If this dead one is here, maybe the other one will come back. And we need to chase down the one that's got Lund. We can't wait here." Healy moved down the line of little windows, confirming Adam was correct and there weren't any more beasts waiting to spring out of the pods.

It was nice to have the wind off his face for a few minutes. Adam slipped his gloves off and flexed his icy fingers. "We will move on. We need to take any opportunity to rest. But I personally can't keep pushing on until I have just a bit of time to come to grips with what just happened over there."

"It feels like that thing is watching us," Reggie said. "Even now. In here. Those fucking eyes are digging into my brain." She was still fully dressed, gloves on, hood pulled up, ready to go. She walked over to see the dead thing through the portal. "Jesus Christ, what the hell is going on? What are they?"

Reggie stood with her back against the wall. Adam joined her, and let himself slide down to the floor once he saw the door was secure.

"No clue." Healy was at the other end of the car, examining a door.

Adam felt a nudge from Reggie. "What about you?"

It occurred to Adam that his native heritage might come into question when it came to strange animals running amok in nature. "I don't know any more than you do. I've heard legends just like you; I've watched television and movies just like you. I didn't really hear more just because I'm a Cree, if that's what you're asking." Adam shrugged. "The First Nations tribes had legends like bigfoot and sasquatch—the other North American tribes did too. I put in power lines further north in Alaska when I was a kid. Up there they talked about the Puk'wis. That was something like bigfoot." He thought long and hard about those stories he'd heard as a young man; how he'd scoffed at the idea of a giant hairy ape-thing. In all his life in the backwoods, the barren lands, the mountains, working for the state and the provinces, even as a constable, nothing had prepared him for what he'd just seen. He'd heard friends and relatives tell stories of their encounters with the strange and unexplainable, but he'd never been able to bring himself to believe them without some evidence: a picture, a recording, *something*. He'd felt out of place in his skepticism, as so many of his friends would accept such claims on faith alone.

Here it was. Proof.

"I wasn't implying…" Reggie began, but pounding on the other side of the car made her stop.

Adam stood in the darkness and stared at the door at the back of the car.

The pounding got louder, and the group moved closer to it. The door was slightly crumpled and jammed. "This isn't leading outside; it's a smaller room, I think," Reggie said. "Is there another one of those things inside?"

"Let's open it," Healy said.

"No." Reggie put her hand up to stop Healy.

Adam thought about it, just as concerned as Reggie. He barely had time to form a cohesive thought when a new sound interrupted. "Hello?" A muffled voice of a woman filtered from behind the door.

"Hello?" Healy responded.

There was another thump on the door. "Can you get this fucking thing open?"

"Hang on," Adam gripped the handle. "We okay with this?"

Reggie and Healy nodded and grabbed the handle and door edges. Together they pulled until it started to give. Finally, they yanked it wide open, with the sound of the metal door scraping across the floor. Inside, a woman was holding a long pole that was glowing at one end. She pointed it at the group like she was ready to stab at them. "Christ. It took you long enough," she said.

ADAM

"My name is Nara," the woman said. She kept the sparking stick in her hand as she sat in the middle of the car among the others. "I'm Doctor Morley's partner." She was young, maybe in her early twenties, comfortably dressed, and very casual about having been in a crash.

Everyone in the room stared at her as she stared back.

"Doctor Morley? He's in charge of this project," Nara said expectantly. "None of you know what the hell I'm talking about, do you?"

Adam and Reggie looked at each other and then at Healy.

"I don't know anything. I was part of the detail helping guard prisoners, I don't know any doctor or project," Healy said. "But I think we need to know a little more of the specs for your operation."

"Of course you don't know, it wasn't exactly for public consumption." Nara took stock of the rest of the car and stood up. "How many did we lose?"

"Passengers? There weren't a lot of survivors in our car," Adam said. "We met up with a few and we're tending to the casualties as best we can."

"We still don't know where everyone is, some cars are scattered over this hill," Healy said.

Nara moved to the viewing slots. "What are you talking about? I need to know how many of the rugaru are still alive."

"The what?" Reggie asked.

"There were four of them in here. The rugaru." Nara moved from one pod to the next, but Reggie stopped her.

"That's what they're called?" Adam searched his mind, but the term meant nothing to him.

Nara nodded. "That's what *we* call them, at least."

The thing looked more familiar to Adam than the term Nara used. "It looked more like the descriptions I've heard of Sasquatch. You get a lot of those stories out here in the middle of nowhere."

"Sasquatch. Bigfoot. Yeti. Call it whatever you want. Rugaru was a term we liked better. It's technically a word for a type of werewolf, but..."

"Look, we saw one of those things –whatever you want to call them- carry a soldier off like he was made of paper. It threw a boulder like it was nothing, and killed a man." Reggie pushed the doctor back. "We need some goddamn answers. What are they? How do we kill them?"

The doctor sighed, more annoyed than concerned. "Kill them? That's tricky. Very tricky. I can't explain that —or what they are. It's classified. Sorry." Nara shrugged and pushed past Reggie to look in the last window. "Muskwas appears to have expired." She stopped and tried to see the creature from whatever angles she could, given the small window space. "That's a shame. He was a terrific specimen."

"Muskwas?" Adam asked.

"I named them. Technically, this one was J04 in the system."

While Reggie fumed over the doctor's indifference, Adam tried to approach the situation from the doctor's clinical point of view. "Three pods opened. That one is dead. So, three escaped?" Adam thought about the one that had attacked them. The idea of three of the things nearly made his knees buckle.

"Shit," Nara said. "Where is everyone else?"

"Right now, we're not sure. All the train cars separated and we're looking for more survivors. There's some in a car we set up as a base behind us," Adam said. "But we were attacked by one of these things. It killed one of the soldiers and dragged another off."

"Well, they'll do that. That's what they do." Nara faced them finally.

"None of us have any clearance," Healy said. She seemed to adopt Adam's tact and spoke quietly and evenly. "But we need to know what's going on. Our lives depend on it. Those other soldiers' lives depend on it."

"And my sister is out there." Reggie's voice still held that angry edge that she couldn't hide.

"Somewhere is another car with Doctor Morley in it, and he has four more of the rugaru with him. Including the Alpha." Nara ran her hands through her hair slowly, her eyes focusing on various points in the car. Adam worried she was breaking down before his eyes.

Reggie pushed forward to the doctor. "What exactly is this thing?" She pounded on the pod window of the dead beast. "If this is your experiment, what are they?"

Nara stood on her toes and peered into the pod where the dead thing lay.

Adam watched her demeanor, surprised that she didn't seem afraid of the thing, but was rather agitated to learn they were gone or dead.

"Look, they're an experiment we were delivering," Nara said. "What are they? They're called rugaru. It wasn't my idea. That's the moniker someone gave them a while back when the whole experiment started some twenty years ago." She walked back to the small room where she'd come from and pulled out a bundle of clothing and threw it on the floor. She sat down on the ground as well and started pulling on a pair of sweatpants over her other pants. "They have chips implanted in them to keep them in line, we don't really control them. They're uncontrollable. But the chips keep them docile at least. The whole train trip, they were doped up and sleeping." Nara slapped the wall. "There are transmitters built into this car that work wirelessly with the chips, essentially telling the rugaru to sleep."

"So why aren't they still sleeping?" Reggie asked. "That would solve a lot of problems."

Hands held up in frustration, Nara laughed. "No power. The crash fucked something up good." She pulled her boots on and tucked her sweatpant legs in. "You want to know what they want? They're programmed to be dropped behind enemy lines, create chaos, kill and survive as long as possible." She unfolded a hoodie and started to slide an arm in.

"The wind and snow are picking up again. We barely made it here. You'd need to find your way down the hill to one empty car, then over to the other, and I don't know how long you'd be able to follow our tracks before they're covered up again. We're freezing our asses off in full cold weather gear, you'll freeze before you even put one foot down out there."

"And we're certainly not guiding you back there," Healy said.

"I'm not going back there at all," Reggie said. "My sister is in one of these cars and I'm not stopping until I find her."

"This car is in better shape than most we've seen. You'd be fine here," Adam said.

"No way I'm staying here alone. I'm leaving with you." Nara zipped up her light sweatshirt and shoved her hands in her pockets.

Adam waited for Nara to say something that would help them; would help *her*, to continue to survive against the beast or beasts that roamed the crash site. As the others checked their suits, it brought a question to Adam's mind. He regarded Nara closely; she was only wearing a button-down shirt over a t-shirt, and jeans with a tracksuit giving her a thin extra layer. "Do you have cold weather gear?"

"I don't know. There might be something in the locker back in that room." She regarded the dead thing in the pod. "I didn't really think I'd need anything. Who really prepares for a train wreck in the Canadian wilderness, am I right?"

Adam shrugged. "To be fair, we were already prepared. We'd been out in the elements. I'm assuming you went from a lab, right to the train, never stepping outside?"

"Exactly."

"I'll go check the locker. If there's no gear, she's not going anywhere," Healy said, walking back to the room where they'd found Nara.

"Who is this doctor you mentioned? Morley?" Adam asked.

A blank look from Nara.

"Classified?"

"Not really. Just none of your business."

Healy returned with a snow suit. “This was in the locker, but it looks huge. I don’t know if it’ll even fit her. Hell, it wouldn’t even fit me, I don’t think.” Healy towered at least a foot-and-a-half over Nara.

“It could help.” Adam gave the suit a quick glance. “But it could also slow her down.”

“Maybe she stays here and we come back when we find a better suit,” Reggie said. “I don’t want to be out there in the middle of the night in a snowstorm with these things. Bad enough as it is, I don’t want to be dragging her around with us.” Reggie stepped close to the pole Nara had left leaning against the wall. “What’s this? Does it control them?”

“It hurts them.”

“Really?” Healy stepped closer.

“Worse than bullets or knives. They’re afraid of it at this point.”

Healy picked it up. “How does it work?”

Nara stared at her.

“You’re safer here than anywhere else. Stay here, let us use this thing, and we’ll come back when we’ve found everyone,” Adam said. He tried to put into words how bad things were outside, but the combination of destruction, the cold, confusion, and monsters, was hard to fathom.

“I need to get to Doctor Morley’s car. I’ll gladly stay put there,” Nara said. “Get me there and I won’t be a problem.”

“I need to get to my sister, and I was here first.” Reggie moved for the door, exhausted with the argument. “We’re wasting time here.”

“I agree.” Healy joined Reggie at the entrance. They both looked at Adam.

“We need to go. That’s a fact.” He tried to appeal to Nara’s good sense. “We could use that weapon out there. But I’m afraid you won’t make it in this gear. Not to the doctor, not even to the next car, wherever that may be.”

“You’re stuck with me. You want this, it comes with me.” Nara snatched the pole away and in an instant, it lit up again. “I’ll layer every piece of clothing I can to stay warm. We’ll cut the suit to fit me and duct-tape it to fit. Take me five minutes.”

Eventually Adam agreed.

MARGO

Margo cobbled her own suit out of things she found in the car, and usable bits of clothing she took from the body at the back of the carriage.

"Good God, you're taking things off of dead people. You're mad. You must have a concussion," Frank said.

"Shut up, Frank." Margo was already feeling queasy about taking parts of the dead soldier's suit. The ski mask and face shield had blood on them, as did the gloves. She cursed herself for leaving her stuff in the other car with Reggie, and hoped that the mishmash she was putting together would hold up outside. Once it was on, she took one of the guns, the knife she'd used earlier, and a small bottle of water. She hoisted a small pack with the water and a little food, over her shoulder, and stepped to the hole in the train car.

"Margo, that thing will kill you. Don't go."

The snow swirled and pushed at her from outside. The second she hesitated brought a thought to her head about Frank. "That thing? You're worried the creature will kill me?"

He avoided her gaze and fiddled with his wound.

"Were you awake when it attacked me? You *were* awake, weren't you? You were fine. You could've done something, couldn't you? You watched that thing attack me and pull me outside and you sat there and did nothing," Margo said. "You just did nothing to help."

"No…"

"You just wanted to save your own ass." It wasn't a total surprise, but she still couldn't believe it. She took a breath and stepped out into the blustering world beyond. *Asshole.*

The wind hit her full on as she walked, first shoving her backward, then coming at her from the side, making balance impossible at some points. Night was drawing close, and what light had made it through the falling snow was fading. She stopped near the spot where she'd fought the monster, right where the other soldier had disappeared. Frank had done nothing to help her. But was her abandonment of the soldier any different? She should have gone after him. That would have been the right thing to do.

She looked around the spot and found only faint indications that she'd been there, and no sign of where the beast had gone.

Beyond, she noticed for the first time, a hill that rose a hundred feet or more. In one direction, she could see the outline of what appeared to be a bridge.

The other side of the hill disappeared into the swirling storm.

In that same direction, she saw a black, rectangular shape nearby, just a few yards up the hill from where she stood. She hoped it would be just as easy to find the rest; and, eventually, her sister.

The climb got steep for a bit as she worked her way to the car, but it leveled off where it had come to rest. The worst part was the wind working against her. Margo breathed heavily and sniffed in the cold plastic of her mask with each inhalation. She was surprised to see the train car she was approaching was a different shape than hers. It was one of the two odd cars at the back of the train that she'd seen at the station before they'd left. One that was expressly off-limits.

She looked up to the top of the hill where she assumed the train tracks were. The climb to this car wasn't even a quarter of the way there. She guessed if she wanted a better view of the wreck, she could get to the top in maybe ten or fifteen minutes if the slope was as gentle as the last. If Reggie wasn't in this car, she'd head there next.

The car was upright on its wheels, with a small metal ladder built in under the door. She ascended, but the door wouldn't budge. Whether it was iced over or locked, she couldn't tell. She clanged on it with her knife hilt, to no avail.

Taking time to look around for anything that could be lurking in the shadows, Margo tried to remain patient. She saw movement up above, maybe three hundred yards up the hill, whatever it was, and it seemed to be coming her way. And fast. Instinctively, she moved around the car for cover and pulled her pistol, feeling better-prepared this time.

The shadowy shape continued in the direction of the car. As it slowed, it split into two distinct shapes —both man-sized— and began sliding quickly down the hill. Once they came to a halt, two people in military coats stood up and brushed the snow from their faces. Though they were wearing the same coats as some of the soldiers, they didn't appear to have any of the other heavy weather gear. They had ski masks, light snow pants and gloves. Both had rifles strapped across their chests.

They gathered themselves and ran toward the car.

"Here," Margo shouted. She waved to the soldiers to get their attention and keep them from going to the other end of the car. They waved back and came toward her.

"Can we get into this one?" one of the soldiers said.

"I don't know. I tried the other end but it wouldn't budge," Margo replied. "Are you two okay?" She checked their gear and found her initial assessment was correct. They were woefully ill-equipped for the weather.

"We just weren't prepared during the crash." The second soldier was a taller, thin woman with scratches across her cheek and forehead. "This was all we could get on before our car started rolling further down the hill."

"We should try this door. We need to get inside." The first soldier moved for the handle, when it suddenly opened on its own. An older man beckoned them inside. None of them hesitated.

In the car it was warmer. Much warmer, despite the fact that they'd just opened and closed the door to frigid temperatures.

"There's heat still coming in through this vent over here. The car has its own generator," the older man said. "Come, come on. Warm yourselves. Is everyone all right?"

Margo nodded and let the two soldiers race past her to get to the vent.

She inspected the interior. Certainly different from the other cars she'd been in. This one had a hall on the left, with a number of bulging rooms, or capsules, on the right.

"I've got a little water. Do any of you need a drink?" The man held up a bottle. The soldiers grabbed it and drank quickly. "I'm Doctor Morley. I'm on the staff at the prison."

The capsules intrigued Margo but some sort of shades blocked her view into them. "What's in here?"

"Experiments," Morley said.

"Experiments?" Clarke asked. She looked through the closest window. "What kind?"

"It's not something I can talk about."

"These experiments, they wouldn't happen to be very tall, hairy and homicidal, would they?" Margo asked the doctor. "I met one of them. I managed to stab it in the neck, and got away."

Morley appeared to understand. "You were lucky. They aren't easy to injure in hand-to-hand combat."

"What is it?"

"What the hell are you two talking about?" Shepard was still hovering over the vent to get warm, but he was listening intently.

"Are all of your monsters still here?"

"Yes."

"Then there was another car full of them?"

"Six. My partner, Nara was traveling in the next car, with six of them. If you were attacked, it must have come from her carriage," Morley said. "Which means there could be more roaming free than just the one you encountered."

"Just wait a minute. Not only is there *one* snow beast, there's a bunch of them? Is that what you're telling us? And we're just supposed to believe you?" Shepard shook his head. "This is crazy."

"Let's see this. Open these shades." Clark knocked on the hard-plastic covers.

"You didn't encounter it? I assumed by the way you were moving down that hill that you were trying to get away from something," Margo said.

"Just freezing our asses off and trying to find shelter before we died," Clarke said.

Shepard nodded. "Any chance you have extra gear in here? In case we need to move on without freezing to death?"

"No." Morley looked sheepish about the answer. "I was supposed to pack a trunk with it, but I needed more room in here. So I stuffed it all into Nara's car."

"Shit." Shepard paced in front of the vent.

Margo watched the two soldiers as they got warm. Clark had unzipped her coat slightly, exposing an orange shirt beneath, which didn't look at all like military issue. "What car were you two assigned to?"

The two paused for a second or two. "We were guarding prisoners," Clarke said.

The answer came slower than Margo expected. "I didn't even know there were prisoners onboard," she said.

ADAM

By the time Nara had made her suit and duct-taped it shut tight, the winds were already buffeting the train car again. “Where are we going?” she asked, when she was finished. It wasn’t pretty, but she’d managed to cut up the large suit, and use material from the bottom of the legs and the ends of the arms.

“Hang on.” Adam remembered the walkie-talkie. “Let’s try to reach anyone that might be close by.” Healy nodded and pulled out the little device.

“You have communications?” Nara asked. “I thought no one was allowed to have their devices on them?”

“Every car had one of these.” Healy held up the little device. “Weak signals, though. Barely covered the length of the train. And we’ve had mixed luck with getting anything in this storm.” She held the little device closer. “Anyone copying my signal? This is Captain Healy. Over.”

Static emanated from the speaker.

“This is Captain Healy, anyone copying? Over.”

The static continued until a faint voice wavered in and out, its words unintelligible.

“Say again, over?”

“This is Margo Hawkins,” the voice said, before fading again.

Reggie turned quickly. “That’s my sister!” She moved to grab the device but was knocked to the ground as the whole car shook again. This time, it continued to tip, sending the whole carriage slowly over onto its side with a crunch. From there, the whole thing slid down the hill on its side, shifting and spinning as it went.

The scraping of metal-on-rock created a hideous screech as the group was tossed around in the confusion. When the train car stopped moving, it remained quiet, except for the loose items that took a moment to settle. It was not nearly as bad a trip as Adam had feared, but he had no idea how far they’d travelled down the slope.

The carriage took considerable damage, mainly from scraping against outcroppings of rocks hidden somewhere beneath the snow. A sharp point of rock stuck through the wall where it had torn into the metal. The car was now on its side, with the cells holding the dead rugaru looming above them, and the rocks below.

“Everyone okay?” Adam asked. Healy was already up and nodded affirmative. It took a minute for Reggie to wave in response. She looked dizzy and off-balance, sitting in the middle of the group. If they were going to try to find the others, it would be more difficult if Reggie had a concussion and difficulties moving. They'd need to wait with her until they were sure of her condition.

Above them, something heavy landed on their car; another bloody screech came soon after.

"Jesus, this thing doesn't give up," Healy said.

"No. It doesn't. The rugaru will continue attacking if they perceive you as a threat." Nara stood and rechecked the gear she'd taped together, and picked up her baton. "Or as food."

"Food?" Reggie asked.

Nara nodded. "Their directives say to create mayhem and survive. Survival means eating. Eating in the current environment means…"

"Okay. We get it. But we're not a threat." Adam was already mapping out the situation, thinking of ways to get out of the car and off to safety. The problem was, he had no idea where they were. "It attacked us."

"True, but we're also in a train car with one of its dead companions. No matter how this thing died, the one outside doesn't care." Nara pulled on her gloves and tested whether she could still hold the baton with her hands covered. "Let's get the hell out of here."

"We can't leave yet," Adam said. "That thing is right outside. Plus, we could be all the way down in the valley or near the river. There's no telling what the terrain is like right now."

"We have to make a run for it now, while there's just one. If his calls bring others, we have no chance." Nara waved the stick around. "This pulse baton will get us out, and once the one outside loses interest in us, we can run while he tries to smash into the compartment that's holding his dead friend."

Healy wasn't buying it. "That will work? Why would it lose interest?"

"Once I zap this a few times, he'll steer clear, or he'll be knocked out." Nara seemed sure of herself.

It wasn't exactly the plan Reggie had hoped for. "Knock it out? Can you kill it with that thing?"

"No. But we can make it think twice about attacking us."

"Couldn't you just knock it out and then the three of us go over and kill it while it's out?" Reggie offered. "What? We need to survive, right?"

"I'm not thrilled about that," Healy said. "How effective are guns against them?"

"Aim for the neck. Maybe you'll get lucky." Nara put her hand on the door handle, which was now sideways due to the orientation of the train car.

"Lucky?" Adam asked.

“Their hides are tougher than you’d expect.” Nara pulled the handle. “Are we ready? No sense standing around. Might as well do it while he’s occupied outside.”

“Hides are thicker than we’d expect? I assumed Bigfoot was a legend until a few hours ago. I didn’t really have a plan for what to expect.” Reggie checked her gun, getting comfortable with it again.

“Lady, if you’re wrong, we’re all fucked,” Healy said. “Pardon my language.”

Adam held the door. “I’ll open it, everyone else get ready to run. Nara?”

“I know, I’ll go first,” Nara said. She held up the stick like a boarding pass.

They all crouched to avoid the door when it swung up, and stood around Nara.

“One… Two…” Adam felt the adrenaline rise in his body as he yanked the door. “…Three.” The door protested as he lifted, then gave way as he pushed it higher above them.

As Nara quickly rose to pull herself out of the door, one long, hairy hand wrapped around her neck and yanked her out into the white static of the storm.

MARGO

“Here’s what you do; see if you can find Nara. She’ll help with the beasts. If you can’t find her, get to the train tracks and follow them in either direction until you find a flat red disk. You can send a signal from one of those.”

“We were told no electronics were allowed onboard the train, and that no gadgets of any kind were to be used on the ride.” It was Clarke, looking intrigued.

“Well, first of all, that wasn’t entirely true. My car and Nara’s were the only ones to have electronics. There’s an array of scientific equipment in here —all state-of-the-art. But… I don’t have anything to communicate with.”

“Well,” Margo said. “All we’ve dug up in the cars were these. They took all our phones and tablets before we could get on the train.” She held up the small walkie-talkie she’d got from the train car and waved it at the doctor. “Did you find the one in your car?”

“No,” Clarke said.

“Didn’t realize there was one.” Shepard shook his head. “Have you tried it lately?”

It occurred to Margo that she hadn’t; not for a while. Maybe their new position on the hill would provide better reception. She keyed the mic and spoke clearly and succinctly; glad Frank wasn’t here to see she was actually following his admonition. “Anyone copy? This is Margo Hawkins. Can anyone read me? Over.” She paused and started again. “This is Margo Hawkins. Is there anyone listening? Over.” There was a moment when the static swelled and took on a deeper tone, but it faded quickly. “Anyone?” she asked. The wondering about her sister was driving Margo nuts. All she needed was a word, just to know she was okay.

The doctor spoke up, breaking the silence and giving Margo something else to focus on. “The red boxes I was talking about on the tracks are monitors. They trace how far the trains have progressed, temperature, et cetera. They’ve likely already transmitted our failure to pass the next marker in a timely manner. Generally, only used by trains carrying important cargo from the Anvil.”

“The Anvil? What the hell is that?” Margo asked.

“The Anvil is White Anvil Prison - it’s a hellish holding facility carved into the side of a mountain where the government holds certain prisoners,” Clarke said.

“This load was all cyber-terrorists and high-profile hackers. They were headed back to the states, presumably for trials,” Shepard said.

"Hellish?"

"You've seen what the weather is like around here," Clarke said. "And since most of their prisoners are computer geniuses, the facility doesn't have any electronics. So, no modern thermostats, no cable, no computers, no telephones, nothing that even resembles today's technology."

"It's like a Russian prison in Siberia, basically," Shepard said.

"But you have a facility there that's ultra-modern?" Margo asked. "How do they keep the prisoners in the dark about that?"

"You heard the woman, the prison side is tough to escape, the prisoners don't know the lab exists, and there's about ten feet of solid rock between the two. They have separate entrances on opposite sides of the mountain. They could get there, but they'd be exposed to the elements, and have to dodge patrols for a long damn time while they found their way around."

"Okay. So, if these sensors you talked about are working, they're sending help already?" Margo asked.

The doctor thought about it for longer than she would have liked. "Well, probably not. Odds are good that the first wave of the storm buried anyone monitoring these sensors, and they'll have a tough time getting unburied anytime soon. *Unburied?* That's not a word, is it?"

"Look, you said we can send a signal from a red disk?" Shepard asked. "How do we do that?"

"Well, the disks can receive signals, so they built in a handset that can be used to send distress signals. It's a small removable keypad that interfaces with the rest of the monitoring equipment," Doctor Morley said. "That could very well be compromised because of the storm, though."

A thud on the exterior wall next to them made Margo jump. "What the hell was that?"

Clarke and Shepard shook their heads. "I don't fucking know," Shepard said.

"Falling ice?" Clarke asked. "Loose snow?"

There was another bang on the wall; this time there were two in rapid succession. It was followed by a low-pitched grunt.

Margo recognized the sound, even if it wasn't the wild screams she'd originally heard. "It's one of them," she said.

On the other side came a similar grunt. This came from one of the pods that contained the monsters.

"Doctor? Are they communicating with each other?" Margo could feel her jaw tighten as she thought about the beast that had grabbed her and tried to drag her off into the swirling storm. She wanted to ask him more, to find out how advanced these creatures really were, but the doctor had retreated to the small room at the other end of the car. He opened a small storage closet and pulled out a pole with a circular metal piece on one end.

"They're very smart," Morley said. "I told you that."

"What's that?" Shepard asked, examining it closer.

At her approach, Morley pulled the staff away from her gaze. "This is a NyCroft pulse baton. Basically, just a stun gun on a stick. But the rugaru respond to the shock and it also emits a particular frequency. The rugaru have become afraid of both. If they get in here, it may be the only thing that holds them off."

"I stabbed one in the neck and it ran off, they can't be too tough to get rid of," Margo said. The image of the thing's face made her flinch.

"You were lucky, they have a thick chest covering of bone and cartilage. Their skulls are particularly thick; you must have brought a knife down at the right angle to miss those defenses. And in all likelihood, you only wounded it. It won't go away."

"The first few times I tried to stab it, the knife glanced off its chest."

"Yes, the skeletal modifications were strongest there —and in the skull," Doctor Morley said.

Clarke leaned in and looked closer at the staff-admiring it by the smile on her face. "What are these things in the pods? I mean, really, what *are* they?"

"Despite our current situation, that all remains classified. I certainly can't discuss it with civilians and low-level soldiers," Doctor Morley said.

It wasn't really a statement that Margo could let go. Not at that moment. "Look, I was nearly killed by one. I barely lived. I think that gives me higher clearance than most." She glared at the doctor, but he looked at the floor.

The soldiers stared as well, waiting for some response.

"This is my project. I decide who gets information and who doesn't."

The banging on both sides increased and the car began to rock just a little as the noise intensified.

"We can't even make a run for it, if there's one out there," Margo said.

"What the hell is 'it' exactly?"

Margo refused to stop looking at the doctor until he met her eyes. "You need to tell them. They need to know. You think you can stay in here and be safe? You can't. They'll destroy this thing; they'll crack it open and drag you out."

The doctor turned and finally faced her. "Don't you presume to tell me what these beasts can do, don't you tell me how dangerous they are. There were four doctors such as me with half a dozen assistants, and now it's just Nara and me." He leaned closer to Margo. "The other doctors did not quit; I can assure you. The government refused to bring any other scientists onto the project because of security." Morley leaned back and pushed a button with his thumb, then pulled down a small lever that appeared. A thin section of the pod, about four inches tall and a foot long, slid down. The doctor looked at the soldiers and nodded his head toward the slit.

Clarke and Shepard approached, only to jump back when something slammed into the wall.

With caution, Margo stepped forward and looked in from a couple of feet back. To her relief, there was still a thin layer of clear hard plastic on the other side of the slit, so nothing would be able to reach through. Just beyond, in a small, completely white room, one of the creatures paced angrily back and forth. It was as she remembered it, but here she could see a little more detail, and it wasn't covered in snow.

The creature had the same sort of long, gray-white hair all over its body, but she could see its chest better; there was some discoloration and a pronounced chest plate as the doctor had described, possibly representing more of an outer skeletal plate, almost like the padding of a baseball catcher. The arms were longer than they should be, more like an ape than a man. Long fingers, long toes. Its face was more flattened, almost like it had been shoved in, though the rest of the head was more rounded; though it, too, was a bit longer than it seemed it should have been.

"Bigfoot. You've captured fucking Bigfoot," Shepard shouted. "There's more of these?"

DENTON

CONGO RIVER REGION - SEVEN YEARS EARLIER

The helicopters were whisper-quiet as they followed the river and zipped past the creature in the water, slowing and hovering a few hundred feet away from it, keeping their distance from the head at the end of the long, swinging neck.

"Who the fuck are these guys?" a voice asked from behind Denton. A couple of soldiers had broken cover and come to stare with him.

"Can't be our ride," another soldier said. "Can it?"

The sleek black 'copters were certainly not those of their extraction team, and Denton couldn't recall ever seeing any like them. They were faster, and a little wider than nearly every one he'd ever hitched a ride on. "I don't know who they are, so let's gather up the wounded and get somewhere reasonably safe while we figure this out."

Denton lifted the captain up and placed him over his shoulder. He walked quickly toward the tree line where the cover was thickest, and set Brewer down against a tree trunk. The two soldiers joined him, one carrying someone, the other empty-handed. "How many more are still alive? Let's get them."

The soldiers shook their heads. "We couldn't find anyone else with a pulse," one said.

"That's not…" There were fifteen people in their detail, and only five remained? Denton didn't believe it. "Let's go back."

A high-pitched hiss over the river was followed by a rumbling explosion. Denton turned to see the 'copters firing stunted missiles at the creature. It roared and swung its head. With speed that didn't seem possible, it twisted its whole body and retreated back toward the water, thick feet propelling it into the river.

The helicopters danced around the beast, hovering in the rain and slowly circling the thing as it went. They fired another round of rockets, which burst on its skin. The long neck and head vanished beneath the water, leaving only the thing's rocky shell visible. Both 'copters barely took a moment to pause before opening up with their chain guns, almost in unison.

With the beast gone, Denton took the opportunity to break cover and move back into the camp to search for other survivors. What he found were vague traces of his fellow soldiers. One hut was missing a roof, and the bare floor inside was drenched in blood —with no sign of where or who it had come from. He turned and shut the door behind him, thinking how strange it was that he would do that —close the door to a building without a roof.

The lump in the river hadn't moved. One of the sleek helicopters was still orbiting it; a spotlight had flipped on, piercing the rain and illuminating the monster. The other craft landed on the shore. A half dozen troops in blue camo disembarked and spread out to comb the area. After a minute, two more people got off the craft. Unlike the soldiers who'd preceded them, these had no military insignia on their dark but anonymous civilian clothing. None of it really seemed to scream that these people were in charge of the unit.

"Hello, mister…"

"Denton. I'm Michael Denton." He felt at a loss for words, and his hands started to quiver.

The man extended his hand. "I'm Doctor Morley, and this is my assistant, Nara."

The woman nodded a hello. "Looks like we showed up just in time to save your ass, Denton." She seemed without a care in the world, oblivious to the battle going on behind her.

"You're just now realizing what happened and how close you came to a creature you can't identify." Denton's hand was visibly shaking. "It's normal for some people. The adrenaline blinds you, keeps you from freaking out when you have every right to. Some people can keep going, others can't." He dropped his hand to his side. "Are you in charge here?"

"No. My C.O. is back at the tree line."

"He couldn't keep going in the face of this, I'm guessing?" Nara asked.

Denton didn't want to say anything bad about Brewer. "What is that thing?"

"Locals call it Mokele-mbembe, though I was expecting more of a dinosaur than this thing," Morley said. "It's glorious, isn't it?"

Glorious was probably the last word on Denton's mind. "How did you find us? No one was supposed to come into this airspace."

With a shrug, the doctor said, "Purely by accident. We were already looking for this beast when we heard your transmission. What were your men doing out here?"

"Tracking a terrorist cell."

Nara kicked some debris, sending it flying into a pile of metal. "Found it, I'd say."

"Are you going to kill that thing?" Denton nodded toward the monster. He was afraid to point at it, lest his shaking hands get worse.

"Not if we don't have to." Morley looked away from the monster. "You like the rain and the heat and whatnot?"

"Not really."

"Me neither. I'll take the cold any day," Morley said. "You like the cold, Mr. Denton?"

DENTON

His trigger finger barely worked in the icy wind, but Denton waited a second, then managed to fire another shot. The shape was only twenty yards from him, but the storm made it hard to make the thing out. It looked to be nearly ten feet tall, and maybe half as wide. It was easy, however, to hear the screams of the person it was carrying, and the voice sounded for all the world like Nara to him. So he aimed high, at the head, and took another single shot, scared to fire the gun in fully automatic mode until he knew what it was, and afraid to hit Nara.

Denton and the two escaped prisoners had moved as fast as they could, backs to the wind, and bundled up using every piece of clothing they had. They'd hoped to get away from the thing that had grabbed their companion, but the horrible racket of metal-on-rock and shouting had brought them running to where they were standing now.

The impact of the second shot sent the beast reeling, and it fell to the ground. Denton ran toward it, the crunch of the prisoners' footfalls in the snow behind. Within a few yards, he stopped running, and was nearly knocked down by Nara as she tried to flee whatever way she could. Denton reached for her and pulled her back. She swung the baton she was holding—one he'd seen her use back at White Anvil—narrowly missing his head.

"Whoa. Wait. It's me. Are you okay?" Denton asked. He held her arms to keep her from swinging again. He was amazed she'd managed to keep track of the pulse weapon through the attack.

It took a second for Nara's expression to soften slightly in recognition. "Michael? Holy fucking shit am I glad to see you." She tensed as the beast got up. "Get back." The staff lit up and took on a blue glow. The monster stood and snarled, reached out with its long arms, and swiped at her with thick fingers.

"Fuck that." Cook mumbled from behind them. "I'll freeze, thanks."

Nara swung the baton with a wide swipe, startling the thing backward. It flinched as the light nearly hit its chest. Denton was surprised the thing would be so afraid of such a small weapon, but he hoped Nara knew what she was doing.

He stepped back and reloaded his rifle, switching the gun to fire full auto, and fired a burst at the thing's chest. The impact sounded like wood being chipped away by a hatchet, but the beast refused to fall.

More shots added to the rip of Denton's rifle and the thing turned again, looking behind it. Blood dripped from its neck and upper back. Whoever had shot it in the back, Denton was happy to have the help.

"Aim for the neck. It's the most vulnerable part," Nara said.

With a quick change of magazines, Denton aimed for the base of the skull, or where he figured the skull might be on the monster. "What neck?" He fired again, not sure if he was hurting it. The tick of a handgun firing joined the racket from his rifle, but the monster seemed only to double its resolve. It snapped its jaws in the air, flinging bloody spittle into the air as it charged at Denton, hairy hands outstretched, ready to tear him to pieces. It continued in that stance until it stumbled, tottered back and forth, and then fell in a heap on its side in the thick snow at his feet. It twitched, and its red-pink eyes rolled back in its head. Beside it, Nara stood with both hands clutching the baton. The fear of being mauled by the monster had made him forget that he wasn't alone in the fight. "Jesus." He could feel his whole body sway as his heart pounded with the excitement and fear of what had just happened.

"You okay?" Nara didn't move.

He could only muster a nod as he stared at the hairy creature at his feet. He took a step back and waited until he was sure it wasn't going to get up, before shouting. "Hello?"

"Hello?" A woman's voice drifted from the heavy veil of snow.

"They're from the car I just left." Nara pushed toward the voice, leaving Denton and the others behind. "Maybe it wasn't so bad a place to hide out after all."

"We need a place to warm up and get our bearings," Denton nodded toward the prisoners he'd picked up. "And I want to get the hell out of the open."

Nara agreed and as they made their way toward the others from her group, he noticed she was keeping her eyes on the beast bleeding in the snow. "How many more are there?" He knew she and the doctor had dozens of cages and pods in their section of White Anvil, but he had no idea how full those containment units were, or how many had been brought along on this doomed trip.

"We each had four. That makes two of them dead from my car," Nara said.

But how many of Morley's were still out and about? It was too much to hope that they'd either all perished in the crash, or they were all contained. Two more of those things were two too many. "Your car had a generator and monitoring equipment."

"All of it was out. The crash fucked it up good. But maybe you can get something useful out of the car." Nara stopped and grabbed Denton's arm. "What's that sound?"

Denton listened and noticed a high-pitched screech like nails on a chalkboard; then it was covered by shouts from the people who were approaching.

The huge shape of the train car tilted and slowly slid down the slope for a moment, then flipped perpendicular. It held for a moment before tumbling on over the side, thundering crunches following as the metal carriage fell onto the rocks below.

It kept tumbling.

MARGO

"I'm afraid we can't leave without that thing," Shepard said. "None of us are going to survive out there without it."

"So, stay here," Margo said. "I'm going out to look for my sister. You have no reason to go."

"We need to keep you safe. Maybe that weapon can help rescue your sister. She could be beset by these monsters, too." Clarke stepped toward the doctor but kept talking to Margo. "I'd think you'd want to be safer, too."

"This car is the safest place, and likely the warmest," Morley said. "Stay here. The battery charge on my generator is getting low - maybe it was damaged in the crash. But if we stay here and keep the doors shut, the heat should last a while." He eyed the man and woman carefully.

The train was buffeted by the wind and shook slightly as the storm brought more danger their way. Margo glanced at Clarke and Shepard, both moving closer to the doctor. The device would be a welcome resource as she searched for Reggie, but it felt to Margo like the two were planning on taking it forcibly if needed. The doctor must have sensed the same, as he moved toward the little room at the back of the train. Taking his cue, she estimated the distance to the door, in case she needed to leave in a hurry.

She reexamined the two soldiers that had come in, disheveled and out of breath. The train crash had taken everyone off-guard, for sure, but they seemed too scattered. She'd seen an orange shirt under Shepard's jacket, and maybe a hint of the color on Clarke, but couldn't make out any sort of uniform like the other soldiers she'd seen on and near the train. If they were injured and disoriented, why take the time to change out of uniform, which would have certainly been more appropriate for the weather?

The doctor moved into his room and grabbed the door, just as the other two made a dash toward him. He slammed it a moment before they threw their weight against it. Margo wasn't ready to leave the safety and relative warmth of the train car, but the situation was even more unpredictable than the weather, and she couldn't allow herself to wait anymore. She moved quickly, even with the equipment she was carrying. Without looking back, she ran for the outer door and twisted the handle.

As she went out, she heard a hiss and a clang from the side of the car. Thuds followed and she was alarmed to find the pods that held the creatures were rolling down the hillside. One was stopped by a group of rocks, another took a wild bounce, and the others bounced off into the snow.

Margo ran as best she could in the snow and wind. Shots cracked from inside the car and hung in the air as she went. Her mind somehow managed to make this all her own fault. The train crash, the monsters, the shooting. None of it would have happened if she hadn't pushed so hard to get on the train in the first place. Even that could have been avoided if she'd just said no to the whole expedition. Things were easier back at the lab in college, but field work was rapidly becoming her favorite thing.

She came to a rocky drop off and looked for a way to get around it without having to linger in the open, when she heard more shots from behind. She saw the outlines of Clarke and Shepard up the hill near the car. Instead of being delicate and strategic, Margo jumped off the top of the rocks and landed in the snow below, which gave way immediately, sending her sliding down the hill. She held out her arms in an attempt to slow her descent, but ended up with snow blowing up around her and causing her to completely lose her bearings.

Eventually, she came to a halt as the terrain leveled and thicker, tightly-packed snow blocked her progress. Disoriented, Margo waited there for any sound of her pursuers —or anything else that might be lurking. She caught her breath and decided there was nothing to be heard over the moaning wind and the rush of the nearby river.

She sat up and brushed the snow off her shoulders and head. It was dark from more than just the storm; she figured it had to be getting late. She pulled on her sleeve, trying to get to her watch, but it was buried under too many layers. How long had it been since they'd crashed? Margo pulled her legs free and stood up, brushing off her legs and doing her best to check herself for injuries. Behind, she found the huge trail she'd left in the snow as she careened wildly down the hill. If the two from the train wanted to find her, she probably wouldn't be too difficult to track. It was an easy decision to get moving. Rather than head for the river, she turned, following the base of the hill back in the direction the train had come from.

The snow was harder to get through; it seemed thicker, though the wind seemed to lessen —blocked by the valley Margo found herself in. There were still tremendous boulders and rock outcroppings; a particular one caught her attention. It appeared like all the others until she got closer. The rock appeared rounded and smooth, though larger than most. She soon realized it was some kind of man-made tunnel, built from concrete. It seemed to be almost like a drainage pipe, though much larger. She came to the front of it and found she could stand easily inside; in fact, once she got past the mouth of the pipe, it was nearly three times her height and even wider, more of an oval than a circle.

She stopped. It was possible that the pipe carried on to the other side of the hill, but there was certainly no light coming in from there. The whole of the tunnel was inky blackness after a few feet.

Margo patted her coat and the rest of her gear, looking for a flashlight or anything that would help, but she realized that anything she may have had was gone—lost in the slide down the hill— except for the knife still strapped to her leg. She'd had it since the creature had attacked, somehow managing to hang on to it through the mayhem.

Margo stared into the darkness, and as her eyes adjusted, she noticed shapes only a couple of yards from the entrance; dark masses on the floor of the tunnel. One was to the right, another to the left. She stopped her progress, and waited for one of them to move. Her heart throbbed harder as she waited, but still nothing happened. She stepped forward, knife drawn, trying to get a better look in the dark. It became clear that the nearest mass on the right was a huge black container of some kind.

She stooped to check it and heard a murmur from just beyond.

"Hello?" she asked. She thought to run then, back out of the tunnel, then down to the river to follow it. It was her only other plan.

A weak voice responded. "Who are you? Hello?" The man's voice was nearly a whisper in the darkness, almost lost in the outside sounds.

Margo stepped closer, seeing him now. It was Major Edwin, who had met them back at the center to say they couldn't take the train. "I'm Margo. We met before the train left. I'm one of the seismologists,"

Edwin nodded slowly, each of his movements accompanied by a faint cracking sound. Margo knelt and pulled a glove off to check his pulse. She found his body not only cold, but partially covered in a layer of ice. "What happened?" His uniform was encrusted and shimmering in what little light filtered into the tunnel.

"When the train went into the water," Edwin said, "we raced for the door to make it out of our car before it submerged. It was a mad rush of people trying to save themselves. The train went under and the two of us grabbed that crate as it floated up." He coughed loud and dry. "We dragged it here, looking for shelter."

"We? Who else was there?" As soon as Margo asked, she saw Edwin's eyes move away from her and fix on the shape on the opposite side of the tunnel. The figure there was much like Edwin; a soldier covered in ice from head-to-toe, face down on the ground. She approached him, hoping there was something she could do. His body heat wasn't sufficient enough to keep ice from forming on his skin, and her fingers cracked a thin layer on his neck as she felt for a pulse. She recoiled and pulled her gloves back on, the coldest she'd been since the crash.

"Did anyone else make it?" Edwin asked.

“A few. But we need to get help or they won’t last long.”

“This is the bin full of all the civilians’ electronic devices,” Edwin said. His mouth barely moved. “I don’t know if you can get reception, but…”

Margo gripped the latch on the front, but was blocked by the padlock. “I hope you have the key.” The lock was icy in her grip. She pulled and shook it a couple of times before giving up.

A single word escaped Edwin before he started coughing again. “No.” When he finished his fit of coughing and deep breaths, he continued. “Lost it, swimming from the train.”

The container was large, and the lock was solid. Margo scanned for any damage it may have sustained in the crash, or in the elements, but it appeared as strong as ever. She stood and kicked it out of frustration. The sensation felt good, and she did it again, smashing down with the heel of her boot. She continued until her legs were tired. It got her nowhere-the lock was just as firmly clasped as it had been when she started. The only progress was that she was slightly less angry with the whole situation, and she was just a little more exhausted. Margo knelt next to the box and put her head on the cold plastic. Her breathing returned to some semblance of normal and she sighed.

“He’s got a sidearm. You can use it to shoot the lock,” Edwin said.

The idea that she could shoot the lock off of anything was dubious to her, and she was tired of taking things from dead bodies. Feeling defeated by something so simple as a lock, she wondered if she shouldn’t just give up and move the officer and the container deeper into the tunnel and away from the harsh weather. It might not be any warmer, but at least they’d be a little safer. And, if she took the gun in order to shoot the lock off, maybe the sound would be muffled enough not to alert the creatures, or anything else that might want to do her harm.

No matter what, the gun was a good idea. She slowly crawled across the tunnel floor anyway and knelt next to the soldier. With a deep breath, she cracked through the ice around his belt and the gun holster. The crunch of the ice reminded Margo of eggs cracking for breakfast back in her tiny apartment, which only reminded her how hungry she was. Her pack was back at the last car, containing her remaining energy bars and water bottle.

She unsnapped the holster with some difficulty. The metal clasps were stuck, and the flap was frozen in place.

“You see? I told you it was a good idea to follow her.”

Shepard and Clarke stood at the tunnel entrance; guns poised.

“What’s in the box, Margo?”

MARGO

Clarke bent down and checked the soldier and Win for pulses but brought her hand away from both, shaking her head. "They're both icicles."

Margo checked Win for any sort of movement; a breath, raised eyebrow, *anything.* She felt her heart drop at his inactivity. "Why did you release the rugarus?"

"Wasn't on purpose, that's for sure. That dumbass doctor tried to get away and bumped something," Shepard said.

A sudden gust blew through the tunnel and everyone swayed against its strength. Shepard pulled his hood back and wiped snow from his jacket. "Any other weapons?" He'd strapped the staff to his back, Margo noticed. She wondered whether that stick would have any effect on people, or if it only hurt monsters. She hoped she'd get the chance to test it out, but not as the subject of the trial.

"No. Both their holsters are empty," Clarke said.

"He told me they'd ditched everything when their train car went into the river, out of fear that they'd drown," Margo said. "I'm assuming that meant they tossed their pistols, too. They held onto this bin for dear life and swam to shore with it."

The look on Shepard's face told Margo he wasn't convinced. "Neither of them kept a weapon?"

"They were struggling for their lives. Probably wanted to drop whatever could weigh them down," Margo said.

"I don't think so. These are soldiers. I don't think they'd give up their pistols for anything," he said. "No. Search her. I bet she..." Shepard choked as his words were stopped by the wide, hairy arms that thrust out of the dense snow and swung at him, knocking him to the ground.

One of the beasts entered the tunnel and snarled at Margo and Clarke. When it stood up, its head nearly hit the ceiling. It swung at Shepard, but narrowly missed. The man rolled to the side and started to scramble toward the two women. Margo moved as quickly as she could, but didn't want to turn her back on the monster so she ended up running backward to get away.

"Jesus, hit it with that stupid stick. We went to all that trouble to get it, now use it," Clarke said.

Shepard listened and pulled the pulse baton from the strap on his back. He didn't take the time to aim; he just swung the weapon. The rugaru dodged backward to avoid being hit, but didn't seem as concerned as Margo had expected.

The creature dodged another swing, but the baton glanced off its hand. There was no shock, and apparently no pain; in fact, it remained unaffected. And while Shepard pulled back to try to land another blow, the rugaru grabbed him by the chest with one massive hand, slammed him to the ground, and then caught his arm. Margo recoiled at the sound of the beast breaking the man's limb, just by closing its massive fist—bones cracked as the man screamed in agony and dropped the pulse baton.

Margo forced herself to move. She stepped back as quietly as she could, pulling the pistol that she'd secreted away from the dead soldier before Clarke and Shepard had shown up. She'd been attacked by one of the creatures and desperately wanted to avoid experiencing the horror a second time. Behind her, the darkness was foreboding, but it beat the alternative. She looked at Clarke, wondering why she hadn't fired yet.

The rugaru reached out and took the long weapon off the ground and pulled it close to its face, seemingly forgetting Shepard and his screams, and ignoring Clarke and Margo. The weapon seemed tiny in front of the beast's face. As it examined it more, it became visibly frustrated, growling loud enough to be heard over Shepard's cries. Its brow creased, and its lips pulled back to expose crescent teeth.

Margo moved faster, not turning her back, but doing her best to fade into the darkness and hopefully from the monster's memory. Clarke saw what Margo was doing and then looked again at what was happening to Shepard. Indecision gave way to what Margo assumed was the logic that Shepard was either a lost cause or that he didn't deserve her loyalty, and Clarke began moving slowly in the same direction as Margo.

Its frustration reached a peak, and the rugaru let out a series of sharp barks. It then easily snapped the staff in half with its huge hairy hands. Spurred on by the sudden display, Shepard crawled on his side to get away, unable to use his broken arm. The rugaru saw, and brought the larger piece of the broken weapon down like a club. It crunched Shepard's already mangled arm, eliciting howls of pain.

"Fuck this," Clarke whispered. She turned and ran into the darkness, abandoning all pretenses of stealth.

The monster hit Shepard over and again until the man stopped screaming. Once those screams stopped, the rugaru grunted and brought the long fragment straight down, impaling Shepard through the chest with ease.

Margo found herself staring at the beast, with it returning her stare from perhaps twenty feet away, all the while, footsteps echoing through the tunnel as Clarke got further away.

She could feel the cold pistol in her hand. She wondered if it still worked after being in the river and then being frozen. If there was one thing she didn't want, it was to point the gun at this terrible monster and have it fail. Seconds passed before the monster finally broke eye contact, took Shepard and the fallen soldier, and made its way out into the snow, dragging both behind it. As the crunch of its feet in the snow faded, Margo turned and ran.

DENTON

"Shit," Denton murmured under his breath as the final bits of the rail car settled, clanging and rattling to the base of the hill.

He heard several of the others gasp as they all got as close to the edge of the drop as they dared. "This whole thing is FUBARed, sir," Healy said. "We just can't catch a break."

Truer words were never spoken as far as Denton was concerned. But the car was gone and standing there staring at it wasn't going to fix anything. They needed shelter, they needed clothing for the prisoners, they needed to call for help. "Alright. First priority is getting out of the cold."

"Up or down, sir?" Healy asked. She scanned side-to-side, surveying the incline around them.

Denton scanned to see if there was an easier way down than the sheer cliff that the train car had just fallen from. There were more gentle slopes further north and south, but there was no telling whether they'd bring shelter or not. About a half mile from the base, another steep slope led up into the mountains. They could follow the natural valley at the bottom and keep out of the wind and snow, which would be blocked by the upward slopes on either side, but there was no telling how far help would be from there, and it wouldn't eliminate the cold altogether.

The top of the hill wasn't all that far away; a slightly shorter distance than the trek down would be. Of course, it would all be uphill, through jagged rock and thick snow. At the top, they might find more survivors, get a better vantage point for finding shelter, and, at the very least, they would know where they were going if they had to set out for civilization; they could just follow the tracks back toward the Anvil or ahead to the nearest town —although he feared both would be too far away to help anyone.

The only one to offer their opinion was Adam. "If it makes any difference, my vote would be to climb up. Maybe the walkie-talkies would get better reception for either side of the hill. And maybe we could actually see other cars to use for shelter, or outcroppings and caves in the mountains nearby. I'm not familiar with this stretch, but back in my neighborhood, there were caves everywhere."

"If it gets us moving and away from the noises that might attract monsters and God-knows-what? I'm all for it," Reggie said.

The group looked to Denton. "Agreed. Stay together. Cover the prisoners as best as possible and shout out if you see anything. Anything at all. We can't take a chance."

“Yes, one is difficult to fight, but any more than that, we’re done for, even with the baton,” Nara said.

“There’s even more of them out there?” one of the prisoners, Cook, said. “*Fuck me.*”

Healy took point, followed by Nara, then the prisoners, then Reggie and Adam. Denton brought up the rear, watching their backs, checking everyone’s footholds in the snow, listening for the slightest sound that might indicate trouble.

The wind had died down again, but the snow still came down at a good pace, covering everyone as they moved. Somewhere in the back of his mind, Denton let himself believe that by some miracle, there would be a safe, warm train car waiting for them at the top. One that hadn’t gone off the tracks, and which was filled to the brim with hot coffee, blankets, and food. And a flamethrower or something to kill the rugaru. That would be at the top of his list.

He forced a deep breath to calm his nerves, but it wasn’t helping. He needed rest and he was sure the others were getting as weary as he was. Behind him, he heard the rumbling sound of snow cascading down the hill.

Denton turned and scanned the area. Nothing moved, nothing stirred.

MARGO

The woman was standing with her hands on her knees, panting heavily, when Margo nearly ran into her in the darkness. Margo stopped, too, her side aching from running in the heavy gear. Her boots were not really meant for running, and the face mask made it hard to breathe with the heavy exertion.

She tried to take deep breaths to calm herself and recover. Clarke's eyes never looked away from her, so far as she could tell. Neither woman went for their gun, though the threat was certainly a possibility.

"Did it follow you?" Clarke asked.

Two heavy exhales before Margo could reply. "First off, if it had followed me, it would have caught me." She swallowed hard and let her lungs fill with air again. "Second, it wasn't like I could've lost it. We went in a straight line, with no possibility of turning. It didn't have to keep up with me or anything." Margo's legs ached. She stepped back and leaned against the wall, afraid that if she sat, she'd be caught unaware —if the beast had indeed followed them. She was possibly more concerned that she wouldn't have the strength to get back up.

"What was in the case? The one you were standing by?" Clarke asked. "Weapons? More of those pulse batons?"

Now, stuck in a tunnel, she felt more comfortable confronting Clarke one-on-one. "Who are you? For real, this time."

"We told you." Clarke pointed to the army jacket she was wearing. "We were on one of the forward trains. We're with the outpost."

"What's with the prison orange jumpsuit I saw under it earlier?" Margo thought about the pistol; where she put it, and how to get to it quickly. "Come on. We're kind of screwed out here. Just come clean and we can get on with this."

Clarke took a deep breath. "Fine. I was one of the prisoners in one of the forward cars. I was arrested for hacking a few things, okay?" she said. "Now. If we're getting to be friends so "We can get on with this," what the hell was in the case?"

There was little room to argue with that. And since Margo had no intention of going back for the container, she answered honestly. "The cell phones of all the passengers, some tablets."

"What?"

"Yeah. Everyone's electronics. They took them before we boarded the train. They didn't tell us why, they just said we couldn't get on the train without giving them up." Margo had no idea whether anything still worked, but she regretted not being able to drag that container along behind her.

"I'm why they took your electronics. Me and all the other prisoners back there with me. We were all hackers and cyber criminals that were stupid enough to get caught." Clarke looked back down the tunnel where they'd come from, staring into the darkness. "Didn't you notice the train was a little short on amenities? The only place with anything in the way of a god damn electronic device was that car with the doctor and his monsters back there."

It had occurred to Margo, but at the time she was angry and desperate to get out of the way of the storm. She didn't really care, back then.

"They were afraid if any of the evil little code monkeys got our paws on a tablet, we'd hijack the train, crash a jetliner, or call the nearest Canadian crime boss to save us with their attack huskies." Clarke sneered, but kept looking into the darkness.

"Can you do any of those things?" Margo didn't want to sound stupid, but if there was any way of getting out of here, she wouldn't mind a ride with a Canadian kingpin to do it.

"Not without a cell phone."

Margo took a second to read the other woman's face, and came away still unsure if she was joking. "Well, you can go back there and retrieve one. I'm seeing what's at the end of this tunnel." With that, she walked slowly on, stepping sideways so as not to turn her back on Clarke just yet.

As she watched Clarke turn, the tunnel seemed to shake as a heavy crunch of metal crashed on their end of the passage. It was still dark, but somehow, what little light had been shining through, disappeared. Margo heard rocks and other material fall on the ground not far from them, as part of the concrete tunnel collapsed in the aftershock of the initial event.

"Jesus. Cave-in?" Clarke asked. "Avalanche?"

It didn't sound like either. Margo had heard an avalanche on an expedition to the Rockies a few years back and studied videos and recordings of them. "I don't think so, unless the avalanche shoved one of the cars down with it. My guess is that a train car came loose and fell down the slope some more." Margo became concerned, not just for anyone who might be in the car, but for her own safety. Her eyes adjusted to the new, low level of light, and it dawned on her that maybe it wasn't temporary. She took a breath and forced herself to move toward the sound.

"What's wrong? Why are you running?" Clarke asked.

Margo almost tripped on a block she didn't see on the ground. "It got darker. Maybe the car is blocking the end of our tunnel. In which case we're screwed and need to go all the way back to the other end…"

"…Where that creature just killed Shepard." The sound of Clarke's footsteps sped up as she followed Margo.

They were closer to the end of the tunnel than Margo guessed. After only a minute or so of running, the passage became more and more littered with larger chunks of rock and ice. Some of it was brick and other building materials from the tunnel. Margo climbed over as quickly as the obstacles allowed her, but soon, she couldn't continue. The entrance was blocked, and there was next to no light breaking through. Once she'd moved a few rocks aside, she found she was correct; she could see a small bit of the bottom of the train car, showing in a gap between snow and rock. Her heart beat a little harder. "See if you can find an area we can squeeze through. Start with places you can see light coming through," Margo said. She stopped pulling on the rock and moved around to another area, looking for a weak spot.

"What?" Clarke asked.

Before she replied, Margo grabbed hold of a large piece of masonry and pulled, trying to dislodge it. "It's a train car. A train car slid down the hill." She pulled harder, her legs braced on other debris, but couldn't move the rock. "And it seems to be covering the whole fucking exit."

"Shit."

ADAM

Adam was regretting his suggestion that someone climb down to the smashed car and see if they could salvage anything. He found himself 'volunteered'.

Reggie had pointed out that she had more climbing experience than anyone, but without her gear and in such frigid temps, Denton was concerned about her safety. Apparently since Denton vaguely knew Adam from the few times he'd been at the station, it made them friends. And it looked like Denton wanted to risk a friend's life rather than that of someone he barely knew. So, everyone else got themselves to cover, under an outcropping down the side of the incline. It gave them some shelter from the wind and snow, but the cold was still bitter.

Adam was concerned with the two prisoners Denton had brought in tow. They were barely clothed to handle the elements and he hoped they'd be able to huddle together for warmth in the protection of the shelter they'd found.

The journey down toward the train wasn't too difficult, but it was slow going. The rocks were buried in snow, handholds were covered in ice, and there was the complete absence of a trail. The snow drifted over ditches and holes, nearly sending him head over heels down the side more than once.

He reached the mass of twisted metal that constituted the largest chunk of the rail car and tested his footing. There was maybe three-quarters of it there; the rest could be seen scattered on the ground in various shapes and chunks.

It appeared the wreckage couldn't go any further. They'd reached the bottom of the slope. Below, there were rocks, and more snow. Opposite was the base of the mountain; more rocks, more snow. If they sought shelter there, it would be more climbing, but maybe a hidden cave could provide them with shelter until the storm blew over and help arrived.

Adam examined the wreck. It was safe from sliding any further downhill, but there was still a chance it could topple over and crash on its side. The only door still attached was on the opposite side of the car, pinned to a rock.

He needed to squeeze through a pinched section of the side. He bent back the most vicious-looking edges of the torn metal as best he could and pulled himself through carefully, flipping on his small flashlight. The car was bare for the most part, with nearly everything it contained piled at the far end. The things that had been stored in a cabinet had been knocked loose and tossed it around until the ride had stopped.

Adam regarded the pile about ten feet below him. "Of course this wouldn't be easy," he said to himself. "Nothing's easy lately." He tested a cabinet on the wall and used it for a foothold when it held his weight. He kicked the open doors to the cabinets until they broke free, and then used the shelves as a ladder.

He stepped lightly onto the floor, listening for any indication that the car was going to fall over. A creaking sound caused him to stop moving altogether and he sat waiting for another. He pulled the walkie-talkie gently from his jacket and keyed the mic. "This is Adam. Over?"

There was a click, and a voice faded in through the static. "Copy. Go ahead Adam, this is Healy. Over."

"It's a mess inside. I'm still trying to move around." He scanned the battered and crushed room. "Good news is, we're at the bottom of the incline. I'm also hopeful about the lower areas of the mountain down here. Could be some shelter there. Over."

"Copy. We're crowded in here pretty good; at least it's helping with body heat, but we could use some room. Over." Healy sounded much like she had the whole time Adam had known her -voice even and measured with no sign of fear- but this time with no sign of hope.

"Adam? Denton. Do you read me? Over."

"Go ahead, Denton."

"Do you see any signs of other survivors? Over."

Adam looked around the confines of the little box he was currently trying to examine. "No." He didn't mean it to be a flippant answer, but he felt it stood to reason that he would have started with that information. "Look, I need all my hands for climbing around so I'm going to sign out for a few minutes. I'll get back to you when I've searched this place and I'm somewhere more stable. Over." He clicked the walkie off and slid it into his pocket. He hadn't heard any more groans of protest from the structure, so he stepped further across the wall of the car below him. He bent to search the piles of junk that had shaken loose in the fall and found most of the objects were exactly that —junk. There were papers, wrappers, chunks of the car's frame, plastics from the interior and tiny bits of other useless debris.

Adam sighed, scanning the other piles for the glimmer of something helpful. There were bandages that had broken loose from a nearby crushed first aid kit. Those led him to a few other medical supplies in a trail from the kit to the bandages. He shoved them into his pocket, disappointed that there was little more than painkillers and anti-bacterial ointment, and nothing of any help to the seriously injured.

He had trouble getting the rolls of gauze into his coat pocket, so he fished in to figure out what the problem was. He pulled out a sheet of paper and unfolded it to find his daughter's sonogram photo. He should have been there by now. It was likely he'd missed the birth by this point, but there was little he could have done. The train crash wasn't really to blame —he'd procrastinated and put off leaving while he helped with minor tribal issues that someone, *anyone* else could have handled.

Rosa had moved to Montana with her mother some eleven years earlier, and he'd seen her only three times since then. One Christmas, one birthday, and one summer break. That was all he'd made time for in over a decade. As much as he wanted to see her, he was more afraid of how much she would hate him. He had missed her wedding to Jim, the weird artist-guy, and her second wedding to Andrew, *who hated to be called Andy*. And now he'd missed the birth of his first grandchild. The cards he'd sent, and the brief phone calls got less frequent and more impersonal. He'd felt the connection slip immediately after she moved with her mother. Now, it was non-existent.

"Hello?" The woman's voice was distant, yet so close.

Adam surveyed what was left of the train car. "Hello?" He felt stupid, because obviously someone had spoken. "I'm here." Of course he was. That's why someone was talking to him.

There was a burst of static and the voice spoke again. "This is Margo Hawkins, is anyone out there? Copy?"

Feeling even dumber, Adam pulled the walkie out of his coat. "I read you. This is Adam. Margo, where are you? Are you alright?"

A squeal broke through the speaker as Margo cheered. "I'm okay. I'm okay. I'm..." She paused. "I'm in some kind of a tunnel under the hill with another... survivor. We're trapped down here and scared that this... this is going to sound stupid... this *monster* is closing in on us."

"We've been attacked too; you don't sound crazy. Not to me," Adam said. "You say you're in a tunnel? Over."

"Yes, there was a cave-in or something. One of the train cars fell and brought a bunch of rocks and snow with it. They're covering the entrance at this end."

Margo sounded more frazzled than anyone from Adam's group, and the fact that she seemed to be deliberately holding something back concerned him. "Listen. I'm exploring a train car that just slid down the slope a half an hour ago, so maybe it is the same thing you saw." He thought about the exposed bricks he'd seen earlier as he climbed into the car.

"I can see part of the car, we're right below it. Hold on," Margo told him. "I can touch the side." There was a faint clanging that came from the roof of the car, which was facing the hill. "Can you hear me? I've got a rock and I'm pounding on the car."

"I can," Adam said. He wasn't sure what good it was going to do them. They were going to have to clear out the rocks and snow around the car to get to Margo and whoever else she had with her. Or if they could somehow cut a hole in the area where she was pounding, maybe they could pull them through. Of course, Adam was having trouble cutting anything, let alone a metal roof. "Hold on, I'm going to try to radio the rest of the people I'm with and see if they have any ideas. Just wait, okay? Over."

A thud was the first reply, and Adam assumed she'd dropped the radio. "You're with a group? Is my sister with you? You remember her? My sister, Reggie?"

"Yes, I remember. And yes, she is with the group I've been with from the beginning. She and I were in the same car."

It was quiet.

"Margo? Did you hear me?"

"Yes," Margo said, close to tears.

"Okay. I have to go. Give me a few minutes. I'm going to try to climb up and get their signal back, over."

"Wait," Margo's voice came back. "Can you make some noise, so I know you're actually there? Just pound on the roof? Something."

It was understandable, Adam supposed. Proof that everyone was where they said they were. He braced himself against the cabinets and kicked the ceiling over and over until Margo came back on the radio. "Thank you."

Adam stepped over the junk strewn about the floor, mentally scanning it for anything else that might be useful. He couldn't remember anything that would be strong enough to cut through metal. It was essentially a medical car, though it was used for something very different than flu vaccinations and cold remedies. He wondered if there were scalpels anywhere and what kind of —if any— actual procedures were done in here, or if they were using it purely for transportation today.

Most of the cabinets were open, but he took the time to check the ones that weren't. He considered himself lucky to find a few breakfast bars and a bottle of water, sliding them into his pocket next to the folded sonogram and putting a foot on a shelf to climb to the exit. His fingers had some feeling back, and he wiggled them. He took a moment to scrunch up his toes as well; there wasn't much he could do if he had frostbite at this point, but at least if he was aware of it, he could try to bundle up any affected area and maybe minimize the damage.

"Denton? This is Adam, can you read me? Over." He wedged himself in the gap leading outside, in the same place he'd managed to find a signal before. “Denton?” He waited. “Margo, how about you? Do you read, over?” There was more silence.

“Damn it.” Adam slid the radio into his pocket and put his gloves on. He’d need to move up the slope some and hopefully get the signal back. He stepped on a jagged piece of metal and used his thick boot heel to bend it out of the way. Outside, the snow was worse and the howling of the wind made him more uneasy.

He tightened his hood and ventured out into the white darkness that had fallen with the night.

MARGO

Behind her, Margo could hear Clarke sliding something around.

"If we're going to wait until everyone else gets here and find a way to cut through the floor, I think we need to set up some sort of fortification," Clarke said.

Margo saw Clarke building a wall out of rocks and ice. She'd started it on top of a decent-sized boulder. It only came up to her waist, but it was already good enough for one person to hide behind. "That's a good idea." She cautiously climbed down from her perch by the car and picked up the first rock she could move, noticing that Clarke had placed her gun on the ground nearby.

"I played a lot of Fortnite before I went away for the big timeout in the Anvil." Clarke kept building. "Damn, I miss video games. Of all the things I miss—New York style pizza, sunshine, Heineken—I miss gaming the most. Just taking that away was punishment enough. They didn't have to put me in that hellhole."

Margo stacked another piece in their wall and considered what to do next. Could she trust this woman enough to stay stranded with her in this tunnel until help arrived, or would she betray her at the first opportunity if it meant saving her own ass?

"I'm happy your sister is okay."

"Thanks."

After a few seconds, Clarke spoke a little louder than before. Matter of fact. "Look. I've explained it and explained it to *everyone,* from the NSA and the FBI to Interpol and Scotland Yard, to my dad and his new girlfriend, and they all agree I'm a shit who deserves what she got," Clarke said. "So, if you're looking for a feel-good story about a poor misunderstood girl that got mixed up with the wrong crowd, you're going to be sorry."

"Well, is it a long story? Because we've got time." Margo looked around. "I doubt we're going anywhere soon."

Clarke was breathing heavily from the exertion of the short work she'd made of the wall. She sat on a rock facing the other end of the tunnel, and Margo watched her scope out the darkness there for any sign, or sound. "Look. I was always good with computers. But all I ever cared about was playing video games. I was good at them, you know? I played online and defeated just about everything easily. So, I started busting onto servers and playing other people's mods and maps. Nothing destructive. I never planted any viruses or stole any information. I just wanted to play. Right?"

Margo nodded, though she wasn't sure if Clarke was really asking.

"You play?"

"Nothing more than Plants vs Zombies and Angry Birds, I'm afraid."

Clarke nodded sagely. "A lot of old people still play those. I was more into all the FPSs. Burning Omega, The Fall of Hetting, Crunch Gun?"

"I have no idea if you're just making those up," Margo said.

"I could be." Clarke smiled a little. "But I'm not. I swear. So, I'm starting college. Business classes. Biology. English. I'm allegedly majoring in poly-sci, but what the fuck did I care about all that? It was what my parents really wanted, and I played along until I started taking programming classes, and some others that made my understanding of computers more complete. Shit, one class accidentally gave me the back door into a number of campus servers. I found class projects, test games, emails with other idiots' passwords and personal shit. I still didn't take anything. Except passwords. That's it. Parents emailed their kids' credit card numbers and bank info. What the hell? How stupid. Anyone knows better, right? But I left that shit alone. That's good. Right?"

"You already said this story isn't going to make me love you, right?"

"True, but I was a model Internet citizen," Clarke said. "Up to a point. I mean, I was learning a lot in classes and I met some… how did the court describe them? 'Like-minded individuals' is what they said. I fell in with some serious hackers who weren't nearly as charitable as I was. We started out playing games, scamming passwords, same as always. But after a while, they moved on to stealing gift card codes from stores and from sites online. I didn't know at first until they started living a little better than a poor, broke college student should. New clothes off certain sites, food deliveries using spoofed Bank of the States pre-paid cards, and no explanation. Seems I was the only one that didn't know for the longest time. Maybe they didn't think I could handle it, or they knew how serious I had been about only gaming and no stealing.

"Look, I won't bore you with the details. But I got over the 'no stealing' thing once my parents cut me off because I'd been skipping and failing classes left and right. I needed money, I needed food, I needed rent. I was a quick learner and started skimming students' meal cards and spoofing their scannable apps for coffee and pizza. Hell, I doubt those guys even looked at their balances most of the time. They never knew."

"So far, none of this stuff sounds worthy of being sent to a secret maximum-security prison in the frozen north," Margo said. She scanned the tunnel behind her, convinced she had heard a noise.

"It wasn't. I'd been doing little stuff, flying under the radar. Getting by. You know? Until one of our group says he has a job we could do for a friend. It would've been cash for a quick hack of a database and a download of a few files. Easy. He stressed it would still be illegal, but we'd be helping this guy out. The database wasn't even on a government protected site, or so we thought."

"You got caught?"

"Big time."

"What was it?"

"This guy's friend was incarcerated for hacking just like us and was tossed into the White Anvil Prison." She seemed embarrassed to admit the finale to her story.

"So, you were thrown into prison for hacking the prison's database?"

"Yeah. Stupid, huh?"

"I don't understand."

Clarke hesitated. "The things we found in those files. I didn't believe it. I thought we'd hacked some video game company. The creatures and experiments they had listed there seemed like out of this world role-playing, like D&D or something. I dismissed it until we were arrested. They rushed through some bullshit trial and shoved me into White Anvil, no questions asked. I still dismissed the stuff we saw until…"

"Until we saw it here firsthand?"

Clarke nodded. "There were files and files —years' worth— on these things attacking us. There were weird dragon-type things, men that resembled moths, devils, insects. These were all experiments or things they were holding somewhere in the prison."

"In addition to actual prisoners?"

"Everyone was a tech criminal, but not all hacked the Anvil itself, from what I could tell." Clarke sighed.

Margo stood; the rocks were freezing her butt. "Look, you're right. You haven't changed my mind about your being a criminal, but it sounds like the punishment didn't really fit the crime." Margo thought about what she just said. Her opinion rested on whether Clarke was telling the truth or not, and of that, she couldn't be sure. It could easily be a convoluted story to evoke sympathy.

Down the tunnel, a faint crunch distracted Margo from asking any follow-up questions. Both she and Clarke stopped moving altogether. The sound echoed from somewhere much further down. The sound was followed by another, and a scrape across the icy ground. Margo held her breath, thinking it would help her hear. Another crunch, and then another reached them, until there was no mistaking that someone —or something— was walking toward them.

"Shit," Clarke whispered.

Margo wanted to agree but didn't want to make a single sound.

DENTON

When they heard about Margo, Denton turned to see Reggie's reaction. Certainly, he'd expected nothing less than the overjoyed reaction on her face. "That's great, Adam, get yourself back into the shelter of the car, if you think it's safe. We'll brainstorm here on how to get them past that train car and join you as soon as possible."

The prisoners were just a few feet away, sleeping, bundled up to use their body heat and what little clothing they had to best effect. They'd had a rough time of it in the cold, beset by monsters, but Denton was slow to find any pity for them; they'd busted out of custody, trying to take advantage of a bad situation, but had only made things tougher for themselves. Maybe if they'd stayed put, they would still be in the car with the others; warm, and hopefully still safe. "Nara, you know those cars, anything that can cut through metal?"

"We didn't exactly pack blowtorches in there to help control the rugaru, if that's what you're getting at," Nara said. "There were some surgical instruments packed away. Scalpels, clamps and the like. There were some autopsy tools —a bone saw should be in there. It would be strong enough to cut through a skull, but I don't know about a metal floor. That's considerably thicker."

"That's a start. But would it work? Is it chargeable, or did it rely on an outside power source?" Even if it wasn't strong enough, maybe it could cut some part of the train floor to allow them to peel it back. Maybe it could cut the heads off of screws or bolts to allow panels to be removed. "I get the feeling there aren't exactly usable outlets on that thing."

"I think it had both, but the battery pack didn't give the blade enough power, so we never used it," Nara said.

Bad news, Denton thought. If it was low power to start with, that battery lowering the juice wouldn't be helpful. "Alright. It's a start. Anything else?"

"Should be a maintenance kit there somewhere. Hammer, screwdrivers, pliers. Not sure what else it had."

A hammer would be helpful; they could use it with a screwdriver like a chisel.

The thoughts were swimming in Denton's mind, and becoming mushy as his own fatigue started to take hold. He didn't want to slow down; he couldn't leave anyone in danger, but he could feel himself fading.

"That could do it. Maybe there's a small saw? There could be a crowbar, for all we know." Reggie's smile faded, just a little, as she tried to contribute some ideas of her own. "A kit like that on a train could have wrenches or other things to adjust the car itself, right?"

"Could be," Nara said. She looked Denton over. "You look exhausted."

It was hard to deny. "It's been a long day, ma'am."

"We can do this on our own," Reggie said. "I'd love to get a few seconds of sleep, but I just can't, knowing my sister could still be in danger."

"We can climb down, catch up with Adam, and find a way through that metal floor. Have it finished before you're done resting. Easy," Nara said. "Gives you more room here. You can stand watch over the prisoners. We'll radio you when it's done, or you three can join us as soon as you can."

"I've got the most climbing experience here, so we'd be safe going down. And once we get there, we'll be with Adam."

"I don't want to break this group up any more than we need to. We just got everyone together," Denton said. "Let's rest and go down together. And what about Healy?" The other military presence in the group had volunteered to take a patrol up on the ridge above their little alcove. She was due back in a half hour. "If we take off, she'll be left."

"Exactly why you should stay." Reggie started pulling tighter on her gear and buttoning her buttons. "Rest, wait for her. Join us when you can. A thirty-minute nap could do you wonders. I want to get down to help with my sister."

Denton couldn't believe they were talking about naps in the middle of the current situation, but his difficulty focusing told him to give in.

Nara asked, "You have your rifle, Reggie?"

Reggie nodded.

"And I have my pulse staff. We're good. Let's go." Once they were bundled up, Nara took Reggie's arm and pulled her out into the cold.

Denton started after them. "Wait a minute. We need a better plan than that. Let's just slow down." He stood at the entrance to the shelter and watched them climb down to a gentler slope, and off into the white nothingness. He couldn't figure out how they'd gone around him so quickly. He was used to all of his orders being taken seriously —even his suggestions were heeded— but here, these two women had ignored him and done what they wanted. It wasn't military, but neither were the two women that vanished down the hill before his eyes.

Denton moved out of the entrance and sat in the shelter; his mind suddenly as numb as the rest of his body. It was like a brain freeze from eating ice cream too fast. He felt himself shutting down and he ached from head to toe. He leaned back and rested his head on the cave wall.

When Healy got back, she'd be sure to follow orders.

DENTON

CONGO RIVER REGION - SEVEN YEARS EARLIER

The doctor wasn't joking. After dust-off in one of the black helicopters, Morley and Nara flew Denton back to the base, had a quick talk with his C.O., which Denton wasn't privy to, and then a small detail helped him pack everything he owned. They left within the hour.

"That thing in the Congo… How did your people finally kill it? Wore it down? Found a weak spot?" Denton looked at his two new friends as they sat strapped in the uncomfortable seats.

"Kill it? That wasn't the idea. That's never been the idea," Morley said. "They used a powerful sedative. Started by numbing it with a mixture they dropped into the water, and when it surfaced for air, they knocked it out."

Nara nodded, but kept her eyes glued on the outside as it passed.

"What? What the hell is it, and why would you want it alive?"

"When we went in to talk to your commanding officer, we told him you'd stumbled across some classified information and we needed to borrow you while we debrief you," Morley said. "Now, had you been in that room, you probably would have been tempted to blurt out some nonsense about a killer behemoth in the river that killed your terrorists and most of your group as well. Wouldn't you?"

Denton shrugged.

"You were probably tempted to talk to someone about it while you waited for us outside the office, weren't you?"

The shock hadn't really worn off enough for him to want to talk to anyone. He was still processing the thing he'd seen in the water —and the bones scattered around it.

"They'd think you were nuts, right?" The doctor glanced at him with a smile. "We all went through it. Members of our own government laughed too, until we were able to give them proof."

"Videos convinced them?"

"No. We took a few to the Anvil," Morley said.

"The Anvil?"

Nara turned from the window and nodded. "The White Anvil. It's a safe lab and holding facility for things that need to be studied a little further, away from prying eyes. It's tucked in nice and cozy in a remote part of Canada. You can only get there by train."

"The airspace is highly restricted and anything that wanders in is dealt with in the harshest manner," the doctor said.

There's a secret government prison in Canada. The thought swirled around in Denton's head as he considered all the black ops prisons he knew of that were run by the United States. The name White Anvil was not on that list. The fact that it housed monsters was secondary. He was more affronted by the fact that he'd not heard of it. "Are you bringing the other survivors from my detail along as well?"

The doctor sighed. "Unfortunately, they are not doing well. They're resting, but your leader in that effort is in a full-blown catatonic state. Hasn't been able to speak or communicate since the incident. The others are being evaluated."

Did anyone else really know where he was? Denton wondered. If they shoved him out of the helicopter to get him to keep quiet about what he'd seen, was there any way his story would ever be told?

"You look uncomfortable," Nara said. "Your detail really *is* being evaluated, and they really are kind of broken about what they saw. They aren't being locked up to hide our secrets or anything." She leaned in and he could feel his muscles tense as he wondered about her intentions. "And we're not taking you out somewhere to kill you, either."

Denton's eyes narrowed.

"How'd I know you were thinking that? I thought the same thing when I was recruited." Nara shrugged. "I'm still here. You will be too."

"Why me? Why am I not being evaluated?"

"You're the calmest I've ever seen anyone after such an encounter. Well…" Morley nodded to Nara, "almost the calmest."

They landed at the Maya-Maya Airport, and were rushed onto a private plane. It all happened very quickly and they were airborne again less than twenty minutes later.

Nara sat down across the aisle from Denton. "I have to admit; you're taking this very well. Quite a few of our recruits go a little crazy getting on the plane, they start asking too many questions."

It surprised him, too. "I don't know. I think I'm just curious at this point. And," he said, "orders are orders, I suppose."

There was a nagging voice in Denton's head. It seemed not to be warning him of imminent danger, but that if he didn't go along, he'd miss something amazing.

MARGO

"I've got about six shots left in the rifle, and a pistol with an eight-shot mag," Clarke said. "Do you have anything?"

Margo nearly forgot that Clarke hadn't seen her take the gun from the dead soldier at the other end of the tunnel. There was no sense in hiding it now, so she pulled the pistol from inside her coat. "It's a revolver, I guess. Six shots."

Clarke nodded.

They both squinted off into the almost-darkness. The crackle of footfalls on ice and rock was sporadic, but still enough to assure Margo that something was coming. Her hope was that it was some*one*, but she didn't want to shout and give away her position, even if it did happen to be a human headed their way. Her hope, or, in this case, *strategy*, was that if it was a blood-thirsty beast, it might be inclined to give up halfway down the tunnel if it didn't hear anything. It was a tenuous plan, one which took very little into account, not least that there was nowhere else to go. It was a tunnel, after all —two ends, two exits, and not a single chance to diverge from the straight path.

"I guess we wait until we actually see something before we shoot." Clarke had her rifle resting against her barricade, pointed down toward the darkness.

There was no guarantee that firing would be any use, from what Margo had seen. The monster didn't seem to have many vulnerable spots. "I guess." She looked behind them at the flat panels of the train car. "I'm still rooting for the others to get here and find a way through that metal."

"I'll keep my fingers crossed, but you may want to be prepared for the worst," Clarke said.

The wait was maddening, especially with the ever-increasing sounds; whatever it was, was coming their way. Whatever was going to happen, she wanted it over with. Better or worse. She tensed with her pistol, ready to fire, when she took a moment to listen to the noise again. "Clarke, it sounds like more than one. The steps are off."

"What?"

Both women went quiet and concentrated hard.

"Shit," Clarke said. "Two. How are we going to do this? We were fucked as it was, fighting against just one of those things."

Behind, a rhythmic tapping emanated from the train, accompanied by the hum of a small motor.

"They're back!" Margo nearly shouted as she pulled the walkie-talkie from her jacket. "Hello? Reggie? Are you there? Over." She waited, listening through the static for a reply. "Adam? This is Margo. What's happening up there? We need help." More static. She clicked the mic again. "Over?" She stayed quiet, afraid to even breathe for fear of missing something. The noise droned on, and she guessed it was a drill of some sort, which they were trying to use to cut the car floor.

A shot startled Margo and a flash of light illuminated the area. She turned to see what was happening, but the corridor was black, her night vision ruined by the flash. The walkie-talkie tumbled to the ground. She fumbled for the pistol again, and once it was free, she pointed it down the tunnel just in time to see the horrifying faces of two of the monsters, lit up by a second shot from Clarke's rifle. Their eyes glowed red with the gunshot and the sight burned into Margo's mind.

And then they were gone. The light faded.

She squeezed the trigger of the revolver and took three shots in rapid succession, giving her a nearly uninterrupted view of the horror that was upon her. The beasts' long arms reached for Clarke, their movements unimpeded by the darkness or the barrage of gunfire that pelted them.

One of the beasts gripped the large rock Clarke was using for cover and threw it aside like it was nothing. A long pair of hairy arms grabbed for Clarke as the tunnel went dark again. Margo turned and climbed the rocks in the dark, making her way up to the train car; all the while, her ears were filled with screams.

She found the cold metal by the sound of the drill and by feeling around, and once she located it, she pounded on the metal panel, producing a muffled thump. She cursed and felt around for a rock, and used it to make a louder noise than her hands could. It got louder and she doubled her efforts, but still the motor sound continued uninterrupted. She tried again and slammed the rock down harder. She shouted for Adam, for her sister, but nothing seemed to get through.

Her ankle felt numb suddenly. Below her, a massive hand had wrapped around her boot and was squeezing. Before she could react, the beast yanked hard, pulling her off-balance. She dropped to the rocks and ice under her, slamming onto the right side of her head. Without thinking about it, she threw the rock she was holding, and it bounced off the thing's rigid head and off into the darkness. Somewhere in the debris, Margo had set her gun aside to pound on the train, and now she frantically felt around to find it as the rugaru began pulling her down off her perch.

The smell —that same stench that had overtaken her the first time she was attacked— met her nostrils, and the memory made her fight that much harder to find the gun. She patted the nearby rocks, knocking pebbles and ice chunks aside, then swiped across the flat surfaces, hoping to hear the weapon slide on the rocks.

As she slid across the cold, stony surface, dragged by the beast, she heard metal scrape against rock to her right as her flailing hands connected with something. She looked behind her and could now make out the outline of the rugaru climbing closer, one hand still around her ankle, pulling.

Margo frantically patted the rocks where she'd heard the pistol fall and after finding loose stones and ice, her hands finally gripped the barrel. She fumbled with it, trying to right it in her hand.

The beast roared and pulled her backward even more. The monster's howl hurt her ears at such a close range, and she could smell nothing but the same rotting sulphur from the first encounter she'd had with it. She gripped the gun and slid her finger through the trigger guard. She turned, and immediately, those blood-red eyes stared back at her. The gun barked and brought with it a bright, blinding flash of red. She heard the rugaru screech in pain and felt the grip on her ankle loosen.

She rolled over onto her stomach and crawled back up toward the crashed car.

She had trouble hearing after the roar and the close gunshot, but the drilling inside the car seemed to have stopped. "Help!" she called. She hoped that someone had heard something. She feared that even if they had, they still wouldn't be able to get through.

Margo blinked rapidly, trying to see anything but the big yellow dot that was in front of her eyes as an after-effect of the muzzle flash. The rugaru was still groaning and growling nearby, but the sound seemed to be fading. "Help," she said. Remembering the walkie-talkie, she patted her pockets to find it.

Far down the tunnel, she heard Clarke scream.

In her hand, the speaker came to life in a mess of static. "Are you still there? What was that sound? Over." It was Adam's voice again.

Margo stared at the darkness that still had a tinge of orange around the outside. Clarke was still struggling and shouting. It was only hours ago that Margo was in her place, stuck in the grip of some horrible beast that had stepped right out of a nightmare. She didn't want to let Clarke go through the same ordeal, but she couldn't move. Her arms and legs wouldn't allow her to climb down the debris and give chase to try to help. All she could do was remember the powerful grip of the thick, long arms—and that stench.

"Margo? Are you there? It's Reggie. Are you alright? Answer me." The walkie-talkie was clear, and the voice a welcome jolt. "Go-go?"

"I'm here, Reggie. I'm…" Margo started to say she was fine, but couldn't do it. "Are you okay?"

“Hey! I’m holding up. Look, Adam is here —and Nara. We’re doing our best to cut through this floor, but the drill is having a tough time. It’s too small to work on anything this tough. We’re looking for other ways, but just hang in there.”

Margo had been holding her breath as Reggie spoke, hoping she’d have good news about getting through, and when her sister was done talking, she let the air out. “There are two of those things in this tunnel. One dragged Clarke away and I think I really hurt the other, but they could come back.”

“What? Margo, is there any other way out?” Reggie asked.

“No. Just the other end of this tunnel.” Margo thought about Clarke. “Look, you’re okay, right Reggie? That’s what matters.”

A different voice answered. “Margo? It’s Nara, I’m Doctor Morley’s partner. Have you seen him? Do you know where he is?”

“I’m afraid he might be dead, but I don’t know for sure. One of the prisoners wanted to take that baton of his. I left before they took it from him,” Margo said. She waited in silence for a moment, the speaker next to her ear.

“Stay put. We’re coming for you,” Reggie said. “Love you, sis.”

“Love you.” Margo put the device in her pocket and climbed down the rockpile to the floor of the tunnel. “Love you, but I’m not staying put.” She looked for anything that Clarke may have dropped, and luckily found the rifle. After holding it close to her face, she was able to see it had only two shots in it. The pistol only had one.

With the thoughts of her encounters with the rugaru fresh in her mind, Margo raised the pistol and ventured into the darkness.

DENTON

WHITE ANVIL PRISON - SEVEN YEARS EARLIER

Nara led the way, with the doctor not far behind, and Denton at the rear. They walked down long white corridors with various codes and arrows built into the floor showing the way. Denton asked himself what this place actually was —and was particularly dubious about what it contained. "Where are we going?" he asked.

"Your gear is headed for the barracks, but we assumed we'd better show you the goods before you started to think we were just making shit up," Nara said. "If you turned right at the next intersection, you'd find yourself at the commissary, and then the exchange, then the mess."

Denton nodded and tried to look interested. He was suddenly not so concerned with monsters and secret bases as he was with getting sleep and finding a shower. Each step felt like he was moving concrete and he was glad he was last in line, so he didn't overwhelm the others with his aroma. The mention of the chow hall reminded him he hadn't eaten since before the failed raid on the terrorist camp. On the journey to White Anvil, he'd managed to dig a granola bar out of his ruck, but that was about it.

Turning away from the commissary, they walked through large automatic doors and were immediately able to step on a moving sidewalk. Each side of the hall had a long, wide, people-mover; the kind Denton had only seen in airports.

"The military likes their soldiers to walk everywhere. Some kind of ridiculous exercise thing, I suppose." The doctor gripped the moving rail at the side carefully. "Fuck that. I'm too old for that. If you want to walk while the sidewalk moves you, be my guest, but I'm going to just glide along, if it's all the same."

Every soldier was acquainted with the notion of walking, hiking, and marching every damn place, but it was a welcome break for Denton. He stepped onto the moving floor and leaned himself against the rail. His feet needed the rest after tromping through a jungle for as long as he had.

"We looked at your files. You seem to have a pretty full background in the military. I didn't see any easy posts there; mostly combat and high-alert placements," Nara said. "You don't like to do anything easy?"

"The only easy day was yesterday, at least that's what they tell us." Denton felt silly repeating a military mantra for the scientists, but he was too tired to be clever.

"Isn't that a Navy SEALS thing?"

"Yeah. I suppose it is."

They'd been travelling the walkway for a while when it finally came to an end much further than he'd expected. "There's more to this place?"

"Now you know why I was insistent on taking the easy way. I'm not as young as I used to be, and that walk is a bitch." The doctor smiled. "But we'll be done in a couple of minutes. Then, we take the elevator up, and we're there."

It wasn't entirely clear where "there" was, but the doctor and his partner seemed to believe it would explain everything. So Denton got off the sidewalk, entered the elevator at the end, and tried to put on an interested face for his hosts.

"Look. You have to know that what you're about to see is classified, and few have seen it. Few even know about it."

Even as the doors slid open, Denton was still sure that whatever they were about to show him was something completely mundane.

He was wrong.

DENTON

Healy's descent to their hiding place woke Denton from his deep sleep. The prisoners were already awake, and had been for a while, as far as he could tell. There was absolutely no sign that they'd tried to escape, or even wanted to.

"Where'd the others go?" Healy asked.

"They made contact with Reggie's sister through the walkie-talkies down by the train car. She wanted to get down there and see if she could help."

"How's the leg?" Healy reached down to pull back the cloth.

"Feels a little better." Denton winced as the cloth and bandage shifted the wound. When he'd sat down to rest, he'd placed a large chunk of ice on his leg, and that had done wonders. Maybe it wasn't really better, but the ice at least made the pain go away. "It isn't still bleeding, is it?"

"Not that I can see. Maybe we need to change this wrap, though." Healy dug into a small pack and pulled out a roll of gauze and a bandage. She was as gentle as possible, but matter of fact about what she was doing. It still hurt.

"I know your answer, but I would be a bad doctor here if I didn't suggest you sit this one out. Maybe you should take the prisoners and make your way back to the train car with Lowenstein and the others. He'd be better able to take care of this than I am, and you could coordinate things better from there. I'm sure it's better protected than out in the open like this."

She was right to present the possibility, and she did it as gently as possible. But she was right. There was no way he was going to stand by and let the others risk their lives. Once everyone else was safe, he'd find time to rest. "Thanks. I'll take it under consideration. Finish up with the field dressing and let's get going."

Once she was finished, he stood and checked if he could put weight on it. He wasn't comfortable, but he could stand. He hoped the cold would help and it would get easier to walk as he went. He leaned out of their little alcove and stared at the steep incline below, wincing. Walking might be doable, but the climb would hurt. "Best get to it."

He checked on the prisoners. They seemed to be doing better than expected. He checked their hands and found their skin white and cracked, but neither seemed to be suffering from hypothermia; perhaps mild frostbite. Healy had come up with the idea of cutting out the linings of coat pockets to make mittens. They were as thick as gloves and allowed some mobility once they were secured. They weren't pretty, but they kept fingers from falling off in the cold.

The car looked about three quarters its normal size; the result of the impact. Denton took a few moments to examine how it was wedged into the rocks; it seemed like the metal had secured itself well, thanks to gravity crushing the car like a soda can.

He leaned in through the gap in the wall and took in the scene. Adam and Reggie were standing on either side of a wide black spot. Bits and pieces of the floor had been chipped away and there were scratches from the drill, but little progress had been made in getting through. Clinging to some cabinets on the far wall, Nara was digging through boxes and bags, tossing whatever she didn't need down into the crushed bottom of the train car where a considerable amount of junk had already gathered. "Are we sure this thing is going to hold us all? Maybe we need to wait outside?" Denton asked. "I don't want to be the one that takes this thing over the edge. Hate to see us all survive this far and get killed because of me."

"It's fine." Adam waved Denton inside.

"Yeah, see?" Reggie jumped up and down and the car barely shook. "We're fine."

Denton took in Reggie's enthusiasm. "You seem cheery for someone trapped in the wilderness."

Reggie shook her head. "Anxious."

"She talked to her sister on the walkie-talkie." Nara stepped down and helped Denton get to level ground. "Margo should be just below us, on the other side of this wall. But last we heard, there was one of those snow beasts in the tunnel with her."

"Below us?" Denton leaned himself against the wall to take some pressure off of his leg. "How's that?"

"My guess is we're over a pass-through for animals. The government started building them under roads and railways to avoid animal strikes. Instead of crossing a busy road and running the risk of getting hit and causing damage, the animals make their way under a dangerous situation," Adam said. "They built a couple out my way to keep the caribou safe during migration."

"Could be. There's a lot of trains with cargo of a sensitive nature that come through here. I'm sure they'd like to keep those trains running and not kill innocent animals," Nara said.

Reggie nodded a little more emphatically than she needed to. If a nod could be sarcastic, this would be it. "This is all fascinating, but how are we going to get to my sister?"

"We can go around to the other end, and catch up with her there," Nara said.

"We're having enough trouble making our way as it is, do we really want to try to climb back up this side and then all the way back down the other?" Healy asked. "Who knows what we'll run into between here and there?"

The floor was solid enough that the tools at hand weren't going to do the job. "We might not have a choice. If we can't get through this, we'll have to face the fact that *over* is the only way to go." The faces glaring back at Denton didn't look thrilled about the idea of more climbing and more of the storm outside.

Reggie took issue with the idea. "Excuse me? My sister is just on the other side of this fucking train. Can we make up our minds here? There isn't time for guessing."

"One way might be just as fast as the other, hell, we might not ever get through this metal," Healy said. "The train was meant to hold prisoners and monsters; I guess someone took their job seriously."

"Hey?" Hall called from higher up in the car. She and Cook had climbed up into the compartment where Nara would monitor the rugaru during transport. "There's a few things we can do in here, maybe. There's communications, controls, plenty of other stuff. We just need power."

"You think that can help our current situation?" Denton was nervous about having prisoners running loose, but figured Hall and Cook were in rough enough shape that they weren't going to try to run away, and, as they'd already trapped themselves in the cold once, he doubted they'd try it again.

"Look," Cook leaned out of the doorway next to Hall. "If we can get power on, maybe we can get some communication going with the rest of the world. Or at least the prison."

"Nara? If I'm reading this right, do these creature containment units come out individually?" Hall asked.

"Yes. They're designed to pop out and attach to their cages back at the base. Why?"

"Well, if I'm reading this right, they separate using an electronic assist. The train car ejects them, in other words," Cook said. "Maybe if we can get the cars to eject from the main car, that force may move the car itself, since we're wedged in here."

The idea spun around in Denton's mind until the full potential hit him. "If the car moves, maybe it'll break free from the rocks and give us room to get into the tunnel somehow?"

"Or knock rocks or ice away, one or the other." Hall's face was a mix of hope and doubt, and Denton understood completely.

"I don't quite follow," Adam said.

Reggie waved her hands around, trying to conjure an explanation out of thin air. "Look, you know Pez? You know Pez?"

"I know Pez." Adam nodded.

"The little candy dispenser? When you pull the head back and it pushes a piece of candy out?" She looked around to see if the others understood, and got shrugs of agreement. "That's what we're talking about. This mechanism will unlock the pod from the car and push the pod free of its housing. Like a Pez."

It seemed to land with Adam as well as the others. "I like Pez. Thanks."

It all seemed like a longshot, and it felt like wasted time even trying while people were still out there. Still, Denton knew the rest of the group was behind it. Maybe because it gave them something to do rather than freezing their asses off out in the elements. It also gave these people a chance to put their talents to good use. He figured it couldn't hurt to explore it. "How do we get power back?"

"It's operated by battery cells. They were fully charged when we left. Enough power for three days or so," Nara said.

"So, if the power cells are intact, it might just be the connections that are off. Fix those and we're good," Adam said. "Hopefully."

Reggie climbed up toward the cabin with the prisoners. "I'm on this. Let me see what the power source and stuff look like."

One of the prisoners raised her hand and waved. "We're good with computers and wiring and whatnot. Give us a chance?"

He wasn't sure if it was a good idea, but Denton did know that if they tried to screw anyone over, they would be putting themselves in just as much danger as the rest of the group. Cook didn't look nearly as sure as his companion. He was rubbing his hands, itching. Did he have frostbite? Was the cold taking its toll on the unprepared?

"Get in there and do what you can. See if you can get something working so we can call for a rescue." Denton watched the three of them climb upward to the operations room.

Healy, Nara and Adam took another look at the metal floor and sighed.

MARGO

The wind screeched in the tunnel, keeping Margo on edge, reminding her of the monsters she was pursuing. As much as she wanted to wait around in the mess of rocks and snow, just to hug her sister, just to make sure she was safe, she felt an obligation to Clarke. The idea that someone else was facing the same fate drove her to launch herself headlong into the darkness, with only one hand on the wall to guide her.

She heard nothing from the tunnel besides the wind. She had no idea whether the creatures had made it out the other side yet, or whether Clarke was alive or dead. Still, Margo was dead set on finding her and she didn't know why. Pity? Compassion? Excitement?

Of the two sisters, Reggie would be the one to race down the tunnel to save someone she didn't know. Not Margo. She'd hope for the best and let someone more qualified handle it. Especially if it involved a convicted criminal. Margo was straight and narrow, all the way. Reggie just *did* things.

Margo was constantly amazed by the stories Reggie would tell at the dinner table when they used to meet at their mom's house for dinner every week. She talked about axe throwing and skydiving, white water rafting, kickboxing —once, she apparently took a course for firefighters, but dropped out after a couple of weeks. It was a litany of high-risk thrills, one after another. Margo was impressed for a time, amazed that her sister was so daring, when she herself played everything safe.

It eventually occurred to her, though, that Reggie didn't stick with anything, and never saw any of her crazy notions through. Dropping out of firefighter school was only one in a long line of failures and fuck-ups. Community college lasted all of six months, the tech start-up dissolved, and who the hell knows what happened to her gig as a tour guide to paranormal hotspots in Saint Augustine. Reggie's career path seemed to be based on fun and circumstance.

At times, it infuriated Margo.

At times, it drove her mad with jealousy.

Margo had graduated from CalTech, thinking California would be a great place to study plate tectonics, earthquakes, and predictive methods. She joined a small research firm, where she met Evan Bertram and others who eventually recruited her to Nycroft Industries, where she'd been ever since. She was all about the stability, whereas Reggie was in a constant state of reinvention. Or was it combustion?

Nine times out of ten, Reggie would be the person most likely to run into a burning building to save a kitten. But today, something was different. Was this how Reggie felt all the time?

Margo was heartened to see signs of light up ahead; whatever glow of the moon or the stars that made it through the clouds and pierced the snow made her passage a level or two easier. At the end of the tunnel, the light was almost blinding for a moment even though it was nighttime, and the wind was still making it difficult to see ten feet away, but compared to the tunnel, it was like a spotlight.

Near the mouth, she stopped to gather herself and prepare for the cold outside, when she noticed something. The two dead soldiers were gone. There were wide trails on the ground that showed where they'd been dragged out into the elements. Blood stained the white of the ground where they'd both rested. Nearby, the big black container full of electronics lay on its side, useless —and still not open.

The scene brought Margo to a halt. The two soldiers. The other prisoner, Shepard. All gone. Were they carried off by the two beasts, or were there even *more* of the monsters? What was she walking into?

She checked the gun, a grim reminder that she had only one shot left. Nearby, she saw one of the pieces of the pulse baton that the rugaru had broken easily in the fight with Shepard, and in her mind she replayed the monster snapping it in half and impaling him with it. The darkness and anonymity of the tunnel behind her suddenly felt welcoming. Maybe Denton had found a way through? She took a deep breath and wondered why she hadn't had faith that her sister might have found a way through, before a perfect stranger.

In the near distance, maybe twenty or thirty feet—at the extreme of her line of vision—Margo could make out two dark shapes; blobs, really. She had to assume they were the rugaru because there was no detail to be made out in the blowing snow. The fact that the two creatures were likely carrying or dragging human bodies along with them likely aided in the confusion of identifying the things. In the moment it took her to pause, the objects moved out of view.

Margo regarded the path the bodies left in the snow, and then the two sets of bloody bare footprints in the middle of them. She pulled her gloves on, sealed them as best she could, fixed her face mask, and tightened her hood tight around her head.

Her chest tightened as she stepped out of the tunnel to the rugaru into the foothills of the mountains.

ADAM

As everyone else was trying to solve the problem of getting through the metal car floor, Adam climbed up to check on the effort to restore power. "Everything going okay up here?" He looked inside the small compartment and found he had been talking mainly to legs and torsos. Both prisoners and Reggie had burrowed into the guts of the car's electronics and communications cabinets. Reggie was on the floor, half-hanging into an area where she'd removed the flooring. The two prisoners had taken the doors off of several cabinets, and were leaning into them on either side of the room.

"Dude. It's kind of crowded in here as it is," Cook said.

It had been quite some time since anyone had called Adam 'dude,' of that much he was sure. "I can see that. Just seeing what I can do."

Reggie shouted from her enclave. "Thanks, anything out there resembling a flat-head screwdriver?"

An array of various tools and objects rested on a tray in the middle of the room. There were medical clamps, syringes, parts of an eyeglass repair kit, scalpels, a roll of medical tape, some nail polish, and some metal screws that appeared to have been removed from the cabinet doors. "I don't see one."

"I'm using one," Hall shouted.

Adam dug through the junk. "How about a scalpel?"

"No. Too delicate. But pass me one anyway, I can use it to cut and strip some of this wire," Reggie said.

There wasn't much that had the flat surface needed to make a screw turn, so Adam started thinking about alternatives that weren't on the tray. "How big are the screws?"

"These are kind of big, why?" Reggie asked.

"Would a penny work?" Adam asked. He started patting his heavy jacket and snow pants, looking for any change he might have.

"Might do."

Adam pulled the zipper down and dug into his uniform shirt, feeling the pockets. He dug out an ink pen and set it aside, then found some business cards they handed out in the community. He thought of all the things that were on his belt that would have been helpful had he not left it back at the RCMP barracks.

His fingers found some change. Possibly better than a penny. "Would a dime work?" He held the coin up in front of his face and examined it.

"Might be better than a screwdriver. Easier to turn in a small space." Reggie's hand shot out and she wiggled her fingers. "Gimme."

Adam placed the coin in her palm and watched the whole arm disappear back under the console. "No problem." He looked around the little room and started to step out once he realized that a Canadian dime was the only contribution he could make. "I'll stay out of the way. Let me know if you need anything."

He barely had time to turn before Reggie responded. "Stay out of the way, but stick around. We may need a lackey to help us out. You know, fetch parts, get us drinks, wipe our brows and whatnot."

Nara, Denton, and Healy were making progress on the hole through the train car, having decided to keep working in case they couldn't eject the pods, *or in case something else went wrong.* There didn't seem to be much room for another person. "Okay. I'm not sure what I can do with all the technical stuff, but I'll stay."

"Keep us company. Sing a song or something. I'm sick of that wind rattling everything," Reggie said. "Make some noise or something."

"Ooh. Music would be brilliant. Know any Aerosmith?" Hall asked.

The other prisoner put in his two cents as well. "Ugh. How about some Common or Ice Cube?"

There wasn't an overabundance of rap played out in the territory Adam covered, and it wasn't exactly his thing, though he was positive his daughter could cite both those artists' back catalogues without batting an eyelid. She was more into Public Enemy, but she didn't like to limit herself. "Sorry, my rap knowledge ends with MC Hammer."

"Who?" Hall asked.

He'd always figured he was getting old, and it was things like this that confirmed it. "Never mind," he said.

"Then tell us a story, anything to break the silence. Come on," Reggie said. "You're on your way to see your daughter? She's having a baby? Talk."

It was a terrible time for a reminder of what he was missing. Adam checked his watch, more to try to waste time than anything. "Yeah. She's due tomorrow, technically. I suppose she could go at any time. She might have had the baby already, I guess." According to his watch, it was early morning—twelve past three. They'd left the station around eleven in the morning the day before. Sixteen hours out of contact with the outside world —and most of that in a snowstorm that buried the rails, the cars, and any hope that someone would find them.

"You, sir, are a terrible storyteller." Hall crawled out of her alcove, pulling a bundle of wires with her.

"Agreed," Reggie said. She also slid out of her work area and motioned for Adam to move aside so she could yell directly to Denton and the others. "Hey. So, there's good news and *less* good news from my end.

This car's gadgets run on four battery cells. Those things power the monitors for the pods, communications, the devices that make the monsters sleepy in their cages…"

"The neural dampeners. The pods have mechanisms that work in conjunction with the chips within their bodies that render the rugaru dormant…" Nara started.

"Not the time for a technical seminar," Denton said, holding his hand up to quiet her.

"Right. It powers everything in here normally. Probably charged up back at base for missions like this one?" Reggie stared at Nara expectantly.

"NOW I can talk?" Nara sighed.

Denton stared at her. "Yes. They're used each time we shuttle something in these particular cars."

"Great. Well, it uses four of those. I found that two were damaged to the point of uselessness. Nothing's going to bring those back. That's the less good news."

Adam spoke up, looking for the silver lining. "You said there was good news?"

"Yes. The other two are intact and functioning. They've both used about forty-five percent of their charge in the journey so far. That means if we use the batteries in tandem, we've got the power equivalent to about one battery. A little more," Reggie said.

"What's that get us?" Healy asked.

"Depends on what equipment works."

"I tore out everything around the communications. I think we can use the two-way. Should have a better range than the little walkie-talkies you guys are carrying." Hall tossed the wires she was holding onto the floor.

Cook leaned out so everyone could hear. "Of the four pods, I don't think we can get more than one to eject. And even then, we'd have to go outside and see which ones will work and which aren't crushed in place."

"I'll go," Adam said. He'd been inside the longest and figured it would be only fair to let the others warm up. "You just need one of those pods that isn't damaged too badly?"

Cook nodded. "That should do. Basically, the area around the rubber seals needs to be as free as possible."

"If we can get the radio working, how about the neural dampeners in the pods? Maybe that would at least keep us safe in here; the rugarus wouldn't be a problem, anyway," Nara said.

"That'll be a priority after we've got everything else working. I want to make sure we don't drain what battery power we do have before we get a call out and hopefully move this car." Denton looked like he was trying to maintain his military control, even though he was now outnumbered by non-military personnel.

Adam felt for him. Not everyone understood the pressure to keep the chain of command in military life. He remembered the old army adage that the chain of command was what they beat you with until you did what they told you to do. At least he *thought* he'd heard it from an RCMP buddy.

Adam stepped carefully on his way to the crack in the car that served as their exit and entrance, stopping only to secure his cold-weather gear. The wind caught him off-guard, forcing him to brace against the side of the car. The precipitation had stopped, but the wind was still blowing snow everywhere, making it tough to tell the difference. The climb up and over the car didn't seem as bad as he'd anticipated. The wind kept the snow off the rocks, but it also managed to make them slippery. Adam was forced to watch his hand and foot holds, while also keeping a watch for any creatures that might be stalking the area.

Those monsters, "rugaru," Nara had called them, reminded him of the stories the elders had told him around the campfire, and which the kids loved to read about on the internet. Back at the barracks, they loved to watch blurry YouTube videos with a splotch of something that was supposed to be Bigfoot, which would inevitably move quickly from view. He'd gone out on more than one call to investigate a noise complaint or intruder call that centered around a hairy monster in the woods.

Looking for monsters seemed to be a thriving pastime on Adam's beat. There were more monster hunters than stargazers in his neighborhood. He himself owned a telescope for looking at the constellations, brilliantly visible in the sky over the Yukon. On the rare occasions someone would come over to use it, the first question they'd ask was if he'd ever seen an unidentified flying object with it. U.F.O.s and monsters were the new mythology, leaving things like Zeus and Nanook in the dustbin.

Working in law enforcement out in the elements, Adam got used to extreme temperatures, but this storm was rougher than usual. The cold seemed colder somehow, the wind a little fiercer. Maybe the fact that the group was being stalked by mythical creatures that were out for blood had something to do with it.

Today, Adam wished he'd listened to a few of the cranks and crackpots he'd dismissed.

With the end of the car furthest away crushed and torn open, Adam assumed that the monsters had probably crawled out through the tears in those pods. The top pod had already launched or come loose, and the structure was already popped out by a foot or so. The second one down had lost part of the wall, but its framework seemed fine, and it was resting up against the rocks of the hillside. It appeared to be the best —and possibly *only* candidate.

Adam braced himself on the rocks and fished out a radio from his pocket. "This is Adam. It looks like number two is our only option. The rest are screwed. Over."

"Got it. Head back. We've got power for now; we'll wire it up to number two and try it after we radio for help," Healy answered. "Over."

"Copy." Adam pushed the radio into his pocket and found he had a hard time letting go of it. His hand was nearly frozen to the handset. After a moment of flexing his hand and closing his fingers of one hand, he did the same with the other hand, trying to get some warmth and motion back. His gloves were thick yet flexible; he'd worn them for years, but now, here, they just weren't cutting it.

The climb back up to the top of the train was tough with his digits behaving as slowly as they were, but Adam made it. He stared back up the slope to the ridge where they'd started and tried to see beyond, but it was impossible. The snow had died down, but the wind was still whipping around, making it look like the storm was still laying it down in blankets.

It would be a short climb down to the tear in the car, but Adam felt his heart sink anyway. His limbs were tired, and his chest ached from the strain on his muscles. He knelt down and placed his foot on the best hold he could find.

From the corner of his eye, he saw a dark object racing toward him from his left. Thinking it was a loose rock, he flattened himself on the ground, hoping it would bounce over his head harmlessly. When he looked up to see what had happened, he found he was face-to-face with a brown-and-white rugaru, hands flexing, claws long and dark, at the ready.

Going on instinct alone, Adam reached for the pistol at his side. The creature was relatively quick, and its long limbs gave it the advantage. It swung an arm, tearing into Adam's shoulder and ripping the jacket across his chest. The sudden burning pain made him drop his weapon, though he'd barely had a chance to clear it from the holster. He recoiled in pain, forgetting that he was already teetering on the edge of rocks.

Adam flailed his arms, trying to regain his balance, but couldn't. He fell backwards and landed on his shoulders on the rocks below and slid down the slope until the side of the car brought him to a halt. He fought the need to black out from the sudden pain, and tried to focus on the shadow that was making its way toward him.

MARGO

The tracks led to a slight incline that went up the opposite side from the train tracks. Margo couldn't help but feel she'd made a mistake in pursuing the beasts alone. The single bullet in her pistol was little comfort faced with the possibility that she could be up against multiple monsters in her quest to help the one woman she knew was still alive.

Hoped was still alive.

As she followed the trail, she began to notice a series of cave entrances in the rocks above. The path she was following ended with the snow just below the caves. Most of the holes in the mountain were too small for anyone to fit through, but she made out two or three of maybe a dozen that the creatures could easily make it through. She climbed to the largest opening and found it wasn't much of a cave after all, and it ended mere feet from where it began. It did manage to offer a place for her to stop and catch her breath and adjust her gear for warmth.

Somewhere nearby, she could hear the howl of one of the rugarus. The enclosure she'd secreted herself into made it a little easier to hear over the winds outside. The sound was close, likely from one of the caves next to her. It spurred her to move on from the comfort of the shelter and on to the next cave.

The cold wind hit her again once she stepped into the open. She climbed easily to the next large opening and accidentally kicked something in her path. On the ground was a torn backpack, like the ones the soldiers had been carrying when they got on the train. Around the pack, she found parts of a broken compass, a green metal flashlight, and a ripped package of gross, pre-packaged army food that she'd heard campers call MREs on several previous expeditions. Margo picked the flashlight up and tested it. It flickered a little when she first turned it on, but it quickly emitted a bright, steady beam of light.

The light illuminated a red trail from the ground next to the pack, and on into the darkness of the tunnel. Another howl echoed out and filled Margo's mind with hesitation again. She feared chasing after Clarke was foolish and was sure to end up with her own death. Still, she refused to talk herself out of it, and took the first step into the tunnel.

DENTON

WHITE ANVIL PRISON - SEVEN YEARS EARLIER

The group of soldiers got off the elevator, following Morley and Nara into a white hall lined with a dozen or so sterile cages with wide plexiglass fronts to them that allowed everyone to see in. In front of every enclosure stood a man or woman with a clipboard, waiting expectantly. As they walked down the corridor, Denton and everyone else leaned over to see what was in the rooms, but they all appeared empty. Morley pointed to the first man with a clipboard and called out, "Taylor? This is Doctor Banfield. You'll be assigned to her. You can start your orientation now." A blonde recruit in a dark camo uniform stepped forward. "Yes, sir."

They continued down the hall, stopping at each person and offloading a soldier to be paired with them. At the end of the hall, Doctor Morley stopped at a room with no scientist posted. "Sergeant Denton? You'll be working directly with Nara and me on continuing the rugaru project."

Denton looked at the door before them, looming like a portal to the unknown. "Continuing?"

"The last security detail moved on," Nara said. She leaned over a pad on the wall and tapped in a code. The door slid open and she stepped through.

"New assignment?" Denton asked.

The doctor followed Nara. "Sure. To a new assignment."

The next room was a narrow hallway that led to another keypad and door. Denton assumed it was some sort of security measure; a double layer of security to keep people out. "So, what is the Rugaru Project? Does it have something to do with those huge creatures from back in the Congo?" Denton could hear the words that came out of his mouth and wondered how he would have been affected by them ten or even five years ago. It certainly would have sent his mind into a tailspin, but now he seemed comfortable asking about giant river monsters.

"No. Not at all. The Rugaru Project is different," Nara said. "Your river monster was one of a kind as far as we know. The rugaru is…" Nara keyed in another password and pushed the door open. "The rugaru is *different*."

Denton walked through the entrance and stopped, startled by what he saw.

The room beyond the door was a large, almost warehouse-sized containment area. It was two levels, with maybe thirty large animal enclosures on each. Each enclosure consisted of two rows of bars surrounded by plexiglass, creating a third row of protection. Denton stood and listened for any sounds, but it was quiet in the room. The smell reminded him of his neighbor's barn from when he was growing up. There was the scent of straw, maybe fresh-cut grass, maybe manure. He scanned the cages, but they were all dark, as was the center of the room. Only a few dim lights illuminated the areas nearest the cages. "I don't see anything."

"Get closer." The doctor seemed amused. He and Nara moved to a bank of computers and monitors on the far wall. From that vantage point, Denton could make out shapes in the cages —rocks, trees, he guessed— all dark outlines of bumpy objects.

"I still don't…" Denton started. At the same time, Nara slid a switch upward. The lighting in the nearest cage came up to reveal that the objects weren't rocks, but large hairy creatures drowsing on the cage floor among fake trees and rubber tires. It was built like a gorilla enclosure at a zoo. "What's that over there? The white one? Is that a razorback gorilla?"

"No," the doctor said.

They all watched as the thing with gray-white hair sat up, still half-asleep. It gazed in Denton's direction. The face was more man than ape; more human than animal. A thick ridge ran from its forehead all the way to the back of its head. The reddish-orange eyes were droopy, but they pierced the low light and seemed to stare right at him.

"That's Elias. The big one. He's the alpha," Nara said. "He's the one to watch out for."

"The others are friendly?" Denton was skeptical.

Morley laughed. "Oh, heavens no. They're all dangerous. But the others will at least kill you before they swallow you."

"Elias would leave you alive just to be an asshole about it," Nara said.

It sounded like a joke, but neither of Denton's new acquaintances laughed or even cracked a smile. "Why Elias? What's the significance of that name?"

"Oh, all the good names have been snatched up. We've started naming the rugaru after features of the Canadian Rockies. Dull, I know."

"Doctor McPherson got to name his beasts after rock stars. The lucky bastard," Morley said.

Nara agreed. "You should have been here when Jagger bit off Starr's head. It was a pretty crazy day."

The sheer volume of things that had been thrown at Denton in the course of about forty-eight hours made him doubt the nature of reality for just a moment, but something deep inside of him righted the world and accepted things as they came.

As the trio stood staring at the terrifying majesty of the strange creature, it stood and strolled to the edge of the containment unit. The beast turned without breaking stride and walked to the far edge of its room, then paced back along the clear plastic wall, staring at Denton the whole time. It walked hunched over, long arms straight down at its sides. Denton stuck with calling it 'The Alpha' or even the file number for the beast in the computer - J20. He was positive he would never get around to thinking of it as an "Elias."

The creature took protracted strides as it moved, easily covering the length of the enclosure in seconds. Its scraggly hair covered nearly every inch of its body, other than its face, palms, and the soles of its feet. It had some sort of thick chest plate that was also hairless, but that was partially concealed by hair from other parts of the monster's body.

"Still not the least bit freaked out?" Nara asked. "I was pretty much a puddle of goo the first time I saw these things up close."

The rugaru stopped and put its two massive hands on the enclosure and balled them into fists and began slowly pounding on the thick opaque walls. Slowly at first, then building in frequency.

"I'm not exactly goo," Denton said. He watched the thing as it pummeled the wall. He could feel his heart beat just a little faster. His lack of a stronger response surprised him as well. He felt strangely at peace with being called out and threatened by a giant monster straight out of urban legends. "You know how you can feel like you belong somewhere? Like you're where you're supposed to be?"

"That's the dumbest thing I've ever heard." Doctor Morley shook his head.

The rhythm of J20 battering the enclosure became more erratic and Denton breathed a sigh of relief that the tantrum didn't last longer. Maybe this would bode well for his tenure at White Anvil.

As he exhaled, he saw movement behind J20 —shadows among the fake trees—- as more of the rugaru emerged from their resting, or *hiding* places. They joined J20, three of them, and began pounding on the wall just as their Alpha had done. One was covered in black hair from head to toe, the other two brown, all of them shorter and smaller in stature than their leader. After a minute, J20 stopped and moved back to his perch. The others continued the pounding at a rapid pace.

One of the black rugaru's hands began to bleed, a long streak of crimson spreading around the area where he struck the plastic undeterred.

"In folklore, the rugaru was sometimes a werewolf-type creature, sometimes a sasquatch, but we liked the name here. It just stuck."

"I'm pretty sure none of them like me," Denton said.

The doctor laughed. “No, *Elias* doesn’t like you. The rest just do as he wants them to.” He laughed again as he stepped out of the room.

The feeling of belonging didn’t fade from Denton’s mind, though several reminders to be well-armed at all times started to seep into his consciousness.

“You think you’re meant to be here or something?” Nara asked. “Like this is fate?”

“Kind of.” Denton shrugged.

“You believe in stuff like that?” Nara asked. “What a weirdo.”

DENTON

The floor was giving way —finally. They managed to peel back a section that led to the housing for the wiring that spanned the length of the floor, and after that, everything started to come up. It was due —in no small part, Denton knew- to Reggie's ability with a homemade tinsnip comprised of two scalpels rigged together.

"Great work, we're nearly through," he said.

"What? Are you kidding?" Nara asked. "We need to figure out how to widen it. We've got room for an arm here and that's it. So unless you're going on a miracle diet, we still have a lot of work to do."

It was true, but Denton didn't want to hear it. He was tired of standing around, *limping* around on the sidelines. He wanted to leave the smashed car behind, climb back up the hill, and down the other side to catch up with the others. That wasn't going to happen with his leg in the shape it was in.

"Denton," Reggie called down. "Adam is on the walkie-talkie. He's telling me to trigger one of the pods."

Healy dug into her pocket and handed her handset to Denton. He took it and cranked up the volume. "Hello? Adam, what's your situation? Over."

The tiny speaker squeaked with static and shouting. "Just eject number two. Number two." He was out of breath and struggling to say anything more.

"Adam, we don't know if that will work. Over," Denton said.

"One of them is here, it's got me. The rugaru has me pinned." Adam still sounded desperate. "It's my only chance."

Somewhere in the background, a growling sound made its way across the speaker, though Denton was sure he heard it coming through the walls of the car. "Adam, we don't know if it'll work. Over." As he waited for a response, he watched Healy climb toward the tear in the wall so she could get out to help Adam.

"What do you want me to do?" Reggie shouted.

Denton put the walkie-talkie up to his mouth again. "Adam? Come in."

"I'm going to try ejecting unit number two. That's what he wants, right?" Reggie asked. "I'm going to do it."

The idea that the power necessary to push the pod out could deplete their entire energy supply was frightening. They might not have any radio, or heat, and possibly no chance of resurrecting the dampeners that could put the rugarus to sleep. It put the group and their rescue in a horrible position.

"Denton, what the fuck do you want me to do?" Reggie shouted her question at him.

"Jesus." Denton looked up at Healy. "Brace yourself." He watched as she put her arms against a cabinet and the torn metal of the wall. When he was sure she was ready, she shouted, "Everyone hold on."

Without further comment or confirmation, Reggie turned and fiddled with some wires she'd rigged up. The convicts moved from their perches, presumably to hold onto something. In a second, Reggie shouted, "Here we go."

ADAM

As he slid himself along on his butt and hands, Adam made contact with the train car. The rugaru climbed down the rocks easily, and slowly made its way through the area next to the car. They were both in a sort of trench with the side of the car on one side and a sheer rock face on the other. For Adam, it meant he was trapped with only two possible exits; one was a good distance behind him, and the other was through the steadily advancing rugaru with the thick, stringy, black hair.

Adam was just rolling over onto all fours so he could attempt to stand and run, when a dull pain spread through his back. He didn't think he'd suffered any real injury when he had fallen, but now, looking at his path, there was a thin trail of red in the snow. "Well, *fuck*," he said to himself, and to the monster coming for him.

Still sliding downhill on his ass as best he could, Adam fumbled around for his weapon. It took a moment, but he discovered it on the ground where he'd fallen, which put it some three feet behind the rugaru, and useless.

In his desperation to find something to save him, he noticed the advancing monster brace itself against the car for balance. The thick hand landed next to the number four stenciled on the pod. It sparked the only idea he thought could lead to his escape. He glanced up just above himself and found the number three. *Three* was the only pod that didn't look damaged and which might actually be removable.

Adam fumbled in his pocket to pull the microphone free. He stopped pushing himself along and held his position. He keyed the mic. "Reggie? Can you hear me? Reggie, it's Adam, over." His hand shook as he spoke. "You have to blow open pod number two. Now."

The dark colored rugaru was only a few yards away. He could smell its terrible dung stench like it was already on top of him.

He argued and pleaded over the walkie-talkie with Denton, before throwing it to the side. He rolled as best he could and pulled himself along, all the while eyeing the seam that indicated where pod three ended and pod two began. He crawled faster, determined to make sure he was on the correct side of that line between the pods.

The rugaru reached out just as a loud click came from the car next to them. Adam pulled his legs away just as the pod ejected in a burst of smoke and the screech of scraping metal. The monster was caught between the rocks and a suddenly launched solid plastic cube like the one that had contained it. Adam watched as the impact crushed the thing, flattening it against the outcropping. The beast let out a startled yelp that ended quickly.

Adam didn't stare long. After he looked at the handful of inches that separated his boot from where the monster's severed hand fell, he let himself shout in relief and sheer terror at what had just happened. Near his head, the walkie-talkie lay half-buried in the snow. He grabbed it without moving the rest of his body, and wiped off the snow that was clinging to it. "Hello? This is Adam. I'm still alive. Thank you." He tried to take a deep breath but the cold air hurt his lungs. "Over."

A reply came from a few feet above his head, rather than the speaker. "Alive, but you don't look so good," Reggie said. She was climbing down the rocks toward him. "Where's the monster?" She had a rifle slung across her back, but didn't seem too concerned about using it.

Adam tried to be nonchalant in his response. He pointed to the hairy appendage nearby, crusted in blood. "He's there. Good timing."

It was then that he noticed Reggie hadn't come alone—Healy was standing at the top of the pod, rifle at the ready, and scanning the area. She locked eyes with him and nodded, then went back to her guard duty.

"Can you walk?" Reggie asked.

"Don't know, been afraid to try." The pain in his back had subsided, thanks to the snow and the freezing temperature. He pushed himself up and Reggie took a look at his injuries.

"It looks like a pretty deep cut on your right side." She moved his coat and burrowed through the layers of clothing. "Doesn't look like anything else. A little to the left and it may have injured your spine."

It was good news, but Adam had trouble celebrating it. "Still stings just a little." He allowed Reggie to grab his arm and help him up.

"I can imagine," she said. "Let's get you out of the cold and get that covered, and stop the bleeding."

He certainly didn't feel like fighting her on that score. As they carefully tried to climb out of the trench, Adam regarded the ejected pod and the blood that was dripping across the rocks nearby. He thought about what it may have cost the group to save him. "Let's just keep climbing up the slope," he said. "Let's go find your sister on the other side." He looked at Reggie. "We're never going to get through that damn car to get into the tunnel. We need to go over and down. It's the only way." It was hard to read Reggie's face with all the gear on and her hood pulled tight, but he tried to see through it all. Light snowflakes danced around them as she turned away.

They were now close enough that Healy could hear the conversation. She nodded at what she heard. "I'm tired of waiting around to get dead. Let's go get them."

"What about the others?" Reggie asked. "I thought the plan was to stay together."

It was the plan. And a good plan. Adam knew it was eating at Reggie more than a little, and he wasn't made for waiting around anymore than Reggie or Healy seemed to be. "If I stay here any longer, my head might explode."

"You aren't in any fit shape. We'd never make it up the hill, let alone over it." She looked up toward the summit.

"Try me."

DENTON

"Where the hell are they?" Denton stared up at the tear in the car.

Nara stood looking out into the snow, pulse baton in hand. "I don't see them."

"They're not responding to the radio," Hall said. "They took one, right? Adam had one. I know he did."

Either they were dead, or their walkie was. Denton favored the latter.

"That little pod trick killed too much power. We don't have enough for anything else, do we?" Cook asked.

Nara turned from her vigil. "We've got a little, but not enough for the dampeners to settle the rugaru if they come around. We can't run heaters long enough to really warm us up."

"So we're fucked, right? What the hell are we going to do? Send more people out for the people that went to save the first guy?" Cook sat up in the control room, dangling his legs over the edge as he sat with the radio in his hand.

That was the question that Denton rolled over and over in his mind. Do they sit and wait? His leg was throbbing, but he was starting to think he could walk without much trouble. "I don't think we can risk going out where Adam was attacked," he said. "That leaves just the hole in the floor."

"Hey," Trudy shouted. She'd stayed out of the conversation and disappeared into a panel when Reggie and Healy left. "Hey. The radio is working. I'm getting traffic on your frequency. Pretty much static right now, but I hear things fading in and out."

"Are you shitting me?" Cook stood and climbed up to her. "She's right. I hear voices drifting around in the mess."

Denton started to climb up to help, only to have the shooting pain return to his leg as soon as he tried to bend it.

Nara saw him wince and pulled herself up to the control room. "I know the communication protocols and all that crap. Why don't you try to widen that hole in the floor? Too crowded in the room anyway."

Denton nodded and watched Nara climb up into the room above them with ease, even with the unwieldy pulse baton strapped across her back. He wondered how much good it would do them, and whether they could make it out alive without it. He took a moment to evaluate their enemy forces; according to Healy's brief message, they'd managed to kill one of the rugaru by opening the pod, he finished one off up on the ridge, and one died in the initial crash. That meant out of the eight they were transporting, there were three known to be dead. That potentially left five for them to face. The idea that Adam's group would potentially face all of them at once was not something he wanted to happen.

After she ran through the authentication codes with White Anvil base, Nara laid their situation out. "White Anvil base, this is Meatlocker. We are in an emergency situation here. The train has crashed, we have multiple casualties, half a dozen hostiles, and the storm is still hampering our efforts. Over." She leaned herself against the console while she waited.

Through the static, a voice gave additional codes. "Meatocker, this is White Anvil base. Your sensors went offline several hours ago, along with all the others. The cold took them all down. We were hoping you guys had made it, and we hadn't received word. As a precaution, we started a plow train to clear the tracks in the middle of the night, but it's been slow going. They could reach you soon, Meatlocker. Over."

"Is that train armed? Are there soldiers onboard? Over." Nara waited for the static to form into a real voice.

"Negative, Meatlocker, it's Big Daddy. They've got Red on lead with the plow, McLaren on the tender engine, and seven crew members. None of them are armed. Over."

Nara looked down at Denton to confirm he'd heard. He nodded.

"White Anvil, that's not going to be all that helpful. The threats I mentioned are courtesy of Doctor Morley. If you don't know who that is, I suggest you get someone who does. In the meantime, can we scramble helicopters? Over."

"Negative. Conditions won't allow it, and I don't have permission to let them into the no-fly zone."

Nara nodded to no one. "Yes. I understand, but we're very, very screwed here. Do you copy?"

Denton suppressed a small smile. It was nice to have someone who wasn't actually with the military, and could say whatever she wanted, *however* she wanted.

"I'm sorry ma'am. Over." The voice grew louder, then faded again.

"You've got other trains to clear the tracks, right? Over."

"Yes. Over."

Nara was nodding again. "Great, hook up any transport carriages you have there, load them up with armed soldiers and send it this way at top speed. Hopefully they can get here in time," Nara said. "Over."

"It could take hours to get that in motion..." The soldier on the other end started.

"Wake everyone up and get them on a train. You have twenty minutes. Out." Nara handed the handset back to Hall. "Thanks."

Nara and Denton glanced at each other, and he knew that they weren't going to last for hours just sitting and waiting for a train.

MARGO

The tunnel widened as Margo continued to make her way in the dim light. She kept her hands on the rough wall to her right, making sure she had some sort of guide as she went. The darkness was so all-encompassing outside of her light, she was afraid the wall would disappear, or widen suddenly, and she'd have no idea what was only a few feet away from her face.

It was then that she panicked and realized that if the wall could disappear, then surely the floor could drop away just as easily. She swung the light downward just in time to see a dark form on the ground in front of her. She stopped moving and took a slight step back, ready to run if the shape ended up being a rugaru on the ground, sleeping or lying in wait. She pointed her light away from it.

The form didn't move. Margo wondered if she'd frightened herself needlessly; that maybe what she was seeing was only a rock formation.

She waited for another minute —a minute that stretched out for far too long— but the shape didn't move. She took a breath and slowly inched the beam of her flashlight back toward it.

When the light fell on the thing, Margo easily identified it as a person wearing a dark parka, stretched across the floor. She inched closer, staying aware of her surroundings. In the distance, a drip echoed through the system of tunnels, possibly close to her, possibly at the end of the caves, or any number of miles away. She stopped to listen for more, for something closer.

Pausing in place, she looked down at the figure on the floor. Finally able to see more of the body, she saw it was Frank, the man who'd been rude in the waiting room back at the station, the man she'd left to watch after Bria in the train. Margo knelt down, but there was nothing she could do for him. As she rolled him to the side, she found his neck had been shredded from his ear to his shoulder by a wide row of claws. His coat stuck to the floor as she moved him, the fabric trapped in a sticky, icy mass of his own blood.

Margo let go of him and sat down on the cold floor. She covered her mouth with one hand, trying to force herself not to scream or cry. The fear that Bria had suffered the same fate was overwhelming and she dropped the flashlight to the ground and slid herself up against a wall to prop herself up. She felt tears slide down her cold face before she even realized she was crying.

The flashlight rolled in a half circle, then back the way it had come. As it went, the light illuminated the wall across from her, and everything around it. She felt her spine tense as she watched the beam shine on more bodies. The spotlight showed the ruined and bloody remains of two soldiers before moving on to a prisoner wearing an orange jumpsuit and a military jacket. Then the device rolled back in the other direction, showing the same two soldiers, and the horrified looks on their faces.

Margo screamed. She couldn't help it. She took the light and swung it rapidly around her, revealing at least half a dozen more bodies, all people she hadn't met.

"Shut up," a voice behind her said. "Be quiet before they come for you."

With a deep, haggard breath, Margo scanned to see who was talking to her, but there was no one there. "Who?"

"Shhhh. It's me, Clarke."

"I don't understand," Margo said. She scanned the room, still repulsed by the bodies all around her.

"Look," Clarke whispered.

Margo stared as three gloved fingers poked out of a small hole more than midway up the wall. It took a moment for her to comprehend that the prisoner was somehow behind the wall peering out. The fingers disappeared and she could see a pair of eyes looking back at her.

The other woman's voice came back quietly. "Pick up your light and shine it to your right. There's a narrow alcove that the monsters can't get through. Follow it back and turn to your right. There's a little chamber back here. Just out of reach. They tried like hell to get me," Clarke said. "They'll be back, I'd wager."

Doing as she was told, Margo grabbed the flashlight and scanned the wall before finding the thin passage Clarke had indicated. "It's narrow." She wasn't sure she'd make it through, as thin as the passage was.

A low growl echoed through the main chamber. It was a rumble she could feel in her spine. Her legs tensed and she couldn't move.

"Drop your pack and go." Clarke sounded as frightened as she was. "Now."

Margo tried to decide which direction the thing might approach from, but she saw only the darkness.

"Move," Clarke said.

Spurred on by the urgency in the woman's voice, Margo let her gear slide off her shoulder and ran for the thin opening with just her flashlight in her hand and the pistol still tucked into her coat. She turned sideways to make it easier to fit, but she found her heavy coat still slowed her as she pushed her way in. Ahead, it looked like the alcove ended in a stone wall, but she kept moving toward it.

Heavy footsteps slapped the rocky passages behind her, but Margo wouldn't turn around out of fear she'd freeze and be caught. She pulled herself along, digging her hands into holes in the rock walls. Just as she was reaching what seemed like the end of the passage, a hand reached out of the darkness and waved her toward the side chamber.

"Over here, keep moving," Clarke said.

Another growl came from the chamber and Margo felt a sharp pain in her arm. She turned her head and came nearly face-to-face with one of the smaller rugarus. The thing's head was spattered with blood, mostly centered around the hole where its eye had been. Margo knew it was the one she'd shot.

The rugaru slashed at her, claws ripping her clothes and tearing into her flesh. She dropped her light and tried to get her hand into her jacket to pull out the gun.

Clarke grabbed Margo's coat and suddenly Margo found herself in a terrifying tug of war between the monster and the convict trying to save her. The rugaru seemed more interested in slashing at Margo than trying to take hold, and Clarke was able to yank her free.

She pulled her into the small grotto she had described earlier. It was indeed small, maybe twenty feet long and six feet wide. No entrances, tunnels, or other means of escape.

"Are you alright?" Clarke asked. She examined Margo up and down before focusing on her shoulder, pulling away the torn, bloody part of her parka.

Margo's attention was drawn back to the long corridor she'd just left, pulled by the snarls of the rugaru still there, clawing at the rock, but still too big to get itself through. "I'm okay." She shrugged Clarke away and reached into her coat to pull out the pistol. She stepped back to the end of the passage and looked at the beast wedged there. It went into a frenzy as soon as it saw her; swinging at her, howling, saliva dripping from its mouth. Margo watched in some sort of terrified fascination. She wondered where this thing had come from before the scientists had got their hooks into it.

"Get back," Clarke said.

Margo raised the gun, glancing at the wound she'd given the beast. The dark crater where its left eye had been bolstered her resolve and reminded her that the monster was not invincible. She squeezed the trigger, and the rugaru seemed to shrug the impact off, swiping out at her. The sound seemed to be the worst part for both of them —they flinched as the thin passage kept the sound ringing in their ears.

The chaotic environment suddenly went quiet as the gunshot, the growls, the shouts ended abruptly. Everything was still happening, but it was now just one long high-pitched tone in Margo's head. When she saw the rugaru lunge forward, she fired again and this time, the bullet tore through the monster's hand, blood and flesh flying on contact and the rugaru pulling back his injured limb and opening its mouth in a soundless howl. Finally, Margo fired a third time, and the bullet bore into the rugaru's face, not more than a few inches to the left of where her first shot had destroyed the creature's eye. This time, the beast slumped forward, still partially stuck in the tunnel.

Clarke's hand gently landed on Margo's arm. Margo saw the other woman's mouth moving, but still only the high sound came steady in her own ears. She shook her head and gripped Clarke, trying to make sense of the movement of her lips, trying to figure out what sounds she was making by analyzing the shapes her mouth was making. "I can't hear you," Margo said. It hurt her to talk. The effort made her light-headed.

Clarke held out her hand and pointed to the blood on Margo's sleeve. The wound from the rugaru was bleeding worse than she'd thought, and her blue jacket was nearly black in places from the fresh, wet blood. In the fight, she'd forgotten all about the injury, focusing instead on trying to get away. Adrenaline had something to do with it, she supposed.

With Clarke's help, Margo moved further into the small cave and they both sat down. Clarke began attending to the wound, pulling the coat's material away and probing closer to the long slashes. The look on her companion's face troubled Margo; there was concern that seemed to go beyond the treatment of just a simple scratch. She tried to read Clarke's lips again, but she couldn't do it.

Pain shot up into Margo's shoulder as Clarke applied a makeshift bandage created from strips of her own thermal undershirt. "Stop," Margo said. "You'll freeze. Use my shirt instead." Clarke held up a couple of long pieces of her shirt, which seemed to suggest it was too late; the damage was already done.

Clarke zipped her coat up tight, then quickly turned to look toward the outer chamber. Before Margo could ask what was happening, Clarke had her finger held up to her mouth for quiet. She moved toward the front, peering out through the slit that looked into the other room.

Margo rose to join her, but was stopped when Clarke fell backward suddenly. Immediately after, the thick hand of one of the rugaru broke through what was a small hole, knocking rocks and stones aside, widening it enough for its hand to smash through up to its wrist. It pulled back the hand and punched in again, burrowing up to the elbow this time. If anyone screamed, or if the monster was roaring, Margo didn't hear it. She certainly smelled the rugaru; whether it was the stench of its breath, or its filthy body, Margo couldn't tell, but the odor seemed to saturate the cave quickly, much worse than any of the other monsters she'd encountered so far.

The rugaru's progress stopped with the hole only wide enough to get the long arm inside up to the elbow, which seemed to anger the creature even more. It tried both arms, one right after the other, then rammed the rocks with one hairy, broad shoulder. Failing still, it stepped back, and walked in a circle, before running at the hole and slamming into it headfirst. A handful of dust fell from the cavern ceiling, and a number of pebbles rolled off of their perches on the wall.

It was obvious from Clarke's face that she was just as terrified as Margo. Margo checked her pistol, only to discover it was empty. She let it fall to the floor and pulled out the knife she'd been carrying since she'd left the car.

Clarke turned away and looked at the hole again. Margo was just in time to see the monster slam its head into the wall again. More dust fell, and this time, a larger rock moved from the impact.

ADAM

Adam was surprised how easily they climbed the steep slope of the hill to the train tracks at the top. The way his back was throbbing with each step wasn't easy, but they didn't encounter any of the creatures the entire way up. It was certainly a welcome change. The weather hadn't given up, though. The wind continued to push the group from side-to-side as they climbed, keeping everyone off-balance.

At the top, Healy walked to the rails and looked both ways before pointing off to her right. "I can just make out the bridge that way, so we must have come from the opposite direction." After a moment, Adam made out the outline of the thick beams of a truss bridge not more than a few hundred yards up the track.

"What's our move here?" Adam asked Healy. "Do we try to find the signal boxes and try to contact someone? Or do we keep after Margo, and hope the others managed to get the radio online?" Reggie's angry stare answered his question. "Okay. We should go pretty much straight down the other side and find this concrete tunnel they were talking about. Hopefully she's still in there, or it's easy to track her from there."

Healy didn't want to argue about it. "I'll take point. Wait a couple of minutes and follow on behind me."

"Can we rest for just a minute? I just need to catch my breath." Adam's back was aching, but he would be able to carry on; he was more concerned about the other two. They both seemed driven to continue, which was understandable in Reggie's case, and Adam figured Healy was just being a hard ass because she was a soldier. Neither of them would admit they needed a breather.

"Just for a minute or two," Reggie said. "We're way behind Margo. She could be inside that tunnel, stranded. Or maybe fighting for her life against one of those things. We can sit for just a minute."

Adam nodded and the pair sat down in the cover of a large rock just off the tracks. It blocked the wind and the snow just enough to allow them to rest without being harassed by the elements too much. Healy didn't join them; she stayed on the tracks and walked off into the distance until she was just at the edge of Adam's visibility. He watched her turn and walk back along the rails again. She scanned the area, still patrolling like this was a normal mission or an ordinary deployment. Despite his wish that she'd take a minute for downtime, he was also happy someone was keeping an eye out for danger.

"She'll be okay." It was all he could think to say. He couldn't make promises about how her sister was doing, or what the outcome of the whole thing would be, so he left it at that. Reggie nodded, just as non-committal and unconvincing as Adam.

Healy was still pacing. She passed Adam and he watched her walk up the tracks, closer to the bridge. There, she paused, looking off down the rails. She walked back to where Reggie and Adam were bundled together, and she knelt.

"Look, if we could round up the survivors, maybe we should consider taking them across the bridge," she said. "I doubt any of these monsters would have crossed it, so if we do, we could easily take up defensive positions. Maybe there's better cover over there, and it seems like there isn't this same sort of hill over there."

It was probably further ahead than Adam wanted to think at the time. He was more concerned with rescuing those people before they could be rounded up and moved across a wide-open train trellis. "It's a good idea, but we're still stuck with a lot of casualties in these cars. It'll be a bitch getting them up the hill. Compared to that, crossing the bridge is a piece of cake."

It was subtle, but Adam caught Healy flinching at those words. He wasn't sure whether she was unaccustomed to civilians contradicting her, if she'd forgotten about the casualties, or if she'd already written them off. "I suppose you're right," she said.

Reggie stood, brushing the snow off her coat and pants. "It's time to go." She held out her hand and Adam took it. She pulled him to his feet and then she started down the slope.

Healy scanned one more time, and followed the younger woman.

Adam took a moment to check his weapons to make sure they hadn't frozen, become packed with snow, or otherwise surrendered to the elements. They seemed good and he strapped his rifle back across his back, re-holstered his pistol and took the first painful steps to follow Reggie.

DENTON

Denton lowered himself through the tight hole they'd managed to cut through the floor and down onto the rocks below. He looked around, but the tunnel ahead was black but for the band of light that came in from the car he'd just exited. He wondered how Margo or anyone with her managed to make it out without running into everything or tripping every few feet.

"This is a bad idea, Denton," Nara said. She handed him the lit flashlight. "We are low on ammunition; your leg is fucked up. And once we get to the other end of this, we're back out in that snow up to our asses."

"We?" Behind Nara, Cook appeared as though he might throw up. "I think I'd do best here. You know, where it's less monster-y?"

"Yeah, there's no *we*," Denton said. He couldn't have agreed more; he was just trying to find a more delicate way to express it. "You two stay here, in case Adam and his group come back. No reason to drag everyone back out into this shitstorm."

"That's hilarious, considering you can barely walk, and I have the baton." Nara was already wrapping her hands in gauze and medical tape, to add an extra layer of warmth. "And that thing isn't leaving without me."

"I can walk just fine," Denton said. "Just stay here."

"No." Nara pushed her way past after slipping through the hole. She flicked on her own flashlight, scurried over the remaining rocks and strode on into the darkness. "You said you could walk, no problems, let's go."

Denton watched her go and suddenly worried that he'd be the one that slowed everyone down.

DENTON

WHITE ANVIL PRISON - TWO YEARS EARLIER

“I thought you soldiers were supposed to be in top condition,” Nara said. She was a good thirty feet ahead of him on the track.

Denton had stupidly agreed to work out with her one morning, and after that, she’d become relentless, joining him every morning and egging him on. The White Anvil facility seemed like a strange place for a world-class workout facility, but the government spared no expense. Apparently, it was an effort to keep the staff engaged and happy. The bleak surroundings didn’t lend themselves to casual morning jogs outdoors. Even the prisoners had an excellent recreation area to stave off the snow madness and cabin fever.

As they rounded the corner and started mile six, Denton took the inside lane and gained on her. They weren’t quite neck-and-neck, but they were in conversation range. “A few of us are going off-base to that little town over the ridge for beers tomorrow; you want to join us?”

“Good luck getting a pass for that,” Nara said. “The administrators are cracking down on off-base activities.”

“What? Why? We’re not really a secret to the locals. I know Ramirez and Miller went just last weekend.”

“That’s different, they’re officers. And they’re good friends with the RCMP officers there.” Nara slowed a bit and let Denton catch up. “Look, if you want…”

She was interrupted by Storch, a soldier who worked in dock twelve with Doctor Madison. “Hey,” he said. “Heard about Topaz Squad?” He started running to keep up with the other two.

Denton knew Topaz was another one of the teams; given the squad name because they had actually gone on several missions. He’d never seen their test subjects, but he’d heard talk of some sort of fishmen, or lobsterlings, or something equally strange associated with water.

“No,” Nara said. “What about them?”

“Shit went sideways. They got wiped out,” Storch said. “Minute they hit the water, their subjects turned on them. Nothing they could do.”

“What?” Denton shook his head. It wasn’t the first time things had gone bad for a squad that was overseeing their creatures, but it still freaked him out when it happened. In his brief spell at the Anvil, he’d come to think of these things as just another normal mission, not leading platoons of snot monsters or brigades of crab creatures into combat. It was directing another asset against a target. “Jesus, that’s rough.”

"No shit," Storch said. "The time will come, Denton. You'll have to take those hairy fucking apes of yours into some bullshit fight and then you'll see how rough it is." Storch peeled off, apparently intent on exercising just long enough to pass on the latest gossip before hitting the showers and finding some other uninformed soul to shout the headlines to.

They ran in silence for half a lap.

"He's right. Things happen when we take these monsters out. Hell, things happen in here with them. You know that, right?" Nara increased her pace until she was out in front again. "We won't take our group out for a couple of years, at the earliest. We'll be ready by then." She put on a sudden burst of speed and got nearly a quarter lap away from him before he knew it. He watched her, slightly in awe of her stamina. This time, he let her move ahead, content to run the track alone with his thoughts.

ADAM

The relative quiet made Adam nervous. It was hard to see again; the wind was blowing the snow off the top of the hill and drawing a white curtain around them. Adam thought he saw shapes, shadows moving around them, but he never heard a sound.

"Anyone see anything? Anything at all?" Reggie asked.

Healy was too far away to hear, but Adam answered, "Snow. And ghosts."

"Snow ghosts? Wasn't there an episode of Scooby Doo that dealt with snow ghosts? Didn't it turn out to be the hotel owner or something?"

Adam laughed. "You seem a bit young to remember old cartoons like that one." Scooby Doo had been a favorite of his. Maybe it was the idea of solving mysteries or having a cool van, or a talking dog, but he had most of the episodes memorized. "Also, I think the ghost was Mister Greenway. Some sort of jewel-smuggling operation, if I remember right." He immediately felt like a nerd.

"Little chance of that happening here, huh?"

That would have been just fine with Adam. Although unmasking the rugaru to find they were just greedy developers rather than bloodthirsty monsters would make all the death even more difficult to handle.

The conversation made him wonder if he had some sort of snow madness, or if his earlier fall had somehow given him a concussion. The look he got from Reggie seemed to be that of amusement, though it was hard to tell with that cold-weather gear covering most of her face.

They all stayed alert for monsters, snow ghosts, greedy developers, and survivors that might have lost their way wandering in the snow.

Halfway down the slope, Reggie slipped on a rogue piece of metal, likely from one of the train cars, and landed on her rear. She suddenly got way out in front of Adam and Healy, unable to stop herself from sliding down on her back. She sprayed snow into the air as she tried to dig her hand through the drifts in order to slow.

Adam ran after her, trying to lift his legs high enough to get over the drifts himself. It was slow going, and he was concerned Reggie would slip out of sight, or worse, slam into one of the creatures. He hopped over a rock and ended up in Reggie's trail of cleared snow. The flatter surface made it easier to run, since there was no snow to slow him down. He stumbled, falling on his chest and sliding a little, but he was able to maintain his control and get up again, barely stopping his forward motion. He tried to keep his eyes on Reggie, but the tumbling, erratic paths they were both taking made it difficult.

When he lost Reggie, he pulled himself to a stop and looked back up the hill to see if he could locate Healy. Unfortunately, she was nowhere to be seen, either.

His chest hurt from the exertion of running combined with taking deep breaths of frigid air. The few moments he took to gather himself weren't nearly enough, but he got up and moved further down the hill, staying in the track Reggie had left.

The bottom of the slope soon came into view and it spurred him to move more quickly, knowing Reggie couldn't possibly go much further. He hoped she wasn't injured; the slope was riddled with rocks she could have easily slammed into if she wasn't able to steer herself out of the way.

Just a hundred yards or so from the bottom, Reggie's trail ended. She appeared to stop, but he couldn't find any tracks to show where she'd gone next. He put his hands to his mouth and took a deep breath to call for her, but he was hit by a snowball before he could utter a sound. From a nearby cluster of rocks and pines, Reggie waved and held a gloved finger up to her mouth, or at least the area where her gear covered her mouth. She waved him over, then ducked back down behind the cover.

Silently pushing through the piney limbs, Adam found Reggie. She was flat on her stomach in the snow and watching something further down the hill.

"There's one of them," she said. "It was directly below me when I was coming down the hill. And it seems like it's heading straight for one of those caves over there." She pointed, and Adam followed her finger to the craggy rocks on the other side. A rugaru with reddish-brown fur moved easily among the boulders there, and it was carrying something easily over its shoulder.

"What's it got?" Adam asked. "Can you tell?"

"Not what, *who*." Reggie shifted away from the monster. "It looks like it's carrying someone wearing camo."

Once she said it, Adam saw she was right. The beast had a soldier slung over his broad shoulders.

"Jesus. That's not Healy, is it?" Reggie said.

Adam quickly looked behind them, remembering they needed to warn Healy if she was coming up behind them. "No. If you saw that thing as you were coming down, there's no way she would have made it to the bottom before us in time to get caught."

"What do we do?" Reggie asked. "Should we follow it? See if they're all holed up somewhere?"

It was a question to which Adam didn't really have a proper answer. "I don't know. Maybe we should try to kill it out here, so that we won't be facing so many of them inside? How many are left, I wonder?"

Reggie was going to respond, but the sound of gunfire stopped her.

DENTON

His relief at finally making it to the end of the tunnel was instantly dashed when Denton saw one of the rugaru lumbering off toward the mountain. From so far away, he couldn't tell anything other than the fact that it had a red coat of fur that made it stand out starkly against the white of the blizzard.

"I don't want to start a fight with this thing, but it might be better out here rather than in a cave somewhere," he said. A cave gave them some restrictions tactically, and Denton was unwilling to go into unfamiliar territory and hope for the best. Outside, he and Nara could spread out and use the wide-open area to their advantage.

"You okay with that?"

Nara nodded.

As they stepped toward the mouth of the tunnel, Nara retrieved the pulse baton from her back and activated the device. It hummed slightly, and a faint blue light travelled from the tip of the baton to the handle and back before fading out. "Okay. Two of us against the big red rugaru. What's the plan?"

"I shoot him, and you whack him with the stick?" He'd come up with better on shorter notice, but he was starting to worry about the burning feeling that was settling into his hands, and the throbbing pain in his leg.

"Not really a plan." Nara held Denton's elbow before he could move to cover. "Be careful. We need to get out of this, so don't do anything stupid."

He didn't want to admit how worried he was about the rugaru. He's seen what the creatures could do, watched them, studied the data over the last several years. The baton gave them an advantage, but he was feeling every injury he'd sustained over the last day or so. "Stupid? You heard the plan, there's no room for stupid in there."

"I'll move around to those trees, so I can charge him after you distract him with cover fire."

Denton dropped himself behind a snowbank for cover. He dialed the monster in through his scope, and then focused on the cave entrances just above the rugaru. There was no sign of any other monsters, or survivors.

Out of the corner of his eye, he saw Nara running through the thin trees, trying to catch up with the rugaru. She appeared to give up any pretense of subterfuge and ran flat-out in the direction of the mountain, parallel with the creature's path.

The monster seemed to have a singular purpose —getting to the cave with its quarry— and didn't try to look around as it went. One of the problems they'd encountered with the rugaru was that they were unable to turn their necks; they needed to turn their entire upper body in order to look around, which gave them a major blind spot. That certainly acted in Nara's favor now.

It got dangerously close to the cave. So close that Denton feared more could come out and attack. He waved to get Nara's attention, and she stopped, crouching next to a boulder.

Denton gave up his own cover; he wanted the rugaru to see him. He sighted the beast in and fired. He felt he was rushing his firing sequence, anxious to bring the monster down and end the long nightmare for everyone. The thump of the automatic rifle pierced the quiet of the snow-encrusted hillside.

He watched the snow fly up around the rugaru where his bullets impacted, and in the middle of those the beast went down. At least one of the shots had pierced the back of the rugaru's leg in just the right way for it to lose its footing.

As it went down, Nara moved in quickly, baton at the ready. She only got a few steps toward it when more gunfire opened up. The rugaru held up his arms to shield himself, ducking lower in the snow and twisting to see where the attack was coming from.

Denton found the source coming from a tree on his far right. Using the tree as cover and to stabilize herself, Healy scored hit after hit on the massive creature. Most were blocked by the beast's thick arms, some by his chest plate, but a few seemed to be getting through, causing the monster to flinch and retreat. As it did, it spotted Nara and charged at her.

"Shit," Denton said. He was afraid to shoot out of fear of a rogue shot hitting Nara. Healy must have noticed the same, because she stopped shooting as well. Denton leapt over the rocks and the snowdrift at the front of the tunnel and ran toward the rugaru and Nara as fast as the terrain would allow.

The rugaru swung its massive arms, reaching out for its prey. Nara was ready and jabbed the pulse baton at the monster's head. It didn't connect, but the rugaru dodged and moved away from her, circling. It was a move he'd seen her do before; something to get the beast's attention and remind it of the power the baton held. Nara had told Denton the baton also emitted a sound only the rugaru could hear, further warning them of what was to come.

The rugaru continued to stalk around Nara, making gunfire dangerous, even for marksmen like Denton and Healy. The rugaru appeared more cautious, but still determined. The body it had been carrying lay in the snow, all but forgotten in the wake of the sudden attack.

Denton wasn't the only one closing in on the scene of the fight; not only was Healy on her way, but out of the corner of his eye, he spied Adam and Reggie sliding down the slope as well. They'd all arrive long after he did, but he was happy to have the additional support.

The rugaru thrust out its arm tentatively, trying to grab the baton without getting hit by it. It's hesitation quickly cost him, as Nara ducked under the creature's outstretched arm and whacked him in his hairy thigh with considerable force. The monster howled and stumbled backward, allowing her to land a jab just below his armpit. Another howl; though this time Denton was close enough to see blood spray from the monster's mouth as it snapped its jaw.

Adam and Healy joined Denton at almost the same time. He was ready to say how glad he was to see them, when the beast swung his arms again in a wide arc. Denton threw himself into the snow to avoid the blow. Out of the corner of his eye, he saw Adam and Healy do the same. Reggie was still far enough out of reach not to worry about the beast's sudden strike. The creature seemed determined to crush Denton, and followed him as he moved backward quickly in the snow.

Denton's rifle strap became entangled in some ground cover and he left it, rather than chance trying to pull it free. Instead, he scrambled toward the thicker rocks, hoping to climb for the opening they'd noticed.

The clatter of an automatic rifle made Denton turn to see Reggie opening fire on the rugaru, which had closed the gap and was within a couple of paces of grabbing him by the leg. A few of the shots went wild, and pinged into the rocks just to the left of Denton. He cringed, covered his head, and rolled himself into a ball, unsure of who to be more afraid of—the monster, or the woman with the gun.

The gunfire stopped, and Adam and Reggie shouted at the monster in what sounded like an effort to get its attention away from Denton. Grateful, he didn't waste the opportunity. He climbed until he found the narrow opening in the side of the mountain. It was only then that he decided to turn around to check on the monster's progress. It had stopped, trying to decide who to pursue.

Before it could commit, Reggie and Adam fired at it, opening up with the M4 carbine rifles they'd been carrying when Denton met up with them. The monster flinched and shied away, though it was impossible for him to tell if they were hurting it or just scaring it with the sudden crackle of automatic rifles.

The sound of another gun made the monster turn. Healy had pulled her pistol and moved to a position less likely to catch Denton in the crossfire. The bark of her Beretta was a welcome sound as she sunk shot after shot into the side of the rugaru's head.

About the time Healy stopped to reload, Nara broke whatever cover she'd found and swung the pulse baton, nailing the monster square in the side. The beast howled, but immediately stopped any struggle or attack. The beast's arms went slack at his sides, and he toppled forward, falling in the snow, face-first.

The others kept their weapons trained on the monster, and Denton could feel his own trigger finger shake in an effort to refrain from shooting. "Nara?"

The small scientist in the ill-fitting snow suit moved cautiously toward the beast, and Denton felt his stomach churn out of fear the thing would jump up and grab her. She moved her hand down the creature's wrist, then took her glove off to feel the area again. "He's dead. I didn't think he'd survive the jolt, but I wanted to make sure."

"Was that J25?" Denton asked.

"Collie was his official code name."

"J25."

The group lowered their weapons and gathered closer. Denton made sure to keep an eye on the caves, just in case another came out to fight. They were loud during the struggle, and he feared the screech of the creature and the rattle of gunfire would attract more of the rugaru.

"Everyone okay?" Reggie asked.

"I'm as okay as I can be," Nara said.

Denton nodded. "Same here." It was hard to say you were fine after battling a giant hairy creature, but the alternative was being dinner for said creature, so it was kind of a sliding scale.

"We need to take a minute to catch our breath before we rush headlong into those caves."

Another scream, this one very much like the one they'd just heard from the dying rugaru, roared forth from the mouth of the cavern. It lasted much longer than the last.

"I think the break is over," Reggie said. "Let's go. My sister is in there."

MARGO

"Let me use your knife," Clarke said.

Margo's head still hurt, but her hearing was slowly improving. Clarke's words were a muffled, far-away whisper, but at least she could hear them.

Margo stumbled, trying to free the weapon from the sheath. "What are you going to do?" She carefully handed it to Clarke just as the beast slapped at the walls with its hands. It reached in, shoving one long, scraggly arm through the hole and swinging it around, trying to reach the trapped women. Both managed to dodge and moved themselves to the back wall of the cavern. Margo flinched and nearly screamed, even though the rugaru's filthy claws were still a couple of feet away.

The monster withdrew its arm and emitted a frustrated whine. It backed up and ran at the wall headfirst again. This time, Clarke jabbed the knife as hard as she could at the beast, using her swing in conjunction with the momentum of the rugaru racing forward to intensify the impact of the blade. Far from burying itself in the monster's head, the blade glanced off of the thing's skull. Along the way, it tore a line from the front of the monster's head to the back, drawing a cut that erupted in blood almost immediately.

The rugaru stepped back and swiped at its face, smearing the blood across the side of its head. It stumbled, and shook. The blood came more freely as it did so. It snarled as it tried to focus on the two women in the cavern. As Margo saw it become angrier, she grabbed the knife back from Clarke, suddenly filled with determination. She stepped to one side of the hole and waited.

"Margo, what are you doing?"

Margo waved Clarke to one side. She still didn't understand everything the girl was saying. "Get out of sight," Margo said. Her hope was that the creature would come for a closer look to find them if they weren't immediately visible through the hole in the wall. She watched as Clarke did as she was told, and then Margo waited for the monster to come looking for them.

The creature snarled and roared, sounding frustrated. It stomped closer, heavy footsteps crunching the snow. Margo was unable to see it as it moved forward and was suddenly gripped by the fear that the thing would outsmart her and reach through the hole. The only other sound she could hear was the deep rumble of its breath as it slowly advanced.

The knife was shaking so rapidly that it took a moment for Margo to realize it was because of her hands. She could barely feel them; she could see them moving rhythmically, making the knife dance. She tried her best to steady them through sheer force of will, but the frigid temperature won out.

A grey cloud heralded the rugaru's breath, and assured Margo that the monster's face was getting close to the hole. The stench from its mouth was fouler than she remembered; rotting trees, manure. It made her turn her head for a second to get away from it, but she turned back to watch for her opportunity. She wanted to wait just long enough that there was no way for the beast to recoil, and with any luck she could drive the long blade right into one of its eyes. It seemed that was one of the few places the creatures were vulnerable, and it was her best hope for stopping this one.

Margo saw what looked to be the ridge of the rugaru's forehead and she swung with all the strength she had in her, taking the knife in a half-circle that ended at the creature's face. Only instead of connecting with one of the beast's eyes, the blade caught it in mid-roar. The rugaru began to screech, and the long knife jabbed the back of its throat, buried almost to the hilt.

The loud growl became a wet gurgle and Margo saw a jet of blood shoot from between the monster's jaws. The dark purple fluid seeped down the corner of the thick lips and wide teeth, as it swiped at the object in its mouth.

A sudden jerk brought Margo to the back of the cave.

"Let's go," Clarke said. It was a shout so close to Margo's ear that she couldn't misunderstand it, even with the ringing in her brain dominating the soundscape. The prisoner pulled her to the narrow passage where she'd come in. The other rugaru blocked part of the passage and they helped each other climb over the monster's body.

As they got to the main chamber, they found the red-haired beast had pulled the knife out of its mouth and tossed it aside. It stumbled with blood oozing from its head, and a thick stream of it dripping from between its lips. It lashed out with its great arms when it saw the women emerge from the passage. A new look of determination replaced the confusion and fear on the beast's face as it advanced.

The women struggled to get back into the tunnel, but the rugaru was too close and Margo realized they'd never make it. She shoved Clarke aside and moved to face the creature on her own, watching the beast's eyes harden in anger as it approached.

There was a faint glow in the dark chamber and then the expression on the rugaru's face changed quickly. Margo watched its eyes close before it collapsed in front of her, landing almost on top of her boots.

Behind her, her sister stood with one of the stout metal stun sticks.

"Jesus Christ, Reggie!" Margo said. "I am so happy to see you. You have no idea how happy!" She stepped cautiously over the beast on the ground and ran to scoop her little sister in a hug. Margo let go after a long minute and realized the hug had transferred a layer of rugaru blood onto her sister, but she didn't care. She hugged her again.

Reggie eventually pushed her off.

"Look, for all we know there are more around here. We need to go," Healy said, standing with her rifle at the ready. It made Margo happy to know that Reggie hadn't had to go it alone to get here.

"How the hell did you end up with the baton?" Margo asked, as her sister started to drag her from the cave.

"One of the other soldiers fell. He'd got a pretty serious leg injury. When we stopped to help him at the mouth of the cave, I snatched the thing and ran in here." Reggie tugged on her sister's arm again.

"Wait," Margo said. In the excitement of seeing her sister in one piece, she'd forgotten someone. She held out her hand to Clarke. "Come on. We need to get out of here."

Clarke nodded, and before Margo could pull her along, she grabbed Margo's face and kissed her on the mouth. Their lips were chapped so badly, Margo barely felt them make contact. After a moment, the woman released her grip and stepped back with a slight grin, before pulling her clothing tighter and stepping away without a word.

Margo stumbled, dumbfounded. Her sister took her by the elbow and led her down the passage.

DENTON

His leg was throbbing, and he could no longer bend it. Each step had become a stabbing pain that he couldn't ignore. Even with Nara and Healy helping him along, it wasn't getting any easier. Despite his better judgement, his training, and his instincts, he sat down at the lip of the cavern and couldn't press on anymore. His vision was cloudy and all he could do was hold still to keep from passing out.

He vaguely heard Nara shout as Reggie took off with the pulse baton to find her sister. The shout from Nara admonishing Healy and Adam to chase after her was a murky echo in his head, and the wind still seemed to be blowing, but it was no longer pelting his face. He had no idea if his face was that numb, or if the wind was blocked by an outcropping.

After that, things were hazy and blank. He wasn't sure if he slept, or if he'd just lost consciousness for a bit, but his eyes opened at a faint sound that fought to be heard over the din in his head. It was a rumble which, at first, made him fear an avalanche or another earthquake, but as he waited, the noise came into focus. The sound was unmistakably a train pushing down the tracks; still in the distance, but approaching. He'd heard that sound often enough around the mountain prison to recognize it even from afar. The chug of the engine echoed through the mountains, carried on the wind, or in spite of it. He worried that he was hallucinating the sound of the plow roaring as it cleared the accumulated snow in its path.

He tried and failed to sit up. "We need to head out. The train's coming to extract us."

Nara stared at him.

"What?"

"You can't even get yourself to a sitting position, and you're ready to 'head out' at the slightest sound?"

Denton reached out and braced himself against the cave wall. He briefly wondered how long he'd been in the cave, and not outside at the entrance, but he let it go. "I can sit up."

"You need to rest," Nara said. "We have no idea how bad your injury is."

"I NEED to get to that train and get everyone out of here." Denton sighed, annoyed, not with Nara for wanting him to rest, but with himself for having to. "We can get to the top of the hill and flag down the train."

"Because they might miss the wreckage of our train strewn across a half mile along the tracks? Or they might not hit the same snow and ice that derailed us?" Nara bundled him up, pulling his hood tighter around his head. "You can take a break." She brushed the snow from his hood and wiped blood from his face.

"No," Denton started to explain why he was so set on getting everyone under his command to safety when they were interrupted by the rest of their group coming back from the cave. He checked everyone was accounted for, including one of his escaped prisoners. "What happened?"

"They killed one of them, sir. That's what happened," Healy said. She seemed impressed.

"Two. We killed two of them, sir." The prisoner, Clarke, corrected Healy.

Healy and Nara helped Denton up. "You think you can walk for a bit, if we take breaks? We need to look for anyone else on this side of the hill," Healy said.

"No, we need to get up to meet that train. I heard it approaching. Even if it doesn't have cars, we can get some people to safety in the engine compartment." Denton could feel his head getting mushy already.

"We can't leave those people vulnerable out there," Reggie said.

Clarke stood apart from the others, following the conversation with concern. "We're not in any shape to help anyone. This guy's got a bum leg, and that dude is limping —and his back looks like it's covered in blood." She pointed at Denton and then Adam.

"She's right," Margo said. She stepped closer to Clarke, so the woman didn't seem so alone.

"Fine, but we need to know what we could be facing. Were any other rugaru in there?" Nara asked.

"We didn't really feel like looking, to be honest," Adam said.

Nara drifted off for a moment. "So, if you killed two in the cave, we killed one out here, one was dead in the original crash…"

"The one up on the hill, before the car went over the edge." Denton waved his hand to keep himself moving.

"We crushed one with a pod," Adam said.

"That's six. There were eight being transported. Any others?" Nara asked, but nobody responded. "There could still be two out there, unless the other survivors killed them."

"Or they could just be dead. Maybe they fell into the river, or got crushed under a car, or ran off to join the circus." Reggie sounded exhausted.

Denton sighed and pulled himself closer to Nara. "We should be so lucky."

Adam nodded and checked his gun. "I'm as optimistic as the next person, but I only have three shots left in the pistol."

They all chimed in with their own dismal ammunition counts. They would be woefully unprepared for another encounter with a rugaru.

Denton leaned back and looked up the hill. The wind and snow had abated enough that he could actually see a good distance; certainly better than before. The slope was daunting and his leg felt like it was being slashed apart by a hot blade.

ADAM

The weather was slowly turning in their favor. The temperature was still abysmal, but the snow and wind were giving the group a break as they made their way up the slope.

Adam hung to the back, taking somewhat of a rear-guard position, with Healy leading the way. Nara and Reggie helped Denton move as best he could. His condition seemed worse than just an injured leg, but Adam could only guess what other injuries the soldier might have.

Whatever it was, it slowed their little squad down, but only just enough to make Adam's own pains a little less obvious. He twisted and turned at every opportunity, working out the ache in his back. It didn't seem like anything was broken; certainly he wouldn't be moving as well as he was if his spine had sustained any damage. His hope for just cuts and bruises remained alive in his every step.

Lost in his self-assessment, he nearly missed the whistle of a train in the distance. When Denton suggested he'd heard the train's approach, Adam hadn't heard a thing, and wondered if it had been a trick of the wind coupled with wishful thinking.

Turns out Denton might have been right, though it was hard to tell how far away it actually was. "Hey," Adam called out to the group. "I heard the train. Did you hear that whistle?" Margo and Clarke acknowledged him, but the others kept their pace up the hill. "Not far away. It has to be close." His gear felt a little lighter at the thought that some form of help, *any* form of help, might be close.

"Do you need some help?" Clarke held out her hand to Adam.

"Is it that obvious?" He grabbed her hand and she helped him up over a rough patch of ice that was hanging off an outcropping.

The woman shrugged. "We all need help once in a while, whether we admit it or not."

Adam got his footing and thought about taking advice from a woman he knew to be a prisoner of the government. He concluded that anyone who'd survived this ordeal was certainly free to dole out wisdom with impunity, at least in his company. Others would have to make up their own minds. "Thanks," he said. "Many times, I've found that to be the case." Though Margo hadn't been a part of the conversation in the least, he noticed her subtle smile at that.

With the newly cooperating weather, Adam could tell that Healy was only a few steps from cresting the hill.

MARGO

Healy helped everyone to the top, and they gathered at the railroad tracks and cleared them off as they waited for Adam, who'd been watching the rear for monsters to follow them up the incline. At this point, it was hard to tell anything had happened. Snow had piled on the tracks and covered the hill. The bridge just a few hundred yards away was nearly a postcard, with icicles hanging from its girders. In the other direction, the trees were just as picturesque, and the rails disappeared into drifts between them. There was a little debris visible on one side of the hill, but snow had blanketed any other evidence.

Kicking the snow from the tracks, Margo thought about the things that had happened in a short day or so. She had no idea what time it was; what day it was. It was impossible for her to guess how much time had passed since they'd left the station.

"Clearing that spot probably won't help anything. The plows can get it done faster," Reggie said.

Margo looked at her sister, completely unaware she'd approached until she spoke. "Just trying to help." She reached out and took Reggie by the hand. She used the added stability to walk one rail like a tightrope, kicking snow as she went. It was funny to her. After the horror they'd endured, it was funny to be holding her sister's hand and playing in the snow, and she wondered if she was crazy.

She was *sure* she was crazy.

Stepping off the rail, she pulled her sister close and hugged her.

Behind them, Clarke suddenly shouted, "Look. Over there. I see smoke from behind those trees." A thick cloud of grey smoke was shooting into the sky from beyond the forest, and was getting closer.

"Anyone have a flare, so we can signal them to slow down before they get too close? There could be track damage, or ice on the rails," Adam asked.

"I doubt they'll be going too fast to miss us, not with the condition of the tracks." Healy took a few steps toward the direction of the train.

"What about whatever it was that derailed us?" Reggie asked. "I mean, it could do the same to them, right?"

Denton agreed with her. "Yeah. If it crashes, we'd be right back where we started. We need to check the tracks up to those woods, now." Healy, Reggie and Clarke moved ahead to start looking deeper into the forest, while Adam, Denton and Nara began scraping the snow aside in the immediate area.

Margo took a deep breath, sucking in the still-frigid air, and did what she could to pull herself together. She scrubbed away the snow from her sleeves and pulled her face mask back on, less to insulate her from the cold and more to shut out yet another possible horror in a long string of horrors.

As she nestled the mask into place, she could see the train come into view nearly a mile away. The grey smoke shooting into the air was joined by a spray of white as the huge rotary plow on its engine flung the snow away in a wide arc.

DENTON

The limp wasn't getting any better. The climbing certainly didn't help, but Denton got a sudden jolt of energy just from seeing the plow train approaching. He moved along the tracks supported by Nara, with Adam nearby. Though he was still mobile, he felt pretty useless.

"Hey," Adam said. "Just out of curiosity, what does that 'alpha' look like?"

"Really?" Denton had a headache, and questions of any kind at this point made it worse. "You've seen as many as I have. You were even up close and personal."

"No. I mean, these have all been relatively similar, but they've had different colors and different heights, and whatnot." Adam shrugged as he peered over the edge of the hill. "What color are the ones that are missing?"

Nara stopped and grabbed Denton. They both had the answer —and they didn't like it. Denton spoke up first. "White. J20 is almost entirely white." He looked at the area before him—it was completely white. The snow covered everything around for miles. Trees were draped with it, the tracks were buried in it, the mountains wore it like a blanket. If that particular rugaru was still alive, it could be standing out in the open and they'd never see it until it was upon them.

Denton looked at the others; their group had moved a good distance away, further than he was comfortable with. "We need to get everyone back together." He let go of Nara. "You need to bring them back, now."

He watched her go, running as fast as she could toward the group in front of them. Doing his best not to fall on his ass, Denton tried to pick up his pace too. Adam raised his rifle and started scanning the hills, following close behind.

Paranoia gripped Denton with each painful step. Everything was white, and the remaining wind kept everything shifting, even if just a little bit. With Adam watching his back, Denton chose to concentrate on Nara and the women she was approaching. It gave him something to focus on, and kept his mind from conjuring things that weren't there.

As he and Adam edged forward, he saw Nara reach the others and wave them back. He breathed a sigh of relief, and stopped to gather himself. Adam passed him, limping. "Adam?" Denton asked. "You do much hunting?"

Confused, Adam replied, "Uh, no. Not since I was a kid. No time for it lately."

"If you *were* hunting, would you attack the larger group of able-bodied prey, or would you go after the pair of injured animals that were lagging behind the pack?" Denton pulled his pistol and scanned the area as Adam did the same.

The drift to Denton's left suddenly came to life as the snow flew into the air, revealing Elias. The creature was already within striking range before he could even turn his gun on the monster. It launched itself from a crouching position and knocked Denton to the ground. He fired off two rounds out of reflex that flew off harmlessly toward the mountain.

The beast was crushing him, its full weight square on his chest. Adam swung at the rugaru, but its long arms easily batted the lawman away. The only good thing about the move was that it took some pressure off Denton's chest.

But the reprieve was short-lived. The rugaru brought its massive hand down over Denton's face. With all the strength he had, he swung at the monster's arm, to no avail. As he became progressively dizzier, he could feel the energy leaving him; his efforts to fend off the beast went suddenly tepid and he felt his arm drop to the snow just as his vision went dark.

MARGO

She flinched when she heard the shots from Healy's gun.

Her hearing was still dodgy from the incident in the cave, so everything sounded distant. But she was so close to these shots, they were hard to mistake for anything else.

The rugaru flinched, and seemed surprised to hear the shots. The bullets seemed to do nothing to it, but it did stand up, releasing Denton completely.

Healy's gun stopped firing, and she held it with both hands and charged at the monster, amazingly agile in the snow. The monster roared, filling Margo's head with what sounded like a faraway foghorn. It held its ground, arms ready to combat the approaching threat.

Healy ducked low and slid under the beast's waiting hands. She deftly jabbed the butt of her rifle up into the exposed part of the rugaru's neck with a quick cracking sound.

The monster stumbled, its cry becoming a hoarse bark.

The train was slowing but not quite as urgently as Margo expected. The rest of the group had engaged the monster, leaving she and her sister to wave in desperation at the engineer of the hulking vehicle. It was almost hypnotic to watch the enormous blades of the plow spin around, sucking in snow and spitting it out in an arc of white.

Next to them, Nara shouted to Denton, but he wasn't moving. Adam was on the ground, crawling toward the tracks, the rugaru and Denton, who was square in the middle of the train's path.

Reggie took off quickly, running toward the train, circling around to the engineer's side. "What the hell are you doing?" Margo watched her sister run next to the engine, reaching for its ladder before finally grabbing it and pulling herself up. It took a moment as her hands seemed to struggle to get a grip, but she made it and was up and into the cabin in a minute. It was a mystery to Margo what her sister thought she was going to accomplish, but at least she was doing something. Margo didn't have any better ideas. She was exhausted, mentally as well as physically, and her mind was as numb as her fingers.

Finally satisfied that Reggie had proven she could handle herself, Margo turned away and ran toward the rugaru to join the fight. Healy was still very close to the thing, swinging at it with the stock of her gun, while Clarke dragged Denton out of harm's way as quickly as she could. Margo ran to join her. "Grab one arm, I'll get the other," she said. A look of relief replaced the desperation on Clarke's face and together they pulled the soldier off the tracks and far enough out of the train's berth.

"Thanks," Clarke said. She got down on her knees and started examining Denton's head for wounds. She pulled open his eyelids and checked his pupils.

"You have medical training?"

Clarke looked up and shrugged. "Sort of, I was in Girl Scouts."

"Girl Scouts? Really?" Margo asked.

"Surprised?" Clarke pulled off her gloves and put her bare hands against Denton's neck. "Man, he's still going, but he needs some help. More than I can give him."

The brakes on the train shrieked as it came to a stop. It was only a hundred yards and the engine groaned in an effort to remain stationary. Clarke yelled something that Margo couldn't make out over the grind and buzz of the plow on the front of the engine. The sheer size of the blades was terrifying and the spinning made her dizzy. While it had stopped its forward movement, it was still sucking in snow like a vacuum cleaner and tossing it away.

The spell that was keeping her transfixed, broke when she saw her sister jump off the train. Three men leapt off behind her; one carried a shovel, another had a pick, and the third carried a very old-looking double-barrel shotgun. At the head of the line, Reggie gripped a large red axe in both hands.

ADAM

He gave up trying to be gentle on himself the moment the monster knocked he and Denton to the ground. It was painful to walk, and he'd tried to move in such a way as to not exacerbate the wounds. When he got up, he had no choice but to fight through the agony.

While the monster was busy with Healy, Adam pushed ahead. "On your right," he shouted at her, trying to ensure one of her wild swings wouldn't come his way. He charged and threw all his weight at the rugaru's torso, trying to knock it off-balance to give Healy a good shot. His plan failed quickly and painfully; ramming the thing's stomach was like hitting his head on a boulder, and that boulder didn't budge. Adam fell to the ground.

"Get back," Nara said. There was a sudden flash as Adam watched her swing the pulse baton and connect with the creature's right leg. It snarled and its leg buckled at the knee, causing it to stumble. A large arm lashed out, preventing Nara from landing a follow-up blow.

With its other arm, it grabbed Healy by the neck and slammed her onto the metal tracks at its feet. The soldier shouted in pain, and the beast picked her up and threw her down again. Healy was silent this time.

The creature appeared poised to do it again, but it was suddenly smacked in the back of the head with a coal shovel. The blow didn't seem to do much in the way of damage, but it certainly got the rugaru's attention. As it spun, it was hit in the calf by the other train tender's pick.

With the beast's attention diverted, Adam ran to Healy. "Hey. Come on. Let's go. Let's get you away from here." He didn't know what to say, but he already knew that nothing that came out of his mouth would make a difference. Her forehead was bleeding heavily already, and as he moved her, he saw sharp bits of her skull breaking the skin. "Come on. You're…"

Nearby, the deep roar of the shotgun broke through the drone of the train's spinning rotor, and the engine's rumble. The beast was unfazed by the blast, other than it getting angrier and angrier the more the attackers continued. It lunged with a terrifying shriek at the man with the shovel, digging into his chest with thick claws. He picked up the tender and threw him over the side of the hill, the man's terrified cries fading as he fell out of sight.

"Get back," Adam shouted. "You're too close." The other train operators scrambled back just in time to avoid a second swing by the rugaru. The one with the shotgun started reloading when he found his legs again. The frightened man fumbling with shells brought Adam's thoughts to other weapons. He knew his own pistol was empty, but he looked at

Healy's; still in her holster at her side. Would she still have any ammunition? Why would she have holstered it, if it was dry?

Adam watched the monster while he pulled the soldier's sidearm. The clip dropped out easily, gun oil filling his nostrils. The weapon was empty. He had better luck once he pulled the slide back, finding a single bullet in the chamber. It wasn't much, but a well-placed shot could make a considerable difference. Everyone was exhausted and doing their best, but the rugaru seemed ready to fight for days.

MARGO

With Clarke at her side, Margo tried brainstorming ideas to help the fight. "Anything at all we can do to help fight this thing other than pelting it with snowballs?" She was crestfallen when she remembered her knife was still stuck in one of the other rugaru's eyes.

"Not that I can figure."

Margo saw Adam grab Healy's pistol and it became painfully obvious that they would all have to follow Healy's example if they were going to get away. She made her way over to Adam and picked up the rifle Healy had been using to pelt the monster at close range.

"That's empty," Adam said.

"I know."

Adam held out the pistol to her. "One shot."

"Keep it," Margo said. "You're better with it."

Adam shifted and offered it to Clarke. She bent down and rummaged on the ground until she came up with a large rock that fit in her fist easily. "I'm good."

With a nod, Adam turned back toward the monster that Denton and Nara knew as The Alpha, J20. "Well, good luck."

Margo gripped the rifle awkwardly until she found a comfortable way to hold it. "Let's go." She ran with the others until the monster was surrounded, and they began circling it. No one wanted to be the one to charge it, or flinch first, but someone was going to have to. Margo prepared to charge when the blare of the train engine startled everyone, including the massive monster in front of them. Steam and smoke suddenly hissed from the sides of the hulking metal vessel.

The sounds spurred the rugaru into action and it dashed directly at Nara and the pulse baton she was holding just a few feet away from it. It appeared Reggie was ready for that, and swiftly swung the axe, burying the narrow point just below the beast's armpit. It howled with surprise, allowing Nara time to crack it on the side of the head with the baton, creating a quick flash of light from the weapon.

The beast stumbled and fell down on all fours, pushing itself partly up and falling back on the ground. It wasn't focusing on anything or anyone around it. The train assistant with the shovel ran forward and cracked the rugaru in the back of the head, taking advantage of the lull in the fight.

"Stay back," Nara said. Her words were lost in the grumbling idle of the engine, combined with the still-rotating plow. "I said *stay back*." Nara tried again, but with no success. It appeared she was playing it cautious, rather than charging in to finish the thing off.

The high squeal of the train's brakes disengaging got Margo's attention and she noticed the engine was inching forward, directly toward the scene of the fight. It didn't have far to go before it would be on her and the others. She was closest, but if she edged away from it, she'd end up nearer to the rugaru. She moved out of the way, stepping to the side, off the tracks.

After a big wind up, the man hit Elias in the head again. Harder this time. His companion with the shotgun moved tentatively closer. As a third swing appeared to be in the offing, the monster landed a chest-crushing punch on the assistant, which knocked the man to the side by half a dozen steps, crashing him into Nara and driving them both to the ground. Nara's baton slid from her hands and rattled to a halt at Margo's feet. The rugaru followed the progress of the weapon and moved toward it.

Just as Reggie planted the axe in the monster's side, Margo grabbed the baton. The axe glanced off part of the rugaru's chest plate, doing nothing but drawing its attention away for a moment. Margo looked down at the pulse weapon; the handle was easy enough to figure out, but there were only a couple of buttons that she could see, and they were buried almost out of sight where the thumb fit into the grip. She pressed the buttons one at a time, but nothing happened.

The plow continued its pace forward, and Margo shouted to the others, "Push it toward the train!" But no one reacted to her. She waved her hand in the air to get their attention just as Adam dashed at the monster and jumped on its back. He hung on long enough to put a pistol up to the thing's neck and fire one shot before being tossed aside.

Margo ran around to the other side of the thing so it was between her and the advancing blades.

Her sister joined her. "Hit it with that thing."

"I don't know how it works," Margo said. She spun it around and showed Reggie the only buttons she could find. "I've pressed them both. Nothing happens."

Reggie shrugged. She was out of breath and looked as though she could fall over any minute. "Try holding them down when you hit it."

As though the monster had heard them, it turned and snarled.

"Let's both hit it." Reggie didn't wait for a response. Instead she ran headlong at the rugaru that wasn't even a dozen feet from them.

Without hesitation, Margo chased after her sister. She couldn't remember the last time she'd done that —followed her sister blindly. Usually, they would run in opposite directions. As Reggie lifted the heavy fire axe, Margo held down the baton's main switch. The red blade of Reggie's weapon sliced into the rugaru's arm at the elbow, just as Margo jabbed the suddenly glowing stick into its chest. It shuffled backward just enough for her to notice that the massive spinning plow was starting to suck snow off the ground from just a foot behind the creature. In fact, she was sure she could see loose snow flying off its shoulders and arms.

The rugaru apparently felt it too, and in its haze from the effects of the pulse baton, it made the mistake of turning to see what was causing the odd sensation on its back. It was dazed such that Margo took the opportunity to attack. She swung the baton again, connecting with the rugaru in the abdomen, her thumb pressed so hard on the button that her whole hand ached. She followed up with one more swipe across the monster's lower jaw. Blood flew from its mouth, and it whimpered in pain.

It was devastating to Margo then when the beast not only remained upright, but stumbled forward, away from the whirling plow.

Until Reggie stepped in, that was.

Margo's little sister ran in with her axe and slammed it into the thing's ridged forehead. While the blade bounced off harmlessly, the rugaru reached out and took the weapon away from Reggie, enveloping it in a thick hand. It appeared ready to throw it away, but it wound up a little too far and there was a sudden clang as the axe was splintered by the blades and disappeared into the plow. The rugaru hung onto the handle a split second too long and its hand vanished in a churning cloud of blood and snow. The monster howled in agony and withdrew what was left of its appendage.

Margo felt a tug at her hand as Clarke pulled the baton away and swung at the rugaru, missing entirely, but then connecting with the subsequent strike, connecting with the rugaru's knee. The injury sent it tottering toward the plow like a falling oak, but as it fell, it reached for Clarke's suit. The monster failed to get a hold on her and toppled headlong into the blades.

This time Margo glanced away, though it was impossible, even with her inadequate hearing, to avoid the crunching sound of the huge body being ground and rattling around in the massive engine-driven plow. She wanted to cover her ears to block it out, but instead used her waning strength to pull Clarke off the tracks and out of the path of the advancing train. As she did, her sister joined in and helped. Once they were clear, Margo sat down on the cold ground and let out a loud scream that was equal parts terror, relief, and confusion. She didn't know what else to do at that point. There was nothing left inside of her. Reggie came over and sat down next to her and they hugged until the shrill sound of the train's brakes kicked in and drowned everything out.

ADAM

Red, the train engineer, helped Adam bring the train to a halt. They could see the snow that the plow threw off suddenly turn red and gray. Hideous sounds indicated the blades were churning something up that was large, thick, and decidedly *not snow*. The thought of it made Adam queasy. He'd seen plenty of unpleasant things in his law enforcement career; he'd prepared small game when he was out in the wilderness; but a body getting sliced up like that was almost too much to handle. Red throttled back the plow and turned it off.

When the train stopped, Adam jumped to the ground with Red behind him. They snatched up Denton and carried him carefully to the crew car behind them and put him inside just to get him out of the elements.

Adam ran to the front of the train and immediately found Reggie, Margo, and one of the convicts, Clarke, sitting at the side of the tracks. They were all staring off at the slope just below them. "You okay?" He didn't direct the question at anybody in particular; he was just hoping one of them would answer.

"Hey," Reggie said, as she looked up at Adam with a groggy swagger to her movements. If he didn't know better, he'd swear she was drunk. "You're okay. I'm so glad." She stood and immediately hugged him too hard and he flinched. "Oh shit. I forgot about your back." She took his arm and pulled at him. "Here, sit down with us."

Adam held up his hand. "No. That's okay. I'm going to check on the others."

"I'll help." Reggie held onto his arm and tried to support him as they walked. She remained there as they checked on the other train crew, the ones they could find. One of them seemed to have a broken forearm, and they both had lacerations and bruises. Once they'd talked to Adam, and had their injuries checked, they took off down the slope, looking for their companion.

"I got word from the Anvil that the other train is hauling ass our way," Red said. "They should be along in a couple of hours or so. I'll go radio them our exact position, so they don't run our asses over or something." He turned back to the lead engine.

"I thought there wasn't supposed to be radio contact or electronics out here, because of the prisoners. Secrecy and all that?"

"It's a rescue mission," Red shrugged. "Anybody gives a shit we're using radios; they can go ahead and kiss my ass."

The sentiment was just fine with Adam, and it made him curious how far the engineer went to make sure he had communications with the Anvil. "Any chance you have a cell phone on you?"

"Now that's REALLY forbidden."

"See, my daughter's having a baby, probably already had it while I was stuck out here with these… *things*." He tried to look as pitiful as possible but had a feeling he looked like hell without even trying.

"Come on." Reggie came alongside Adam and propped him up again. "Help the guy out. We certainly won't tell anyone." She smiled at Red, but it came out a little creepy to Adam, considering she was covered in blood and had scratches across her face from falling and fighting.

Red apparently saw fit to pity one or both of them. "Come with me. I'll show you where you can climb up to for decent reception."

"Thanks," Adam said. "I appreciate that."

"Just don't bleed all over my iPhone. It's new." The engineer led them to the engine where he handed over the latest technology and helped Adam up onto the tender train behind it.

Dialing from memory, Adam punched in his daughter's number and listened as it rang.

MARGO

As the survivors sat in the cramped tender car with Denton, Red and the other able railway men made their way to the crashed cars that were visible from the top of the hill. The snow had stopped for the time being and a few of the cars were easy to spot. Red had pulled together as many weapons as he could from the engine, including rusty chains, pry bars, the shotgun, Reggie's axe, and other found objects. When they returned from a car with two people that made it, Red also brought back a number of fully loaded weapons that had been stockpiled while the soldiers waited. Each trip saw Red and company better equipped.

It was quiet. No one wanted to talk, or even make a sound, it seemed. So it was a surprise when Red came back shouting.

"What is it?" Nara asked. She was suddenly thrust into a leadership role with all the high-ranking military incapacitated. "What's going on?"

"There's one of those things down the hill a ways," Red said.

It was almost too much for Margo to bear. She leaned back from the entrance to the small car and squeezed her sister's hand tight. "Did it attack your men? Are they alright?"

"They're fine, the thing didn't attack anyone. It's almost dead."

Nara moved toward the door. "*Almost* dead? What do you mean?"

"Looks like it got beat to hell and crawled into a car for shelter. Still breathing, though." Red shrugged. "Bleeding a lot."

"Let's go see it."

"I'll go with you," Clarke said. "You'll need all the help you can get." She stood and moved toward the front. For some reason, Margo felt her chest ache suddenly as Clarke made her way to the back of the car.

"I need you to stay and help guard the train. I've got all the help I need and…" Nara thought about it for a second. "And honestly, everyone here has been through enough, you should stay and help here." She grabbed Red's coat. "How far away is this?"

"Pretty close."

"Show me," Nara said. She took her pulse baton and jumped off the back of the car. "Let's go."

DENTON

He woke with a start, thinking he was in the middle of a battle with one of the beasts, but Nara's was the first face he saw when he opened his eyes. "Where the hell are we? What's going on?"

"Easy." Nara put her hand on Denton's arm. "You're fine. We're on a train headed for civilization," Nara said. "Well, *America*. It's the closest thing we could find."

The car swayed and rocked as Denton sat up. He was on a stretcher on the floor of a dirty train car next to Nara. There was a tube in his arm that led up to a plastic bag hanging on the wall. At the other end of the car was a large shape under a long grey tarp.

"Is that…"

"Yes." Nara cut him off before he could even form the sentence in his head.

They sat in silence, hypnotized by the rhythm of the train.

"I obviously missed the end of the whole thing, what happened?" Nara filled him in on the battle and what had happened to Elias —and how Red and his men gathered the survivors and discovered the beast under the cover.

"Which one is it?" Denton asked, as if it mattered.

"Hector."

"You mean J32?" His eyes fluttered and he did his best to keep them open. He felt like sleeping for a few more hours –if they would only let him. He reached out and patted Nara's hand, and together they stared at the barely concealed rugaru. The lump of creature plastic was huge.

Denton watched the pile rise and fall slowly with the creature's breath. "We need to kill it."

"We should save it." Nara's voice was flat and dispassionate. "We created it. We should be the ones to help it. It isn't this beast's fault it's here."

"You don't believe that. You want it dead, too. He's not a pet. All the shit we just went through?" There was more than one moment that Denton felt sure the beasts would stand up and begin killing again —starting with Nara and himself. She was adamant that that wouldn't happen, but Denton kept his pistol close and the pulse stick in sight. "Where would you take it? Would anyone else let you take over where Morley left off?"

"I don't want it dead. I'm just thinking it *should* be dead. You know? I don't *know* what comes next. Does someone else take over? I've been afraid of what a change in lead scientist would bring. What would they want to do with one of these?" Nara said. "We don't even know if White Anvil Prison was damaged in the storm or the earthquake. We could start over there if we had to. If all the equipment is still intact, we could make a new start. Figure in ways to control it." She trailed off as she spoke. "And all that shit we just went through was kind of the point. That's what we were training, building them for."

"Yes, that's what they were supposed to do, just not to *us*."

Nara nodded.

"I'm out," Denton said. "I don't mind guarding prisoners, but I think experiments like this are way out of my comfort zone. Maybe I can get transferred to some nice desk for a bit. Perhaps in the tropics."

"That doesn't sound like you. You get bored in hot temperatures, remember?"

Denton nodded. "I wasn't bored. I was fine there."

It was quiet, and they both went back to staring at the form of the beast.

ADAM

The train ride was rough. If they were in an actual car, he'd tell them to have the shocks repaired —the way they swayed and dipped was near dizzying. But as it was, they were in a train car that wasn't meant for high speeds, high tailing it for the nearest base or town, or wherever they could get shelter. Adam hadn't bothered to ask where that might be, or when they would get there. He lay on a workbench, which, judging from the smell of oil and grease, had been the home for any number of tools that railway workers had cause for; all hastily tossed to the workshop floor when the poor souls left behind at the White Anvil got the call that they were needed.

Next to him, Lowenstein, the only survivor with medical training, sat on an overturned box and leaned over two soldiers placed on the floor for lack of a better place to put them. They seemed to be in bad shape, and Adam wasn't ready to ask about their conditions.

"You okay?" Reggie stood at the foot of his bench and grabbed one of the many straps hanging from the ceiling for workers to steady themselves. "I mean, I know you're not *okay* okay, but you're going to live, right?"

"Yeah. I'm fine. But not *fine* fine." Adam was surprised in that moment how much Reggie reminded him of his daughter —dark hair, daring, tough, and hard to understand sometimes when she spoke.

"Good. That's good," Reggie said. "I don't know if I'll see anyone from this train again." She looked around the crowded car and her gaze landed on her sister. "Well, I don't know if I'll see you again, so I just wanted to say thank you for everything you did back there to get me to my sister. That's certainly one person on this train I'll see again, and again and…" She shook her head, looking self-conscious. "Anyway, thanks." She put her hand on his foot and patted his boot awkwardly and started to pull away.

"Wait." Adam couldn't let her go without returning the sentiment. "Thank *you*. I didn't get to my daughter in time to see my grandson's birth, but I'll get there eventually. You did a hell of a lot to make that happen."

"You're really a grandfather? You look too young," Reggie said with a smile.

Adam wasn't sure how to react to that, but could feel his face grow hot. "Thanks, but after what we just went through, I'll be surprised if my hair doesn't turn grey overnight."

Reggie drifted off toward her sister, careful to step between the people on the floor.

Adam watched her go, then leaned his head back on his makeshift pillow of a folded-up coat. He stared out the window, letting the still-blowing snow lull him to sleep.

MARGO

Margo sat near the rear of the car and pulled her coat tight against the cold. This train ride wasn't nearly as luxurious as when they'd left the station the other day. These carriages were meant to take workers to and from job sites along the rails, evidenced by the equipment and gear hanging from the various hooks and compartments around the car. The seats weren't as comfortable, and they were torn in places and falling apart in others.

It was colder than their first transport, Margo was fairly sure of that. There was a chill lingering from the sting of the storm they'd been stuck in. The wind still rattled the windows and a few flakes still fell, but it was nothing like before.

"You want to maybe start doing research somewhere warmer?" Reggie sat down in the seat next to Margo and leaned close, putting her head on her sister's shoulder. "They have earthquakes in the Bahamas, don't they?"

"I don't think so." Margo really hadn't studied up on the plates in the tropics. "Not with any regularity."

"That's something we could investigate, right? Why there aren't any quakes there? Why are the tectonic plates so stable?" Reggie half-smiled. "Our first paper could be: How do gallons of margaritas affect the stability of non-earthquake susceptible land masses?"

A smile forced its way onto Margo's face as well. "That sounds like an actual paper. You mean you've been paying attention when I talk about that stuff?"

"Not really." She was fast asleep in minutes.

Margo stared out the window to follow the mountains in the distance. It was peaceful and serene, like a Christmas card. She watched the scenery pass without a sense of safety. Though the ordeal was over, she felt she needed to scan each hill and pine for something moving, something watching.

THE END

THANKS

To my wife and kids for patience and inspiration
To my mom and dad for years of help and love
To the Greater Columbus Arts Council for support
To CM Franklin for editorial assistance and helpful snarkery

Visit www.mattbetts.com for more about the author and to say hello!

Leave a review of White Anvil at Goodreads or the online retailer of your choice!

CHECK OUT OTHER GREAT CRYPTID NOVELS

SWAMP MONSTER MASSACRE
by Hunter Shea

The swamp belongs to them. Humans are only prey. Deep in the overgrown swamps of Florida, where humans rarely dare to enter, lives a race of creatures long thought to be only the stuff of legend. They walk upright but are stronger, taller and more brutal than any man. And when a small boat of tourists, held captive by a fleeing criminal, accidentally kills one of the swamp dwellers' young, the creatures are filled with a terrifyingly human emotion—a merciless lust for vengeance that will paint the trees red with blood.

TERROR MOUNTAIN
by Gerry Griffiths

When Marcus Pike inherits his grandfather's farm and moves his family out to the country, he has no idea there's an unholy terror running rampant about the mountainous farming community. Sheriff Avery Anderson has seen the heinous carnage and the mutilated bodies. He's also seen the giant footprints left in the snow—Bigfoot tracks. Meanwhile, Cole Wagner, and his wife, Kate, are prospecting their gold claim farther up the valley, unaware of the impending dangers lurking in the woods as an early winter storm sets in. Soon the snowy countryside will run red with blood on TERROR MOUNTAIN.

Printed in Great Britain
by Amazon

61758451R00132